The newspaper stories were familiar enough but the people of Ambleford never imagined that they could apply to them. Among the usual headlines were such startling revelations as:

Daughter of Vicar on Drug Charges
Teenager shoplifter arrested
Actor's son steals cars
Titled youth on rape charge
Schoolboy had arms cache

Ambleford was a quiet town in the Weald of Kent, surrounded by farmland and open country and bounded by the river Amble. Scattered about the country outside were substantial houses in their own extensive grounds whose occupants came into Ambleford to do their shopping.

The chief attraction of the town was its very wide main street which ran through the centre of the town. It was bounded by a wide grass verge planted with flowering cherry trees that made it a photographer's delight in the spring and reproductions of the scene were to be found on most calendars. Tall, elegant detached houses set back from colourful front gardens lined the street. It was in these houses that the well-to-do residents lived, red brick and solid like themselves.

The houses in this main street were called Cedars, Firs, Poplars and so on. All except one, which was called Number Three, not in figures but in letters and so called because it happened to be the third house in the road.

The only person who appreciated the idiosyncrasy was the postman. The other residents considered it typical of the owner, John Rossiter, and the allusion was not entirely complimentary.

John Rossiter was known as a 'character', a title he was not slow to relish since it gave him an excuse to behave after his own fashion and defy convention. Today he was considered irascible and unpredictable but he was a retired lawyer and pictorial evidence of him in earlier years showed him in wig and gown, an immaculate and important figure in the law courts. He had been the senior partner in a large and successful law firm in the City and had amassed a considerable fortune acting as leading Counsel in some of the most famous trials in the country, trials that attracted the media who created a 'star' out of the man. He chose early retirement to Ambleford because of his wife's prolonged illness.

He was 60 years of age when his wife died. She was 51. She had been ill with cancer for a long time and John nursed her throughout and looked after her right up until the end. She was a very attractive woman and they were a devoted couple. He regarded her as his own precious property and even resented the inevitable intrusion of the funeral directors.

John was tall, handsome and of distinguished appearance. In the eyes of the people of Ambleford he was regarded as something of an eccentric. He called himself a pin-striped rebel. The fact was that he had definite likes and dislikes in both people and things and was not averse to voicing his prejudice. Among his likes were good food and wine and what he considered a misnomer, the working class. Among his dislikes were what he called toffee-nosed snobs and social climbers and, in particular, his sister-in-law, Susan, whom he could barely tolerate.

She was married to his brother, Frank, a successful stockbroker, and they had a daughter, Karen, who was at university. Ever since her inception into the family she had tried to run it as if she were some self-appointed

4

TWO INTO ONE

TWO INTO ONE

Peter Rogers

The Book Guild Ltd
Sussex, England

First published in Great Britain in 2003 by
The Book Guild Ltd
25 High Street
Lewes, East Sussex
BN7 2LU

Typesetting in Baskerville by
Keyboard Services, Luton, Bedfordshire

Printed in Great Britain by
Antony Rowe Ltd, Chippenham, Wiltshire

A catalogue record for this book is available from
The British Library

ISBN 1 85776 791 8

CONTENTS

The Empty House   1

I'll Die if it Kills Me   115

THE EMPTY HOUSE

matriarch. She and Frank lived outside Ambleford in a thatched house surrounded by several acres where she kept horses. Of course, John would say, with her it had to be horses. Horses were somehow further up the social scale than other animals.

She and John could never meet without quarrelling over something or other and poor little Frank, the exact opposite in appearance and temperament to his brother, flapped about and whined ineffectually in his efforts to keep the peace. Susan was 50 years of age, dark-skinned to a kind of olive with jet black hair pulled back tightly and held in a black bow. Half-gypsy, declared John. She also had a loud voice that irritated him. Comes from talking to horses, he decided.

Her husband, Frank, was a hen-pecked, insignificant little man. Susan always said he was 'something in the City', a title she preferred to stockbroker which she considered somehow common. John said at that rate he might be a lavatory attendant in Lombard Street. Actually, the bespectacled 55-year-old tweedy Frank dealt in what was called commodities and had cornered the market in pepper, of all things, to his great financial benefit.

The latest quarrel between John and his sister-in-law was over the death of John's wife, Dorothy, known affectionately to all her friends as Dot. All the time that she was ill Susan would visit as often as possible, considering it her duty, until John actually told her to stay away. He told her that she disturbed his wife with her know-all manner of telling everybody what they should do. She would sit beside the bed and tactlessly recite instances of cancer that she knew or heard of with no regard to the sensitivity of the patient. When Dot died she wanted to see her in death, as it were, but John refused. He would not let anyone look at his wife, lovely as she was once the ravages of the illness had vanished with her soul, as he called it. He used to sit by her on his own and when he went to bed he said goodnight to her.

John hated funerals. He used to say that the only funeral

he would attend was his own. He made an exception in the case of his wife. He always felt he wanted to re-write the service as it appeared in the prayer book. As he walked behind the coffin with the church bell tolling monotonously and the vicar intoning wearily he felt further away from Dot than he had ever done in his life and he would have liked to run back home where he thought she would be. He could not feel that she was in the procession. It was a lovely sunny day in May and he could hear a lark singing high in the sky. He looked up but couldn't see it. He and Dot used to see who could spot the lark first when they heard one. Now she could even be up there with it.

He complained about the funeral service to his brother.

Susan, who happened to overhear the remark said, 'Oh, you're never satisfied, John. You always want to change things.'

'I wish I could change you,' John retorted.

The verbal exchange took place at what was called 'the reception' at the Bear Hotel and Susan even had to quarrel about that.

It happened the day after Dot died. They were having tea at Number Three. Susan wanted to take over the funeral arrangements and relieve John of the responsibility. John had other ideas. He had already contacted the undertakers and had reserved a room at the Bear Hotel for the reception after the funeral.

'You can't do that!' protested Susan.

'Do what?' asked John, innocently.

'Herd all your friends and relatives into a stuffy room at the Bear. They should come back here to your house.'

'I don't want them here.'

Dot was lying upstairs at the time and Susan and Frank had called to commiserate with John. As they sat in the large, elegant drawing room with its tall ceiling and decorative cornices the strident, corncrake voice of Susan cut across the peace of the room.

'It's very rude to push them off to a hotel, virtually a pub,' she insisted.

'So long as they get something to eat and drink they won't care where it is,' said John.

'Well I do.'

'It's nothing to do with you, Susan, You just happen to be Frank's wife, otherwise you wouldn't be there at all.'

Susan turned to her meek little husband, all five feet five of him, and complained, 'Are you going to let your brother talk to me like that?'

'If he wants the reception at a hotel then he wants it at a hotel,' replied Frank. 'What does it matter?'

'It matters a lot,' countered Susan. 'It's bad manners.'

'Susan,' explained John, patiently, 'I don't want their loud chatter, their cigarettes, their pipes, their cigars disturbing the atmosphere of this house.'

'Why not?'

'Look at the mess there'll be to clear up.'

'You've got Norah and her husband to do that.'

Norah was the cook-housekeeper whose husband acted as chauffeur-handyman.

'I still won't have them here. What happens when they've gone? Silence. A nasty silence. Not the nice silence there is when nobody comes. That would be completely shattered.'

'You're mad,' concluded Susan.

'Good. I prefer to come back here as it is now.'

'Oh, let him have it at the Bear and get it over with,' interrupted Frank.

'All right, then,' conceded Susan, 'Frank and I will come back here with you afterwards.'

'I'd rather you didn't,' said John.

'What!' exclaimed Susan. 'John, you really are bloody rude.'

'Susan,' asserted John, grimly, 'when I leave the Bear I will come back here alone. I don't want either you or Frank with me. Is that understood?'

'Yes,' said Frank. 'That's understood.'

'By you, perhaps, Frank,' said Susan. 'But not by me.'

'Who cares what you understand?' exploded John.

7

'Well!' exclaimed Susan, indignantly.

'The thing I can't understand,' John went on, 'is how Dot managed to put up with you. When she was confined to her bed she had little option. Until I decided to stay home and look after her. Then she was relieved of your so-called good intentions.'

'I've heard people say you're the rudest man in Ambleford and I can sympathise with them,' said Susan.

'I couldn't care less what people say.'

'If you go on like this you'll be ostracised. You'll end up a recluse. It was only Dot who saved your bacon with the neighbours.'

'Dot was always the sociable one, bless her,' mused John.

Frank, in an effort to restore some kind of peace between his brother and his own wife, decided to change the subject.

'John,' he declared. 'What are you going to do about Falcon House?'

'Yes,' added Susan. 'What about that place?'

Falcon House was an attractive Georgian style house a few miles out of the town which John Rossiter had bought before his wife became ill. It was their intention to move out of the town because the traffic passing by Number Three had increased so much. It was something that they were both looking forward to but now, with Dot's death, all that was changed.

'Oh, I think I'll sell it, Frank,' said John.

'Sell it?' echoed Susan, in alarm.

John ignored her. But she went on, 'The best thing you can do is sell this place and move into Falcon House.'

'Why?' asked John.

'Start afresh. Put all this behind you. The bad memories.'

'What are you talking about, woman? What bad memories?'

'Why, Dot and all that.'

'I can't move into Falcon House because there is nothing of Dot there.'

'That's the whole point. Isn't it, Frank?' Susan suggested, turning to her husband for support.

8

'Don't bring me into it,' protested Frank.

'There's nothing for me there, Susan,' explained John. 'Dot died here and I'm staying here.'

'I thought you'd want to get away from it all,' urged Susan.

'No. Thank you.'

For one magical moment there was a silence between them. Frank and Susan drank their tea in their usual genteel manner while John seemed to ignore his.

'Your tea will get cold,' said Susan.

John came out of his reverie to drink his tea. Because her brother-in-law did not react aggressively to her remark she ventured to voice something that had been on her mind since Dot died.

'What are you going to do with her clothes, John?'

'Nothing.'

'Won't you send them to Oxfam or the Salvation Army?'

'No.'

'I know a dressmaker who...'

'They're staying where they are, Susan.'

'They'll rot away.'

'So will I. And one day, happily, so will you.'

Frank frowned a warning at his wife to drop the subject but she went on, 'I wouldn't mind her mink coat.'

'Do you think I want to see you going about in my wife's clothes?'

'Only the mink.'

'Nothing.'

'Do you intend to keep this place as a museum, then?'

'I don't know what it has to do with you.'

'You can't live in a large house like this on your own.'

'Why not?'

'You'll close some of the rooms, surely.'

'Close them? Why?'

'You can't use them all.'

'How do you know? I may have drunken orgies and fill the place with dancing girls.'

'You're mad.'

9

'So you said.'

'I could help you...'

'I would be grateful, Susan, if you would leave me to lead my own life. I would be even more grateful if you would finish your tea and go home.'

'All right. I know when I'm not wanted.'

'If only you did,' muttered John.

Susan stood up indignantly and Frank pulled himself wearily to his feet. John remained slumped in his chair. He didn't even get up when the other two went out of the room, he was that tired. He heard the front door close with a bang. He smiled resignedly to himself. He didn't mind bumbling old Frank but he had never been able to stomach the man's wife. He couldn't explain what it was about her. She just put his back up, as they say. Dot used to laugh at his fixation. There would be a slanging match as soon as he and Susan got together. It wasn't just because he considered her a domineering snob with an infuriating habit of correcting people, including her own husband, she had an aura of repulsion for him. He didn't even like the clothes she wore or the way she stomped about on her heels when she walked.

In the car on the way back to their own house Frank said, 'You always manage to rub him up the wrong way.'

'He's impossible.'

'He always has been. You know that.'

'I could slap his face.'

'I thought he was going to slap yours.'

'Then I hope you'd knock him down.'

'Don't be ridiculous, dear.'

'Wouldn't you?'

'Wouldn't I what?'

'Hit him.'

'He's my brother.'

'And I'm your wife.'

'You don't need to remind me.'

10

'Runs in the family,' muttered Susan.

She was furious that John was not prepared to move into Falcon House. She could then have moved into Number Three herself. She was keen to move into Ambleford proper. She felt out of touch socially in her present set-up with the horses. She could still keep the horses in the country while living in Ambleford itself.

True to his intention, John returned to Number Three alone following the funeral 'bun fight', as he called it, at the Bear Hotel. Although he had managed to shake off Susan he was quite sure that it would not be long before she was on the phone. He would warn Norah to tell her that he was out.

He was sorry that Dot was no longer in the house in her comfortable-looking coffin on the trestles in the bedroom. He used to go and look at her from time to time until the undertakers put the lid on the coffin on the day of the funeral and took her away. He didn't like that bit. He knew that Norah, too, used to look at her when she thought he wouldn't notice. He knew that she was fond of his wife. Was he being foolish? Susan would think so. He couldn't help himself. It was typical of him. In spite of what people called his legal mind he had a heart and at heart he was extremely sentimental.

The day after the funeral he walked to the estate agents, Hillier and Morgan. He always walked erect, looking neither to right nor left. People who saw him smiled to themselves for, in spite of the loss of his wife whom they all loved, the old devil, as they affectionately dubbed him, cut a fine figure in his panama hat, black jacket and light grey trousers. He carried, as always, a malacca cane.

Derek Hillier, the senior partner of the firm of estate agents, was a long-standing friend and he and John had done business together over a number of years. He was a stout, florid character, the epitome of a country auctioneer, complete with loud check suit.

'What can I do for you, John?' he beamed as John entered his office.

'I've decided to sell Falcon House,' announced John.

'Oh, I thought you wanted to move there out of the town.'

'I did. Now I don't. I'd have moved there with Dot but not without her.'

'Understood.'

'I'd like you to deal with it yourself.'

'No problem. You haven't had it long so you shouldn't lose on it.'

'I would like it sold as soon as possible. Auction if necessary. I don't want a lot of people traipsing all over it. They're only curiosity customers. I leave you to pick out the serious buyers.'

'Leave it to me, John.'

That was all. Derek knew better than to mention John's wife. They shook hands and parted. On the way home John called in at the newsagent to pick up a copy of the *Ambleford Gazette*. There would be a report on his wife's funeral but that was not his reason for buying it. It was a regular order and it amused him to read about local council meetings and, in particular, readers' letters. This week the front page story concerned the tragedy of some old tramp who had been pulled out of the river Amble which flowed beside the town. His identity was so far unknown.

John was not to know that a few other people were reading the same story with more interest and concern than his. He was to meet them later in ominous circumstances.

Just as Norah came into the drawing room with John's tea and toast the telephone rang. Without thinking that it might be Susan John picked up the receiver.

'Hello.'

'John?'

'Oh, hello, Derek. Back from the house already?'

'Yes. And there's something I don't understand.'

12

'What's that?'

'There's a lot of damage since I last saw it.'

'Damage? What kind of damage?'

'Nothing structural. Superficial. Decorative.'

'It was ready to move in, for Heaven's sake,' complained John.

'That's what I thought,' agreed Derek. 'It looks as if squatters have been in there. There's graffiti on the walls and litter everywhere. You'd better come and have a look.'

'I will. I'll just finish my tea and meet you there.'

'Right.'

John put the phone down and began to pour his tea. 'Bloody vandals,' he muttered.

While he was waiting to drink his tea he crunched on the toast. He tried to drink the tea but it was too hot. He stood up. He became impatient. Who could have done that to Falcon House? He nearly scalded himself on the tea.

He put it down, walked into the hall and called, 'Norah!'

Norah, small, dumpy, middle-aged, came hurrying from the kitchen area.

'Yes, sir?'

John walked back into the drawing room with Norah following him. He picked up the cup of tea again and found that he could drink it now.

'I have to go out, Norah,' he explained. 'Something's happened at the other house. I don't know what. Vandals. Sorry I can't finish your nice tea.'

'Don't worry, sir. I'll make some fresh when you get back.'

'Thank you, Norah.'

She followed him to the front door and opened it for him.

'Will we be moving, sir?' she asked.

John paused in thought.

'No, Norah,' he said. 'We're staying here.'

'Oh, good, sir,' enthused Norah. 'We'll be nearer to madam, won't we?'

Funny woman, mused John, as he went down the wide steps that led to the front garden path. Kind woman, though, he decided as he realised that she echoed his own feelings.

He got the car out of the garage and drove to meet Derek Hillier at Falcon House.

Falcon House was a square, three-storied, red-brick building in the Queen Anne style with a pillared porch at the front and latticed shutters at the sash windows. The shutters had been made secure during the time that the house had been empty and as John drove through the gates and up the long gravel driveway he could see that they were still intact. No damage there.

Derek Hillier was waiting beside his own car as John pulled up at the front door.

'Looks all right at the front,' said John. 'No shutters missing.'

'None at the back, either,' Derek told him. 'But come inside.'

Derek led the way to the back of the house. As they came to the back door, which was half-timbered with a glass panel at the top, they stopped.

'That looks all right,' said John, standing back.

'Push it,' suggested Derek.

John pushed the door gently. It opened wide.

'The lock's been tampered with,' Derek explained.

'Professional?' asked John.

'Someone experienced, anyway. I'll have it done for you. Come inside.'

The estate agent led the way into the house. The lighting was dim because of the shuttered windows but there was nevertheless enough light to judge the condition of the rooms. Their footsteps echoed on the bare boards as they made their way to the kitchen area. Here there was evidence of people having prepared food and eaten at the kitchen table. The sink was full of empty cans and cartons of take-away food. Newspapers and magazines and more cans and cartons littered the floor. Empty beer cans and bottles of wine were to be seen everywhere. As they progressed to the other rooms they found sleeping bags, candles, quite a few candles, a portable radio, more cans and cartons. There was evidence of the inevitable condoms. When they came to the lavatories and bathrooms the sight and smell was disgusting because the water had been turned off so the toilets could not be flushed. As the house had been empty for so long all the services, such as water, gas and electricity had been disconnected, hence the abundance of candles.

John became more and more angry and depressed as he followed the agent over the building. The stench and desecration was sickening. There was less damage on the upper floors except, again, in the bathrooms and lavatories, so it was obvious that the squatting was confined to the ground floor. That was a slight relief for John who remembered how immaculate the house had appeared when he last went over it with Dot. That was a long time ago, of course.

On the way out of the house John kicked against something on the floor. He thought at first that it might be something nasty but he could just about see in the gloom that it was a grubby wallet. He picked it up gingerly. When he got outside in the light he examined it more carefully.

'This may give us a clue,' he said.

'What is it?' asked Derek.

'Looks like somebody's wallet. I kicked it just now.'

'Anything inside?'

John opened the wallet and took out the curled up, faded papers that were inside. They were photographs. One was of a group showing a bearded man, a woman and two children, a boy and a girl. The others were single pictures of the same children.

'Whoever owns this will probably come back looking for it,' suggested John. 'In which case we should get the police to keep watch.'

15

'What are you going to do about the damage?' asked Derek.

They began walking down towards their cars which were parked in the front of the house.

'I'll get in touch with the insurance people,' replied John. 'Breaking and entering and damage.'

'You'll need a decorator,' added Derek. 'You'll also need a cleaning company to clean the place and fumigate it.'

'I'll see to that,' John told him. 'I obviously can't sell the place until that's done and I can't have that done until the insurance is settled. A bit of a lost journey for you, Derek, I'm afraid.'

'Not at all. I can go ahead preparing the particulars. A good job we discovered it in time. I'll hold off the actual selling until I hear from you.'

'Yes. All right. I'll call at the police station on the way home and show them this,' said John, flourishing the wallet.

He flourished it again at the police station. He had been shown into the office of Detective Inspector Waller who examined the wallet with interest, particularly the photographs.

'Ah! Yes,' he exclaimed. 'That's him. He didn't always have the beard.'

'You recognise him?'

'You know who this is, don't you?' asked the Inspector.

'No idea,' admitted John, blithely.

'It's the tramp we pulled out of the river.'

'I was reading about that in the local. So he's the one who's been squatting in my house.'

'Looks like it.'

'That's the end of it, then,' concluded John.

He stood up and held out his hand.

'Don't go yet, Mr Rossiter,' said the Inspector. 'I don't think this is the end of it, as you say.'

'No?'

John sat down again.

'More like the beginning,' added the Inspector.

'Oh?'

'There's something I think you should know.'

John waited expectantly.

'The tramp we pulled out of the river wasn't drowned.'

'Wasn't he?'

'No. He was strangled before he went in the river.'

'Foul play, you mean?'

'Looks like murder, yes.'

'Could he have been murdered in my house?'

'If this wallet is anything to go by, yes.'

'I see.'

The lawyer in John Rossiter told him that he had a problem on his hands. Not only could he not repair the damage to Falcon House until the insurance claim was agreed he now had to wait for possible extensive investigations by the police murder squad.

'I'd better get a team together and have a look at your Falcon House, Mr Rossiter,' said the Inspector.

As John had expected. That meant fingerprint experts and possible forensic.

'By all means,' agreed John. 'I'll meet you there.'

He stood up.

'You coming now?' he asked.

'Right behind you,' the Inspector told him.

John drove back to Falcon House with mixed feelings. He was both angry and anxious. Once the story got out about a murder he would be faced with the possibility of a media invasion of the house and grounds, which didn't please him very much and would probably affect the eventual sale. And then there was the doubtful prospect of finding a purchaser. Who would want to live in a house where a murder had been committed?

He arrived at the house before the Inspector and paced about outside. What would Dot think of it all? he wondered. He didn't go inside for fear of disturbing something that might assist the police. The Inspector drove up on his own.

'I thought you were bringing a team,' John remarked.

17

'Fingerprint and forensic are following,' explained the Inspector.

John led the Inspector to the back door and showed him where the lock had been tampered with.

'Typical,' murmured the Inspector.

As John led him through the ground floor rooms the Inspector did not seem very impressed. He examined the sleeping bags, the candles, the bottles, the cans.

'A lot of candles,' he said.

'That's because of the shutters,' explained John. 'It's dark in here at night.'

'This is not Old Bill's scene, you know,' mused the Inspector.

'Old Bill?'

'The tramp. That's what he was known as.'

'Come upstairs,' said John.

John showed the Inspector the overflowing bathrooms and lavatories as they continued on their way to the attic rooms at the top of the house.

'This is more like it,' enthused the Inspector. 'This is more like Old Bill.'

Something about the orderliness of the remnants and belongings told the Inspector, from experience, that this is where the tramp would have made his quarters. Not for him the careless untidiness of the squatters.

'You think this is where Old Bill hung out?' asked John.

'No mistake about it,' the Inspector assured him. 'He was well known to us. He was no trouble in the summer months but always managed to get himself taken down during the winter. He couldn't stand the cold, you see.'

'Poor devil,' said John.

'That's his wife and family in the photographs. Taken a long time ago, of course. The children must be grown up and married by now.'

'And the wife?'

'Either dead or married again.'

'Nobody wanted him, I suppose.'

'Just the reverse. He didn't want them. He couldn't settle down. At least, that's what he always told us.'

'And you think he was murdered here?'

'Not necessarily here in the attic. In the house certainly. Probably downstairs where you found the wallet.'

As they made their noisy way down the bare stairs John said, 'You said he'd been strangled.'

'That's right. With a nylon rope.'

'Motive?'

'Anyone's guess.'

'Couldn't be for anything he had.'

'That's for sure.'

They reached the ground floor.

'I can't do anything,' complained John. 'I can't redecorate if your people are going over the place looking for clues, as you call them.'

'A few days should do it,' the Inspector suggested.

'Think so?'

'Hope so.'

'What about the squatters?' asked John.

'They've probably moved on.'

'If they have they've left their sleeping bags behind,' John pointed out.

'We'll keep our eyes open,' said the Inspector. 'But it's not really our province, squatting.'

'I know. It's the council. Thanks all the same.'

'I'll wait for the boys now.'

'I'll leave you to it, then.'

And so they parted, not knowing that they would meet again through extraordinary circumstances.

John was glad that he could dispose of Falcon House even though the actual date was some way ahead. As he drove home he was thankful that he didn't have to tell Dot about the vandalism to what was going to be their dream house. She certainly wouldn't have wanted to live there if she thought someone had been murdered in the house.

His visit had taken him longer than anticipated and

when Norah asked him if he would like some more tea he declined.

Norah could see that he was worried so she asked, 'Have they done much damage, sir?'

'I'm afraid so,' he replied.

'The devils.'

He didn't tell her about Old Bill. She would read it in the local paper soon enough. Instead of going into the drawing room John went into his study. He thought he'd go through the photo albums and pick out a snapshot of Dot to have enlarged and framed. As he sat turning the pages memories came flooding back to him, memories of holidays in the sun, in the walled garden of the present house, first attempts at taking photographs indoors. The whole exercise was a form of masochism, perhaps, but he enjoyed the moments of nostalgia that it evoked. He came across an already enlarged picture of Dot's head and shoulders made from a snapshot he remembered taking in the South of France. It was a happy, laughing picture but for some unknown reason she never liked it so it was never framed. He remembered that, according to Dot, the hair wasn't quite right but he liked it nevertheless. He decided to frame it and hang it there in his study. He took it out of the album and held it against a blank part of the wall. That's where he'd hang it. He'd do it now. There was an empty frame in the cupboard in the study. It was the one he was going to use in the first place before Dot's veto. He found the frame, put it on his desk and inserted the picture. He then went in search of a hammer and a picture hook. He did not want to bother Norah or her husband. There was a cabinet at the top of the cellar stairs where various tools were kept. He rummaged about in the cabinet, found a hammer but could not find any picture hooks. Disappointed, he returned to his study. He held the picture against the wall once more and studied it. He'd go down to the hardware shop in the morning. He knew what he wanted, one of those sharp nails that go into the wall at a slight angle to hold the hook.

In the meantime he had to go to bed. That was something he dreaded these days. He suddenly disliked the
night. He didn't sleep very well. He would keep going over
in his mind the last days with Dot and wondering if he
did enough for her. Although sleep evaded him he was
too tired to do anything else, such as reading. He actually
wished the night away. Dot's bed beside him was still made
up and turned down for her to get into. He insisted on
that routine with Norah. It was the interminable darkness
and being too tired that upset him. He fell asleep, however, without knowing it. His last thought was of his visit
to the hardware shop, a mundane enough experience for
a successful lawyer. He was not to know that the visit
would eventually tax his professional expertise to the limit.

The hardware store in Ambleford was owned by a
bearded old man named Steven Harcourt. It had been
established for so long that nobody could remember when
it wasn't owned by a Harcourt. It had been in the Harcourt
family for generations and each generation of ironmon-
gers, as they called themselves, sported a full beard. It was
their trademark. The store sold everything from a shovel
to a nail. The wooden floor of the shop was so well worn
that knots and smooth nail heads protruded to trip the
unwary. Behind the long, crowded counter was a range of
fitted drawers and old Harcourt knew what was in each
one of them. Items for sale hung on the walls and from
the ceiling, to say nothing of the goods displayed halfway
across the pavement outside the shop – dustbins, buckets,
mops, wheelbarrows, roofing felt.

When John Rossiter entered the shop there were no
other customers and old Harcourt was nowhere to be seen.

John called out, 'Shop!'

Very soon the old man, all of 80 years of age, came
shuffling from somewhere at the back of the shop.

'Hello, Mr Rossiter,' he wheezed. 'Sorry to keep you
waiting.'

'That's all right, Mr Harcourt.'

'What can I do for you?'

'Well, now. What I want is a picture hook.'

'Just one?'

'Well...'

'Do you want the kind of hook that goes over the picture rail?'

'No. I'd like the kind that goes into the wall. The nail has a very sharp point that goes through the hook at an angle to hold it.'

'I know. They come in packets.'

'All right. I'll have a packet.'

'Hold on.'

Stephen Harcourt shuffled off down the counter in search of the required hooks. While he was waiting John wandered about the shop looking at the enormous variety of gadgets and innovations to help housewives in the kitchen and amateur carpenters in the tool shed.

'It amazes me that you know where anything is in this Aladdin's cave,' remarked John.

'I know where everything is,' replied old Harcourt. 'All I have to do is remember where.'

He came to John with the packet of picture hooks.

'That suit you?' he asked.

'Just the job.'

John saw the price on the packet and put his hand in his pocket for the money.

'I suppose people buy some of these new-fangled gadgets,' commented John.

'Oh, aye. You'd be surprised. Nothing lasts in stock very long.'

John noticed two or three common white candles in an open box on the counter. He recalled the candles that had been left behind by the squatters at Falcon House.

'You don't sell many candles these days, do you?' he asked.

'Candles?' echoed old Harcourt. 'I'm almost out of stock. Didn't think I'd need to stock many these summer months. Sold a whole packet a little while ago.'

'You did?' said John, suddenly interested.

'I thought it odd at the time.'

'Why?'

'Light evenings. No power cuts.'

'Do you remember who bought them?'

'Some girl. Don't know her name. Local. Seen her about.'

'Would you recognise her again?'

'Oh, yes.'

'What was she like?'

'Student type. Shirt and jeans.'

'Anything on the shirt?'

'No. But she filled it well,' grinned old Harcourt.

Fat lot of good, thought John. Eliminate all flat-chested students. On the other hand, does it mean that the squatters were local? Their sleeping bags were still in the house. Surely they would have taken them away if they were itinerant squatters. John leaned towards the old man conspiratorially.

'If you see her again let me know,' he confided.

'Let you know?' asked the old man, puzzled.

'It's rather important.'

'All right, Mr Rossiter. If you say so.'

'Don't forget.'

'I won't.'

After John Rossiter had left the shop the old man wondered why on earth the lawyer should be interested in a common student and her candles. He felt quite perplexed.

Nearly as perplexed as John Rossiter himself. He just couldn't believe that the squatters were local. What would be the point? There were no homeless in Ambleford. And it was obvious that the unknown student-type was local because old Harcourt said he had seen her around the town. The student squatters that he had heard of were permanent and usually protesting about something. They didn't indulge in squatting picnic-fashion as would appear to be the case at Falcon House. He would pass on his suspicions to Inspector Waller.

He called on him at the police station on his way home.

'There were certainly a lot of candles about the place,' admitted the Inspector. 'Because of the poor light in the house at night, as you said.'

'It's obvious they came from Harcourt's.'

'Not necessarily. Coincidence. I doubt if old Harcourt could recognise them. After all, a candle is a candle. It's circumstantial at the moment.'

'I can take one to show him.'

'That's up to you. I can't do anything about squatters, Mr Rossiter. You know that. Squatting comes under the local council. I'm only concerned with the murder of Old Bill.'

'The squatters may know something about it.'

'I doubt it.'

'I'll keep a watch on the place tonight and see if they come back. That way, at least, we'll know who they were.'

'Let me know how you get on.'

'I will.'

Not very helpful, decided John, as he left the station. If the squatters were student types, as old Harcourt's observation seemed to suggest, then he would agree with the Inspector that they could know nothing about the murder. What connection could there be between them? If the squatters were local students, as seemed likely, the whole escapade might be a game. They weren't crooks and murderers. A youthful dare was one thing, cold-blooded murder was another. Nevertheless he would drive up to Falcon House after dinner and see what was going on.

Once home John busied himself with the task of hanging Dot's picture, about 18 inches square, showing her relaxed and laughing in the sun, just as he liked to remember her. Her laugh was always encouraging. That was the word for it. He couldn't understand why she didn't like the picture. It was completely unposed. He found the facial expression carefree, almost childlike. He felt happy when he looked at it. He called Norah to look at his handiwork.

'There,' he declared. 'What do you think of that?'

'Oh, very nice, sir,' enthused Norah. 'Just like her.'

'Isn't it?'

Of course it's like her, he nearly told Norah, because it happens to be her. Rather than upset the poor dear he let the remark go unsaid.

'Will you be in to lunch, sir?' asked Norah.

The mundane request brought John down to earth from his reverie.

'What? Yes. Oh, yes. Of course.'

He was still gazing at the picture when Norah went out of the room.

'Very nice, sir,' repeated Norah as she closed the door.

Lunch, thought John. What did it matter? The poor woman had to have a routine, he supposed. She ran the house and had her husband to think of. He didn't fancy sitting in the dining room on his own, though. She was probably cooking something with vegetables. He didn't fancy that, either.

He went to the door and called, 'Norah!'

'Sir?' came the answer as Norah backtracked on the way to the kitchen.

'Could I have a tray in the study?'

'Of course, sir.'

'Thank you.'

He went back into the study and closed the door. He sat in his favourite wing chair, which was a recliner, and studied the *Times* crossword. He felt sleepy. He pushed the chair into the semi-reclining position and dozed off. He had noticed that lately he had become sleepy both before and after lunch; before perhaps, because he needed food and after, perhaps, because he had eaten it. The phenomenon amused him.

At any event, after dinner that evening he drove out to Falcon House to see what was going on – if anything. And nothing was going on. He took a torch with him and went over the whole building. It was completely deserted. There was still the evidence of squatting that he had pointed out to Inspector Waller but nothing else. The story of the tramp being pulled out of the river may have frightened them away. News of the murder had not yet been released so it couldn't be that. John returned home none the wiser.

However, one morning a few days later old Steven Harcourt was standing in the doorway of his little emporium watching the world go by, just looking up and down the street out of mild curiosity. It was close to midday and any moment he would be busy with customers making their purchases during their lunch hour. The shop opposite was called, simply, Angela, and dealt in ladies' requirements – dresses, underwear, stockings and so on. It was a double-fronted shop similar to his own.

He saw a white, drop-head sports car pull up outside the shop. It was driven by a handsome young man wearing a striped woollen scarf of inordinate length and a yellowing straw hat. A typical student, decided Steven Harcourt, knowing from experience that the universities were still on holiday. The young man sounded the horn in a rhythmic, staccato fashion and continued to do so until the door of the dress shop opened and a young girl came hurrying out and got into the car which drove away with a roar, driver and passenger laughing happily.

'Where did you find this?' asked the girl.

'Saw it outside the King's Head,' the boy replied.

'Whose is it?'

'God knows.'

'Where are we going?'

'Bert's.'

'How long are you going to keep it?'

'I'll take it back after Bert's. No one will see me then.'

Borrowing cars for short periods, as opposed to stealing them, was the latest game some of the students played while they were 'down', as they called it. They invariably got away with it, the owner being completely unaware that the car had been taken away and returned while he was at a meeting or even at work.

Steven Harcourt recognised the girl as the one who had

26

bought all those candles. He was able to make a note of the number of the car. He moved back inside his shop and made for the telephone. He looked up John Rossiter's number in the directory and dialled it. John answered the call himself.

'Mr Rossiter?'

'Speaking.'

'I've seen her.'

'Seen who?'

'The girl who bought the candles.'

'Oh, good. Where is she?'

'She went off with a man in a sports car. I've got the number.'

'I've got a pencil. What is it?'

Steven Harcourt pronounced the number clearly and carefully.

'L52 GCF.'

'L52 GCF,' John repeated. 'I've got it. Thanks.'

'I can't tell you any more. Except the man looked like any other student. Long scarf and straw hat.'

'Thank you, Mr Harcourt.'

'That all?'

'Yes. Thank you.'

'Thank you,' repeated Steven Harcourt and put the phone down, still wondering why John Rossiter was interested.

John, on the other hand, immediately rang Inspector Waller.

'Inspector,' he announced happily, 'I've traced the girl who bought the candles.'

'I told you, Mr Rossiter,' said the Inspector, patiently, 'squatters come under the local council. Vandalism we can deal with, squatters no. Unless, of course, they cut up rough and we're called in.'

'I know all that, Inspector, but these squatters, who appear to be mere students, must have had some contact with your Old Bill if they were all in the same building.'

'That's true.'

'I would have thought it was worth having a word with the girl.'

'Where do I find her?'

The Inspector appeared to be coming round to John's way of thinking.

'That I don't know,' admitted John, who heard the Inspector's gasp of exasperation. 'But according to Steven Harcourt she went off a while ago in a white sports car driven by another student type. Registration number L52 GCF.'

'What? What was that number?' asked the Inspector, suddenly interested.

'L52 GCF,' repeated John.

'Hang on,' urged the Inspector.

John waited for the Inspector to resume the conversation.

'You there?' he asked.

'Yes.'

'That car's just been reported stolen.'

'Ah!' exclaimed John.

'Thank you, Mr Rossiter,' concluded the Inspector. 'We'll go after them.'

'Good luck,' said John.

He began to see a pattern of student behaviour, a pattern of 'dares'; squatting and stealing cars for joy riding. But he still didn't think that the murder of Old Bill could be among their little games, though they may be able to throw some light on it.

Steven Harcourt was surprised to be visited by the police. A patrol car pulled up outside his shop and two police officers entered.

'Morning, Mr Harcourt,' said one of the officers.

'Hello, Harvey,' cried Mr Harcourt, in surprise. 'What are you doing here?'

28

'You said you saw a white sports car drive away from here.'

'That's right.'

'Which way did it go?'

'Straight out of town. Like a rocket.'

'Thanks.'

Again, to Steven Harcourt's surprise, the two policemen hurried out of the shop, got into their patrol car and drove away.

It did not take them long to find the stolen car. It was parked outside a roadside cafe frequented by lorry drivers and known as Bert's Caff, about four miles outside Ambleford. It was little more than a lock-up shack with no accommodation but managed to produce popular food and snacks. It opened at six o'clock in the morning and did not close until dusk. It was owned by Bert Whittle who ran it with his wife. He was a burly ex-circus pugilist. In recent months a few students had adopted it as a meeting place where they would sit drinking coffee and making it last as long as possible.

The police car spotted the sports car outside Bert's. Both uniformed officers entered the building.

'Morning, Bert,' said one of them to the owner who was serving up sausage and mash behind the counter.

'Morning, Harvey,' returned Bert.

A couple of lorry drivers sat at one of the tables drinking strong tea. At the far end of the room sat the two students. The boy was still wearing his straw hat and the scarf that trailed on the floor.

Harvey, the patrolman, called out:

'Is the owner of L52 GCF here?'

Nobody answered.

The patrolman approached the two lorry drivers.

'What's the number of your vehicle, mate?' he asked one.

'UMG 756,' the driver replied.

'And yours?' he asked the other driver.

'KDC 486,' was the reply.

The patrolman approached the young couple at the far end of the room.

'What's the registration number of your car, sir?' he asked.

The young man looked up and regarded the officer disdainfully.

'I beg your pardon,' he said in his best drawl.

'What is the registration number of your car?' the officer repeated.

'To tell you the truth, officer,' said the student, 'I don't really know. I've just taken delivery of it, you see and I haven't memorised the number yet. Why? Is it in the way?'

'For your information, sir,' explained the officer, 'the car is stolen.'

'What!' exclaimed the student, indignantly. 'The man who sold it to me...'

The officer interrupted the young student.

'Nobody sold it to you, sir. The car was stolen an hour ago from the King's Head car park.'

'Oh,' remarked the young man. 'Was it?'

He turned to the girl who was looking rather frightened.

'What do you make of that?' he asked, innocently.

'I think you'd better come with me to the station,' suggested the officer.

'What station?' asked the young man, insolently.

'The police station, sir,' explained the officer, patiently.

'Oh. That one. Why should I go there?'

'You are in possession of a stolen car, sir.'

'Inadvertently.'

'Come along, sir. If you please,' urged the officer.

'Yes. All right,' said the student, standing up, wearily. 'Anything to oblige.'

You, too, young lady,' added the patrolman.

'What do you want me for?' protested the girl.

'If you don't come willingly, miss, I'll have to arrest you.'

'Come on, Karen,' urged the young man. 'It could be fun.'

He helped her to her feet and took her arm as they followed the policeman out of the cafe.

Once they'd gone one of the lorry drivers called out to the owner, 'What's that all about, Bert?'

'Kids,' scoffed Bert. 'They get up to anything these days.'

'Know 'em, do you?'

'Yes. They're often in here. They and the others. I wish they'd stay away. They think it's fun to come to a place like this. Sometimes they nearly fill the room. They don't spend much.'

'Who are they?'

'Students.'

'Oh,' conceded the lorry driver. ''Nuff said.'

At the police station, apart from giving the police his name and address, which was Tom Parker, The Vicarage, Ambleford, the student would give no other information. He was passed from the duty officer at the front desk to Inspector Waller in one of the interview rooms where he lounged nonchalantly in a chair with his legs crossed. He was a handsome young man of 19 years of age with fair, wavy hair, something of a baby face and a weak mouth.

'Evidently you're not prepared to help us with our enquiries, Mr Parker,' said the Inspector.

'I'm not prepared to help the police in any way whatever,' declared Tom Parker.

'We know that you are the son of the vicar of St Augustine's and that you live at the vicarage with your parents when you are not at university. Apart from the present charge of car stealing are you prepared to tell us what you know about the goings on recently at Falcon House?'

'No.'

'We suspect that you and your friends have been squatting there but that's not our concern. That's local council business. What is our business, though, is the sudden increase of joy riding, stealing cars and leaving them abandoned, as in your case, Mr Parker.'

'I didn't steal the car. I borrowed it. I wasn't going to abandon it. I was going to take it back.'

'So you say.'

'I told Karen. You can ask her.'

'It was still taken without permission.'

'A quibble.'

'A crime.'

There was a silence between them.

'By the way,' said the Inspector, at length, 'do you want us to tell your parents where you are?'

'Not necessarily.'

'Won't they worry?'

'Why should they?'

'Up to you. You know, this car stealing business only seems to happen when you and your friends are down from university.'

'Really?'

'Don't you find that a coincidence?'

'Not particularly.'

'What is your relationship with the girl in the car?'

'None of your business.'

'Her name evidently is Karen Rossiter. She is at present being questioned by my sergeant.'

'She doesn't know anything. She wasn't with me when I took the car.'

'You went with her to Falcon House, though, didn't you?'

'No comment.'

'You know that Falcon House belongs to her uncle.'

'Does it?'

'You also know that a tramp known as Old Bill was fished out of the river recently.'

'Was he?'

'Didn't you read about it in the paper?'

'I don't read papers. Load of rubbish.'

'Everyone presumed he was drowned.'

'Did they?'

'But he wasn't. He was strangled before being thrown in the river.'

'Was he? Hard luck.'

'He was murdered.'

'Sounds like it.'

'We think he was murdered at Falcon House.'

'Why?'

'Because he was dossing there. Where you and your friends have been squatting lately.'

'Really.'

'There are sleeping bags and the usual squatters' clobber up there still.'

'Is that so?'

'And a lot of candles. Candles which, we believe, were purchased by Karen Rossiter at Steven Harcourt's shop.'

'Oh, yes?'

'You've nothing to say about all that?'

'Nothing at all.'

'I think you and your friends are spoilt, vain and conceited.'

'How kind of you.'

'I'll have some more questions to ask you later on. In the meantime, you will be locked up, of course.'

'Please yourself.'

He stood up and waited to be escorted to the cells.

In another interview room Sergeant Skinner was questioning Karen Rossiter. She wasn't at all arrogant. She was actually frightened. She was an attractive, dark-haired girl of no more than 18. Her figure was hidden in a shirt and jeans.

'I wish you'd tell me what I've done wrong,' she insisted.

'That depends how much you were involved in stealing the car,' explained the Sergeant.

'I told you. I was in Angela's dress shop when Tom tooted outside. I simply got in and he drove away.'

'Pre-arranged?'

'What do you mean?'

'Were you waiting for him?'

'No. It was a surprise.'

'How did he know you were there?'

'I probably mentioned it the evening before.'

'Had he done it before?'

'Done what?'

'Surprised you with a stolen car.'

Karen hesitated, troubled.

'I don't want to get him into trouble,' she said, quietly.

'He's in trouble already.'

'He'll manage. He doesn't actually steal cars. He borrows them. Then he takes them back.'

'I'm not concerned with that at the moment.'

'What are you concerned with?'

'Candles.'

'Candles?'

'Yes. You bought a large packet of candles from Harcourt's store.'

'Yes.'

'Why?'

'Because I wanted them.'

'What did you want them for? It's summer. Light evenings.'

'I thought they'd make a nice show.'

'Where? You didn't take them home.'

'How do you know?'

'You took them to Falcon House, didn't you?'

'Well, yes. As a matter of fact I did.'

'Your uncle's house.'

'Yes.'

'Why did you choose that house in particular?'

'I didn't think Uncle would mind. It was family, anyway.'

'What did you take them there for?'

'Light, of course. It was dark with the shutters closed. With the candles we could read and play music.'

'We?'

'Yes.'

'Who is we?'

'Me and Tom.'

'Who else?'

'I can't give people away. You should know that.'

'A gang of you?'

'Sort of.'

'All students?'

'No.'

'Who broke in? The door was tampered with.'

'I don't know. It was open when we got there. We were going to put everything right when we left. It was Uncle's. He wouldn't have minded.'

'What about the graffiti? Would you put that right, too?'

'Yes. We'd clean it up before we went back.'

'To university.'

'Yes.'

'There was someone else in the house, wasn't there? As well as you lot.'

'We didn't think so.'

'But there was, wasn't there?'

'What? Yes.'

'Who?'

'I can't answer any more.'

Karen took refuge in tears which caused Sergeant Skinner to hesitate before pressing on with the interrogation. He waited patiently until she had finished what he called 'her wee cry'. He was convinced in his own mind that the tears were an attempt to put him off his line of enquiry.

When she stopped crying and blew her nose he said, 'Can we go back to the candles?'

'What about them?' she snivelled.

'Why did you buy so many?'

Karen took a sharp breath to save herself from crying again.

'I told you. It was dark in there because of the shutters. It was dangerous. Tom nearly fell down the stairs once.'

'The stairs.'

'Yes.'

'All the sleeping bags were on the ground floor.'

'We didn't stay on the ground floor.'

'That's what I mean. You moved about the house.'

'Of course.'

'In that case, did you meet anyone upstairs?'

'Only our own gang if we had a picnic.'

'You didn't meet an old tramp?'

'No.'

'You're sure?'

'I didn't meet anyone.'

Sergeant Skinner didn't believe her.

'You're quite sure?'

'Quite sure.'

'You read about the tramp being fished out of the river, didn't you?'

'Yes.'

'He wasn't drowned, you know?'

'It said he was.'

'The post-mortem showed that he'd been strangled before being thrown in the river.'

'Oh, no!'

'You're surprised?'

'Of course I'm surprised.'

'Everything points to him being murdered.'

'Murdered?'

'Well, he couldn't strangle himself and then fall in the river, could he?'

'No, of course not.'

'What's more everything points to him being murdered as Falcon House.'

'Where we were?'

'Yes. He was dossing there.'

'Where? I didn't see him.'

She's still making out she didn't know he was there, noticed the Sergeant.

'He was on the top floor.'

'I didn't go up that far.'

'You're sure?'

'Quite sure.'

'You know, you can distort the truth in your statement to me but once you get into court that distortion becomes perjury and the penalty for that is a prison sentence.'

'Court? I don't have to go to court, do I?'

'As a witness, yes.'

'Witness to what?'

'The stolen car.'

'I didn't see him steal it.'

'He told you he'd stolen it, didn't he?'

'He told me he borrowed it.'

'Same thing. You knew it wasn't his car and you were the passenger.'

'Yes.'

'It wasn't the first time. You were used to him turning up with a different car every now and then.'

'Well, boys are like that about cars, aren't they?'

'They didn't all steal them.'

'He always took them back. I told you.'

'Did anyone else in your lot borrow cars, as you call it?'

'I don't know.'

'How many of you used to meet at Falcon House?'

'I don't know.'

'You're not being very helpful, are you, Miss Rossiter?'

'I've told you all I know.'

'I don't think you have.'

'I have! I have!' shouted Karen, in a temper. Sergeant Skinner ignored the outburst which brought on more tears.

'I'm afraid we'll have to keep you here for further questioning, Miss.'

'Keep me? What do you mean? You can't do that!'

Karen stood up, defiantly.

'Got a lawyer, have you?'

'Yes. My uncle.'

'You'd better get him on the phone.'

Karen produced a mobile telephone from her pocket and dialled a number. It wasn't her uncle's number, it was her mother. Sergeant Skinner sat casually listening to the conversation or, rather, what he could hear of one side of it.

Susan Rossiter took the call in the hall.

As soon as she recognised the voice she cried, 'Karen! Where are you? Why didn't you come home to lunch?'

'I'm at the police station, Mummy.'

'Police station? What are you doing there?'

'I've been arrested.'

Susan made a noise that was more like a shriek than a cry of alarm. She dropped the telephone and sank into the chair beside the table. The phone dangled from its cord.

'Hello. Hello,' repeated Karen.

A very faint Susan returned to the telephone.

'I'll get in touch with your uncle,' she said weakly and hung up.

'Mummy's ringing my uncle,' Karen told Sergeant Skinner.

'Good,' muttered the Sergeant. 'Let's play Happy Families while we're waiting.'

John Rossiter was enjoying his usual afternoon tea in his study. He particularly enjoyed Norah's home-made jam tarts. He cast occasional glances at the photograph of Dot and wondered what she would say if she could see it there. It wouldn't be there if she were still alive, of course. She would never have allowed him to hang it. He was studying the picture when the telephone rang shrilly, disturbing his peace. He picked it up, reluctantly.

'Hello.'

'John!'

Oh, God, he realised. It's Susan.

'Susan, what are you shouting for?'

'Karen's been arrested.'

'Has she?'

'Is that all you can say? Has she?'

'What am I supposed to say?'

'I want you to help her.'

'How?'

'Go to the police station and get her out, for God's sake.'
'I can't do that unless I know why she was arrested.'
'Her boyfriend stole a car.'
'Who's her boyfriend?'
'Tom Parker.'
'The vicar's son?'
'Yes.'
'Vicar's son steals car. I can see the headline.'
'Karen was with him.'
'When he stole it?'
'No. Oh, I don't know. Help her, John. Please.'
'All right. I'll go and see what I can do.'
'Oh, thank you, John. Thank you.'
'Mind you, if they stole a car they deserve to be arrested.'
'She didn't steal it.'
'How do you know?'
'She told me.'
'Judging by her present behaviour one wonders if she's telling the truth.'
'John, I assure you...'
John suddenly became impatient with his sister-in-law.
'Oh, get off the line, for God's sake, woman,' he cried, 'and let me see what I can do.'
With Susan sill spluttering at the end of the line John put the phone down. He finished his tea at his leisure and set off to see Inspector Waller.

'What can I do for you, Mr Rossiter?' asked the Inspector as John sat down in his office.
'You've got a niece of mine here,' said John, without aggression.
'That's right, Karen Rossiter.'
'She didn't steal the car herself, she says, so she's at worst an accessory after the fact. If that, since she was only a passenger in the car.'
'She is also the girl who bought the candles.'
'What!'

The Inspector laughed at John's reaction.

'Steven Harcourt recognised her getting in the car outside Angela's. Evidently a little gang of them have been camping out in your house.'

'The buggers,' muttered John.

'Oh, according to my Sergeant they were going to clean up the place before they went back to university, but I'm more interested to learn what they know, if anything, about Old Bill.'

'Of course,' agreed John.

'Interesting, isn't it?'

'Very.'

John allowed a moment of silence before he said, 'In the meantime, I'm prepared to stand surety for my niece so that I can take her home.'

'That's all right. She's not all that important. It's her boyfriend, Tom, who holds the key to our questions. He stole the car but refuses to cooperate.'

'Bad sign.'

'Certainly is. From his point of view. I want to know who made up the gang and where they are now. If they were all in the house together they must have met Old Bill. Tom Parker won't tell us.'

'Karen might help us if I talk to her nicely. But not here.'

'That's an idea. See what you can find out.'

'Stupid buggers,' muttered John again.

John visited Karen in her cell, a confinement that he thought both unnecessary and illegal. As soon as the cell door opened the girl, who was sitting dejectedly on the trestle bed, jumped up and ran to him, flinging her arms round his neck.

'Oh, Uncle John!' she cried. 'I'm sorry.'

She burst into tears for the third time since her arrest.

'Tears won't help, dear,' said John.

He led her back to the bed and sat beside her.

'We need to talk, Karen.'

'Yes.'

'But not here.'

'They won't let me go. They want to ask me more questions.'

'I'm asking them now.'

'You?'

'Yes. I'm taking you home first.'

'You are?' Karen asked, excitedly.

'I'm afraid they won't release your boyfriend.'

'He's not my boyfriend.'

'Whatever he is. They're keeping him because he refuses to cooperate.'

'What do you mean?'

'He won't answer their questions.'

'Oh, he's like that. Can you help him?'

'I haven't been instructed.'

'I'm sure his father would want you to.'

'I can't take that for granted.'

'Can you ring him and find out?'

'No. Unethical.'

'Oh, really!'

'Yes, my dear. Really. Just as it is unethical to borrow a car without the owner's permission. In any case, your mother asked me to help you, not your boyfriend.'

'They won't let me speak to him.'

'Of course not. That's called collusion.'

'I might have been able to persuade him.'

'They're keeping you apart so there's no collusion in your statements.'

'How awful.'

'Never mind. Let's go home.'

'Can we?'

'Trust your Uncle.'

He took her hand and led her out of the cell and out of the station, waving a cheery goodbye to the duty officer at the desk.

In the car John said, 'I suppose we've got to suffer the

41

reunion with your mother. All the questions and answers and reasons, whyfores and wherefores.'

Karen knew what he meant and laughed.

'So I suggest,' John went on, 'we put up with it and then, when things settle down, sometime after dinner you come over to my place and talk. You're not off the hook yet, you know.'

'No,' Karen admitted. 'I know.'

Karen was very fond of her strange uncle. She had spent her life listening to her mother complaining to her father about him, his terrible manners, his language, his drinking, his outrageous behaviour, how he was always letting the side down, whatever that meant. Considering that her father was more Rossiter than her mother, Karen thought her mother's criticism was misplaced. Karen, at least, knew which side she herself was on.

Susan Rossiter greeted her daughter as if she had been abducted, raped and forcibly imprisoned. She had, in fact, been away from home only a few hours and had missed lunch, which she did most days. Susan wept and wailed.

'Oh, thank you, John,' she cried. 'Thank you for rescuing my little girl.'

'You mean I've done something right?' asked John.

'Oh, John,' moaned Susan, 'this is no time to bicker.'

Frank Rossiter arrived home from the City to find some kind of conference taking place in his drawing room and, of course, he wanted to know what it was all about.

'Susan will tell you, Frank,' said John, eagerly. 'In a nutshell, Karen has been playing silly buggers with her student friends and had a brush with the law and I'm going home. Goodbye.'

'Won't you have a drink?' Fred asked, as if it was a social visit his brother was making.

'No, thanks.'

John let himself out of the house, relieved not to be part

of the family post-mortem that was surely about to take place.

He hadn't been home five minutes before the telephone rang. He answered it. It was Susan.

'You again?' he asked, irritably. 'What now?'

'Will all this be in the papers?' she asked.

'How do I know?'

'Oh, John,' she went on. 'It would be terrible. Think of our reputation as a family. What would people say? You know the editor of the local rag. Couldn't you get him to keep it out?'

'Have you finished?' asked John, patiently.

'John, I'm worried.'

'Susan, the vicar's son may be in the paper if he's charged with stealing cars but Karen hasn't been charged with anything.'

'Hasn't she?'

'Not yet.'

'Not yet?' echoed Susan, in alarm.

'No.'

'Then why did they arrest her?'

'They didn't arrest her. They invited her to the station as an accessory for questioning.'

'But she was locked up.'

'She wasn't. She waited in a cell because there was nowhere else for her to wait. All the other rooms were occupied. The cell door wasn't locked.'

'Talk to her, John. Try to find out what it's all about.'

'That's what I'm trying to do and it doesn't help for you to keep putting your spoke in.'

'Oh. All right.'

She put the telephone down abruptly and John sighed with relief. He began to piece the items together on paper, items that he had so far gathered from his meetings with Karen and the Inspector. He was convinced that there was no malice behind the stupid adventures of his niece and Tom Parker. The car borrowing, a kind of student dare, had obviously gone wrong. Presumably, in the past, the boy had managed to return the cars without their having been missed. Was Karen always the passenger on the joyrides or were there other girls? She had said that the vicar's son was not her boyfriend so that meant that there was nothing permanent in their relationship. When the police patrol caught up with the car the passenger could have been any other girl, any other member of the gang. Who? And how many were there? If they all met at Falcon House they must have come into contact with Old Bill. It was tempting to visualise Old Bill as a ragged, bearded character, wearing several waistcoats and overcoats. But according to the pictures he'd seen the man was tall, upright, bearded certainly, but clean with it. A misfit, one who'd given up on society. John didn't think for one moment that Karen, in particular, had anything to do with Old Bill's murder or even knew of it. Did any of them? Then why was Tom being so tight-lipped? Was that student defiance? After all, car stealing was straightforward. There was nothing mysterious about it, no reason for him to be so uncommunicative. Perhaps he was merely sulking. None of it would do his family's reputation any good, of course. The vicar, the boy's father, would know how to cope with that in his profession. More than likely his congregation would increase out of personal sympathy. Susan's reputation can only be slightly affected since Karen was only a passenger in the car. Knowing Susan, that would be enough to turn her into a recluse but Frank wouldn't worry. Girls will be boys, he'd say.

When Norah came into the study to tell John that dinner was ready he told her about the goings-on at Falcon House.

'Stupid idiots,' he concluded. 'Evidently my niece and some of her student friends have been making free with it.'

'Oh,' said Norah. 'You mean Tom Parker and that lot.'

'You know them?'

'I don't know them, no,' admitted Norah. 'My Harry and I have seen them about. Six of them.'

'As many as that?'

'Always together, they are. We didn't know they were using your house. We never knew where they went. They were always noisy, larking about and pushing each other as they went along. Like a lot of hooligans.'

'Hooligans is right,' agreed John, as he sat at the table.

Very revealing, he thought to himself as Norah went out of the room. He could imagine the gang 'larking about', as Norah put it, forcing people off the pavement in their exuberance. John could name two of the gang. Who were the other four? That's what he must find out.

After John's solitary dinner Karen arrived, not in her usual jeans and sweater but a blue skirt, silk stockings and a blue jacket over a white blouse. Obviously her mother had advised her to try to make a good impression.

'Come in, Karen,' John greeted her. 'Make yourself at home.'

Karen sat in one of the armchairs by the fireplace in the study and John sat in the other. Karen crossed her legs elegantly and John recorded in his mind how attractive she looked.

'Would you like a drink, dear?' he asked.

'No, thank you,' replied Karen, in a small voice.

'Now then,' John began. 'Let's start at the beginning.'

Karen told John that she was having a cup of coffee in Bert's Caff with Tom Parker when the police came in and started asking questions about Tom's car.

John didn't interrupt but this was not what he wanted to hear. Tom had taken the car, she explained, as a dare. He had done it before. It was a joke. He always took them back after a couple of hours.

'Are you sure he took them back?' asked John.

'Oh, yes. Positive.'

'Sometimes they were abandoned, weren't they?'

'Not abandoned. It wasn't always possible to return them to the exact spot.'

'Why not?'

'People about. That sort of thing. But they were returned as near as possible to where they were taken.'

45

'That was a mark of honour, was it? Returning them to the same spot.'

'You could say that, I suppose.'

'It's all rather puerile, isn't it?'

'You could say that, too, I suppose, depending how old you are.'

'Except that car stealing is illegal.'

'Tom didn't call it stealing.'

'Borrowing. I know. It's still illegal.'

'It was only a dare. Nothing criminal.'

John decided to stop Karen's inconsequential prattle with a sudden shock question.

'What were you doing buying all those candles from Harcourt's store?' Karen was momentarily nonplussed but she soon recovered.

'You, too?' she asked.

'What does that mean?'

'The police kept on at me about candles.'

'You know why, don't you?'

'No.'

'There were candles all over the place at Falcon House.'

'We needed them because it was so dark inside.'

'Why pick on Falcon House for your silly japes?'

'Because the others said I knew the owner, which was you, so we wouldn't be had up for trespass. I didn't think you'd mind.'

'You didn't think I'd mind you desecrating my property.'

'We were going to clean it up before we went back. It was all in fun.'

'Fun? Meeting your boyfriend Tom and making love by candlelight.'

'We didn't...'

'Don't try to deny it, dear. There were condoms all over the floor.'

'I wasn't denying it. I said Tom is not my boyfriend.'

'Fine. So while you were making love in the candlelight with your boyfriend, whoever he is, Tom was making love in the candlelight with his girlfriend, whoever she is.'

'Something like that.'

'Did you ever see anything of a tramp known as Old Bill?'

'I don't know anything about a tramp.'

'No?'

'No.'

'You're lying.'

'Uncle John!'

'Go home.'

'What?'

'Go home. Tell your mother to find another lawyer.'

Karen burst into tears. John stood up and moved to his desk and started shuffling papers unnecessarily while he was waiting for her to leave.

'You've got nothing to worry about,' he said, grimly. 'When Tom Parker's case comes up you'll be called as a witness and that'll be the end of it. So go away and tell your mother what I said.'

Karen stood up and hurried over to her uncle and clutched his sleeve.

'Uncle. Please,' she pleaded.

John turned and pushed her away.

'Go and sit down.'

Dutifully Karen returned to her chair while John paced up and down the room.

'There's more in this Falcon House business than appears on the surface. I'm convinced of it. This is not just a case of trespass and borrowing cars.'

He stopped in front of Karen's chair and looked down at her.

'I'll give you one more chance,' he said. 'I want the names of all the people who went with you to Falcon House.'

'I can't do that.'

'Why not?'

'I can't.'

'It's no good snivelling and saying you can't, you can't. You're just a handful of kids pretending to be gangsters with a code of ethics. Mustn't give anyone away. Is that it?'

'I don't know.'

'A man has been murdered. You know that, don't you?'

'The Sergeant mentioned it.'

'The Sergeant mentioned it,' repeated John, with irony. 'Like mentioning the weather. He was squatting in my house and you didn't see him.'

'No.'

'You had no idea he was there.'

'No.'

'So you couldn't have done it, then, could you?'

'Murdered someone?' cried Karen, aghast. 'Me? Good grief!'

'But you might know who did,' persuaded John.

'No. I've no idea.'

'You're a liar, dear.'

'Again? I'm not.'

'You were unaware that someone was dossing on the top floor. If he heard your music he would have come down out of curiosity. All right. He may not have wanted his presence known so he could have hidden as he watched you. But you're not going to tell me that your lot and he, occupying the house for as long as you did, were not aware of each other's existence.'

'That's just what I'm telling you.'

'Yes. You're telling me that but I doubt if it's the truth.'

'It is.'

'Inspector Waller is in charge of the murder. I only come into it because it appears the man was murdered in my house and you stupid urchins have complicated the issue with your squatting.'

'I'm sorry.'

'You don't know how sorry you and your friends may yet be.'

'What do you mean?'

'Forget stealing cars. You could all be accessories before and after the fact. The fact of murder.'

'I don't know what that means.'

'It means that some of you must have known what was going on.'

'We didn't.'

'Karen, you're being mistakenly loyal to your fellow idiots. This has gone beyond your japes. I have discovered since I took you home to your mother that there are six of you. My own housekeeper and her husband have seen you lot together. They put your behaviour down to high spirits. Sometimes all of you would pile into one small car and drive out to Bert's Caff. I daresay even then the car was stolen. If not by Tom Parker then someone else. Who else? Who, Karen?'

'I can't tell you.'

'Well, that's a change from I don't know.'

'I can't.'

'Three boys and three girls. Is that right?'

Karen did not answer.

'You all went to Falcon House and paired off. Is that what the candles were for?'

'Yes.'

'Who broke the back door?'

'I don't know. It was already open when we got there.'

'Old Bill, as they called him, could have done that, of course.'

'I suppose so.'

'The tramp you say you didn't know was there.'

Again Karen did not answer.

'Is all this silence to protect Tom Parker?'

'No.'

'As a loyal gang member you refuse to give any information. Is that it?'

'If you like.'

'You could be arrested again, you know.'

'Why? I haven't done anything,' Karen protested.

'The candles. Remember?'

'I have every right to buy candles.'

'Of course you have. And the police have every right to

suspect that anyone in the least way connected with Falcon House at the time of Old Bill's murder could provide them with information.'

'I didn't do it.'

'No. But you could possibly lead them to the person who did.'

'How?'

'By judicious questioning. That is something for you to look forward to.'

'When?'

'At the convenience of the police.'

'What do I do in the meantime?'

'Nothing. Go home. Tell your mother to find another lawyer.'

'Aren't you going to help me?'

'No.'

'Why not?'

'Because you're not helping me.'

'How can I?'

'By telling the truth.'

'But I have.'

'My dear, as a liar you're a bloody amateur. Now go.'

'But...'

'Go.'

Karen slunk out of the house, close to tears once more. John heard the front door slam shut. Stupid little cow, he thought. Trying to protect some feckless youth, even though he may be the vicar's son and even though he wasn't her regular boyfriend. He wasn't so angry about the damage to his property which was superficial. He would make sure the gang, whoever they were, put that right. He was more angry at the apparent indifference of his niece to the murder of Old Bill, who was not all that old but was nicknamed Old Bill because of his drooping moustache which was reminiscent of a famous cartoon character.

He knew what would happen next. His sister-in-law would be on the telephone begging him to help her daughter and he would refuse. Like mother, like daughter. He had never taken much notice of the girl before. She was just another student, rather scruffy and untidy, dark-haired with a figure disguised by jeans and sloppy jacket. She was supposed to be studying history. Let her get on with it, he decided. Let her stew in her own juice.

In disgust, he needed a drink to calm himself. He poured himself a whisky and soda and sat in his wing-chair wondering why he was so angry. Was it because he thought that the interview with Karen was going to be easy and the girl had thwarted him? Was it nothing more than frustration? He gleaned nothing from the interview that he could pass on to Inspector Waller, nothing except to confirm that it was Karen who bought the candles and that the gang consisted of six people, two of them being Karen herself and Tom Parker. Nothing that helped solve the problem of who killed Old Bill. Surely the kids had nothing to do with it themselves. They may indulge in dares but that would be going too far. There couldn't be any motive, anyway.

He looked at the clock on the mantelpiece and saw that it was eleven o'clock. Resignedly he decided to go to bed. Before he got to the door the telephone rang. It was Susan.

'John?' she asked.

'Who else could it be? I was just going to bed.'

'Karen came home in tears.'

'When?'

'Just now.'

'Where'd she been since she left here?'

'I don't know.'

'It's time you started finding out.'

'She said you refused to help her.'

'That's right.'

'Why, John? She's your niece, for God's sake.'

'Don't blame God.'

'Why won't you help her?'

'Because she's not honest.'

'What!'

51

'Your daughter is a liar and she's lying to protect the vicar's son and all the other silly farts in the gang.'

'That's not true.'

'How the Hell do you know?'

'Please, John. Don't let her down.'

'She's letting herself down. Besides, she's not charged with anything yet.'

'What do you mean, yet?'

'Exactly what I say. The girl's been playing with fire but she won't tell us who fans the flames.'

'Won't you give her another chance?'

'I did. This evening. But the result was the same.'

'If I talk to her and tell her she's got to tell you everything, will you help her?'

'What makes you think you have any influence over her? You're a parent. Kids like Karen don't believe in parents. They're rebels for the sake of it.'

'Please, John.'

John hesitated.

Then he said, 'If she knocks on my door and says she's prepared to tell me everything, including the truth, then I'll reconsider. That's as far as I'll go.'

'Oh, thank you, John. I'll tell her. If she...'

'Good night.'

John put the phone down without listening to anything else his sister-in-law might have to say. On his way to bed he smiled to himself, imagining Susan having any power over a student rebel like Karen who was obviously controlled by the unknown boss of her little gang. They were evidently playing their games quite seriously. He was quite sure that there would be no knock on the door in the morning.

But he was mistaken. At exactly eleven o'clock the next morning Norah, the housekeeper, came to his study door and told him that Karen Rossiter was in the hall and wanted to see him. He was working on a report he intended to present to Inspector Waller on the goings-on so far at Falcon House. He put it aside and got up from his desk to greet his niece.

52

'Hello, Karen,' he cried. 'I didn't expect you.'

'I don't suppose you did,' answered Karen, with a guilty smile.

'Come and sit down.'

He turned to Norah.

'Would you bring us some coffee, please, Norah?'

'Certainly, sir,' said Norah and left the room.

'I see you've reverted to your uniform,' observed John.

'That's right,' agreed Karen.

John was calling attention to the fact that instead of her more feminine clothes that she had worn the previous evening she now appeared in her scruffy jeans and T-shirt.

'Good,' said John. 'Now what?'

'It's true,' said Karen. 'We do go around in a gang when we come down.'

'What happens to the gang when you go back?'

'It breaks up.'

'And comes together again at the next vacation.'

'Yes.'

'I get it. How many of you?'

'Six.'

'The six of you get together when you come down and decide to create mayhem to amuse yourselves.'

'Something like that.'

'Was six the limit?'

'Yes.'

'Who was the leader, Tom?'

'No.'

'Who?'

'Harvey.'

'Harvey who?'

'Harvey Winter.'

'The mayor's son?'

'Yes.'

'The vicar's son and the mayor's son. Very distinguished.'

'His father owns the off licence down the road.'

'Yes. I know. Where was Harvey when you and Tom were picked up by the police?'

'I don't know. We were all going to meet up in the evening.'

'The evenings were the usual thing?'

'Well, yes. We all went about our personal business during the day.'

'For instance, you were at Angela's buying tights or whatever, when Tom suddenly makes up his mind to borrow someone's car. How did he know you were there?'

'I'd said the evening before that I was going there in the morning. I'd said it to everybody generally, as you do. We usually waited until the evening before we thought about cars. They weren't missed so much then.'

'You think it all out, don't you?'

'The boys do.'

'Tell me. Was Harvey voted your leader or did he just assume it?'

'He assumed it. He thought up the idea.'

'As a lark.'

'Yes.'

'Some lark. Turned out a bit of a cuckoo, hasn't it?'

'We never did any harm.'

'I'll send Harvey the bill for redecorating Falcon House.'

'I keep saying we were going to clean the place up.'

'You still can.'

'We will.'

'If you're not all in gaol.'

'Why should we be?'

Norah arrived at that moment with the coffee on a tray. She put it on the table beside John's chair and went away again.

'Shall I do it?' offered Karen.

'Thank you,' said John.

Karen began to pour coffee for the two of them.

Once they were both seated again John asked, 'Are you prepared to admit now that you knew about the tramp?'

'Yes,' said Karen. 'We knew about him.'

'At last.'

'I'm sorry.'

'This is the dangerous bit, you see. Your contact with him. The age-old question: When did you last see the deceased?'

'I see.'

'We talk about Old Bill but he wasn't old, was he?'

'No. He told us he was forty-five.'

'You spoke to him?'

'Oh, yes. He used to come down and join us when we were having a picnic.'

'Poor devil. I expect he was hungry.'

'He was.'

'He was tall and strong, though, according to the autopsy.'

'Yes. He was big.'

'So you couldn't have strangled him yourself.'

'I couldn't and wouldn't.'

'He had a family, you know. A girl and a boy. I suppose there's a wife somewhere but nobody seems to want to claim him.'

'He was always talking about them.'

'I wonder what the motive was for the murder.'

'You're sure it was murder?' Karen asked.

'Quite sure. And I have an idea that you know it was, too.'

'Why do you say that? He wasn't part of us. When we went home anyone could have come in.'

'You were the only people who knew he was there.'

'But, Uncle,' Karen persisted. 'If he could break into your house, as he did, to kip down then another tramp could do the same. They probably go looking for empty houses for shelter.'

'Rivals, you think?'

'Something like that. A quarrel.'

'Go on.'

'I can't. I don't know what could have happened.'

'I think you do.'

'I don't,' protested Karen, almost tearfully.

'You wouldn't tell me, anyway.'

'I can't tell you what I don't know.'

'The six of you and him,' stated John. 'There's no evidence of anybody else.'

'There must have been.'

'Never mind,' said John. 'That will come to light eventually. Tell me more about the members of your little gang. You said Harvey was the boss. Who did he pair off with at the house?'

'Eva Thomsett.'

'Who's she?'

'Her father's the manager of Barclays Bank.'

'Oh, yes. I know him.'

'She works at Angela's, the gown shop.'

'Oh. So when Tom picked you up there in the stolen car were you conferring with a fellow gang member or were you a customer?'

'I was a customer. I didn't see Eva. She was in the back of the shop somewhere.'

'Who else?'

'Who else what?'

'Gang members. Remember? You're not giving anyone away so you needn't worry.'

'There's Little Fred.'

'Little Fred? Who's he?'

'Chap with glasses. His father owns the garage at the crossroads.'

'Oh, yes. Fred Miller. I know. He's not a student, Little Fred.'

'No. He works for his father at the garage.'

'And his partner in crime?'

'Gillian. Gillian Curran. She works at the supermarket. She's some kind of supervisor at the checkout.'

'Her father's a magistrate.'

'That's right.'

'Very useful. And that's all of you?'

'Yes.'

'Half and half. Three students and three workers. Were there any rules?'

'Rules?'

'Apart from the one you're so scrupulously observing, which is not to split on a fellow gang member.'

'No. There are no rules.'

'Why aren't there more of you? Why only six?'

'We thought six was enough.'

'You mean Harvey, the boss, thought six was enough.'

'Yes.'

'Was it always six?'

'Yes.'

'Right from the beginning?'

'No. Not the very beginning. It was only four to start with.'

'Which four?'

'Me and Tom and Harvey and Eva.'

'Three students plus one.'

'Yes.'

'I'm fascinated by the mixture of students and non-students.'

'Why?'

'It's rather like oil and water.'

'It didn't feel like it.'

'On the other hand, I suppose, it's useful to have what you might call a home-grown product to make contact locally and to look after the shop, as it were, when you returned to university.'

'We were all friends.'

'In a way, perhaps.'

'What do you mean?'

'Not exactly dinner guests by your mother's standards.'

'That doesn't matter.'

'How did the other two, the non-students, get in?'

'I don't remember.'

'They don't go to university and come down and play silly games. They're working.'

'Yes.'

'So they're only with you during the holidays.'

'Yes.'

'And since they're both working they can only join you in the evenings.'

'That's what I told you. We only came together in the evenings. Any of us.'

'Even when you were only four?'

'Yes.'

'Now. Something else. What was the magnetic attraction of Bert's Caff?'

'Well, it's like a coffee bar or disco.'

'Bert's Caff?'

'To us, yes. It was rough and ready. Full of atmosphere.'

'A bit of slumming in other words.'

'You could say that.'

'Was Bert himself anything to do with you little lot?'

'No. I don't think he wanted us there all that much. We put his real customers off.'

'What did you do there?'

'Talked. Smoked.'

'Planned escapades?'

'Sometimes.'

'But it's way out of town. On the main road. How did you get there?'

'By car.'

'Stolen car.'

'Borrowed.'

'That was the meeting place, was it?'

'No. How could it be without a regular car? No. We met at the King's Head. We made our way there separately. Then, when we were all together, we would decide what to do.'

'Such as making free with my house. Who thought of that? You?'

'No. Tom.'

'Knowing the connection as between you and me.'

'I suppose so.'

'There were a lot of wine bottles on the floor. Who provided those?'

'Harvey, of course.'

'Pilfered from his father's off-licence.'

'Naturally.'

'The qualification for entry to your little gang appears to be a certain skill in stealing.'

'I didn't steal the candles.'

'How long were you all there before you met up with Old Bill?'

'Oh, some time.'

'Days? Weeks?'

'Days. The vac's not all that long.'

'I see.'

'That's all I can tell you.'

'It doesn't amount to much, I'm afraid.'

'What! After all that?'

'You've talked a lot, I agree, and I'm grateful. But it's more background than evidence.'

'I've given you names.'

'Yes. I'll follow them up.'

'Do you have to?'

'Oh, yes. I'll ask them a few questions. I intend to carry out my own investigation and pass on what I think is relevant to the police.'

'They'll arrest them all, then, won't they? If you tell them.'

'No. Question them, yes. Not arrest them.'

'You'll question them first?'

'Yes. Talk to them. See what they have to say. Not an inquisition. Provided they don't clam up on me like you we might get somewhere.'

'I haven't clammed up on you. That's not fair. I've told you everything.'

'Except what I want to know.'

'What's that?'

'Who killed Old Bill.'

'I don't know.'

'Well I can't make you tell me.'

'I don't know.'

'I don't believe that you don't know. I'm not suggesting that your friends are murderers. Nevertheless he was strangled and thrown in the river by someone. Someone you might have seen.'

'Why do you think he was strangled in your house?'

'Because his wallet was found on the floor by the back door. I kicked against it when I was there with the house agent. I would guess that it fell out of his pocket as he was carried out of the house.'

'Not necessarily. He could have dropped it any time.'

'Not with those precious photographs in it. He would have tried to retrieve it.'

'Have you finished with me now?'

'Yes.'

'What do I do now?'

'Go home. Or visit your friends. Tell them what a terrible ordeal you've been through. You won't be able to tell Tom. He's still in custody and likely to be until he decides to cooperate. There's a limit to how long they can keep him, of course, but they can let him out and bring him in again.'

'What about me?'

'All you can do is sit and wait.'

'Wait for what?'

'If and when whoever is responsible for the death of Old Bill is arrested and charged. There is no doubt you will be called by the prosecution as a witness.'

'But I didn't see anything.'

'Then tell them so. You will probably only have to admit that you knew Old Bill stayed there. Simple.'

When his niece had gone John sat down at his desk and scrutinised the notes that he had made during the interview. He now had a list of the names of all the members of the gang. He would attempt to question each of them in turn. He had no authority to do so officially but as the owner of the property he considered that he had a right to ask questions on a social level. Did they continue to meet? he wondered. He suspected that they did as Karen must have been somewhere between the time she left him the evening before and her arrival home. Perhaps they met at the King's Head, as Karen said. They certainly couldn't use Falcon House any more.

He picked up the telephone and dialled his brother's number. Susan, of course, answered.

'Karen there?' he asked.

No preliminaries. He never bothered with all that how-are-you nonsense.

'She's just come in,' said Susan.

'Put her on.'

'Is anything wrong?' Susan asked, nervously.

'Put her on. She'll tell you.'

He waited while the phone at the other end of the line was transferred to Karen.

'Hello,' said Karen.

'Karen, do you still meet up? I meant to ask you.'

'Well, no,' explained Karen, 'we can't really. We've all scattered since the police came on the scene.'

'You're only one short. Tom Parker.'

'I know. But it's not the same.'

'I thought you'd gone to meet the others when you left me yesterday. You were a long time getting home.'

'I know.'

There was a silence between them.

'Understood,' said John, eventually. 'Can you come back, dear?' he asked. 'I want to ask you some more questions.'

'Can't we do it on the phone?'

'No. You never know who's listening.'

'Oh. All right,' conceded the somewhat aggrieved Karen.

She put the phone down. John could imagine Susan questioning the girl and the girl fobbing her off. But if it meant another visit to her uncle Susan would presume that he was helping her and all would be well. John was impatient with himself for not questioning the girl further about the other members of the gang. The more he thought about Old Bill the more he wanted to ask questions. Even though his instinct told him that Karen was holding something back she was the only one who could answer his question at the moment. He wondered how much he should tell the police. He didn't want them to go charging about like the proverbial bull in a china shop. They would question Harvey for a start, as soon as they knew about him. He anticipated that Harvey and Tom appeared to be the dominant members of the gang. Either or both could have strangled Old Bill. But why? And where did Little Fred fit in? He was the odd man out, being neither student nor socialite. By socialite John meant the normal dinner party exchange that went on in Ambleford.

When, during the afternoon, Karen returned to his study he was able to get a clearer picture of Little Fred's involvement. It was he, evidently, who gave the order to scatter. Karen was talking more freely now, she was more relaxed. Any idea of telling tales on her friends appeared to be forgotten. She may not have spoken so openly to a stranger, certainly not to a detective. John Rossiter was not only a close relative, he had been a distinguished lawyer, famous for defending seemingly hopeless cases and achieving an acquittal.

'It was funny,' said Karen, as a prelude to her revelations about Little Fred. 'Well, not perhaps funny. Lucky.'

'I'm glad luck comes into this story somewhere,' commented John. 'Fun certainly doesn't. Go on.'

'Little Fred had to take the breakdown van to pick up a smashed car somewhere. You know he works for his father at the garage.'

John nodded.

'Evidently he had to pass the gates of Falcon House and saw police cars going in and out.'

'That must have frightened him.'

'It did. He phoned Harvey from his mobile and warned

him that something was afoot. Harvey then rang round to all of us telling us to stay away and keep our mouths shut.'

'Including you?'

'Including me.'

'He rang you personally.'

'Yes.'

'Why had you to keep your mouths shut?'

'In case the police questioned any of us.'

'Why should Harvey expect the police to question you if you were only squatting? You could have said I gave you permission.'

'I didn't think of that.'

'Unless Harvey thought you might be questioned in connection with Old Bill. He wasn't to know that I'd picked up the man's wallet.'

'I don't think he thought that,' said Karen, glumly.

'You're not prepared to accept that the boys might have had anything to do with the murder?'

'Of course not. Certainly not.'

'I exclude you girls. I can't see you girls strangling a big chap like that with a nylon rope.'

'I can't see any of us doing it. Boys or girls.'

'Although you don't mind talking about individuals in the gang you stick to your guns on that.'

'I certainly do.'

'Going back to Little Fred giving the alarm, it's unlikely that any of you would go to the house on your own, isn't it?'

'Yes. We always went as a gang.'

'Did you continue to meet after the alarm?'

'Only once.'

'Where?'

'Bert's Caff. We'd seen the story about Old Bill in the local paper and we met there to talk about it.'

'That was when he was fished out of the water?'

'Yes.'

'Before it was known that he had been murdered beforehand.'

'Well, yes. That never appeared in the paper.'

'Why were you all so interested in the story?'

'Because we knew him.'

'You're all prepared to admit that now, I suppose?'

'All? I'm the only one you've spoken to.'

'I intend to contact the others.'

'On your own?'

'On my own.'

'Not with the police?'

'No. See how far I can get.'

'John Rossiter, private investigator,' suggested Karen.

'Something like that,' laughed John. 'So you all steered clear of Falcon House since Little Fred gave the alarm.'

'Yes.'

'I still can't have the place cleaned until the police close the case and they can't do that until they've apprehended the murderer or murderers.'

'Murderers? Plural?' questioned Karen.

'Yes. More than one person must have been involved. An accessory of some sort. One man couldn't have strangled him with a rope and carried him out of the house.'

'That sounds horrible.'

'Doesn't it? Makes your little games rather ominous, doesn't it?'

'We didn't mean any harm.'

'But harm has been done.'

'We were going to clean the place up. I keep telling you that.'

'Yes. All that rubbish was yours, not his?'

'What do you mean?'

'Tramps are tidy people. They have to be. They carry their world on their backs.'

'I'm sorry. That's all I can say.'

'If I were a judge when this case comes up I'd put you all on community service. That is, the ones who are let off.'

'Let off what?'

'Prison, dear.'

'What!'

'In other words, those not charged with murder or accessory to murder. You know what accessory means, don't you?'

'Yes, I think so.'

'You can be an accessory before the fact merely by condoning or looking on. You can be an accessory after the fact by agreeing to keep quiet about it.'

'I see.'

'Go away and think which part you and the other girls belong to.'

'But...'

Karen began to protest but John interrupted her.

'That's all,' he said. 'We've talked enough.'

Karen didn't think that they had. She was convinced that her uncle was on the wrong track and wanted to tell him so. None of the boys in the gang could ever have committed murder. Admittedly the man known as Old Bill had made himself a bit of a nuisance by interfering in their affairs and Harvey had said that he could strangle the bastard but, in the end, the boys had persuaded him to stay in his own quarters. They may have threatened him but that's all. The girls were in another room when it was discussed. She hesitated to tell her uncle all that in case it incriminated the boys.

Karen and John parted without a word of farewell, Karen feeling peeved and frustrated, John quite convinced that she was still holding something back.

It wasn't surprising that the local paper should make a front page story out of the arrest of the vicar's son. The vicar had pleaded with the editor to keep the story out of the paper but his pleas were of no avail. When the story broke everybody felt sorry for the poor old reverend and his wife. The vicar had expected some kind of ostracism but, strangely, his congregation increased, whether out of sympathy or curiosity it was hard to tell. It was hardly likely that he would condemn his own son from the pulpit.

65

The newspaper hinted that the boy was part of a gang of local youngsters of both sexes and this intrigued the townsfolk more than ever. The gang had been seen together so any gathering of young people was now suspect. The only other person who had seen all six together, apart from Norah, the housekeeper, and her husband, was Bert of Bert's Caff.

John Rossiter decided to call on him.

The cafe was empty when he arrived and Bert and his wife, Gladys, were relaxing in canvas chairs outside in the sunshine. Bert was an ordinary, shirt-sleeved, working man of middle age with close-cropped hair. He would not stand out in a crowd. Gladys was a large, happy soul, friendly and warm but standing no nonsense. When Bert saw John Rossiter arrive he found another canvas chair so that he could sit with them.

'Hello, Mr Rossiter,' he cried, happily. 'We don't see you out here very often.'

'No, Bert' John answered. 'It's not on my beat.'

He turned to Gladys.

'Good afternoon, Gladys.'

'Hello, Mr Rossiter. Would you like something?'

'No, thank you. I've come to have a chat.'

'Something bothering you, Mr Rossiter?' asked Bert.

'You know the police picked up Tom Parker here a few days ago,' prompted John.

'Oh, yes,' agreed Bert.

'Stupid little fool,' muttered Gladys.

'The whole gang of them came here sometimes, didn't they?' John asked.

'Yes,' admitted Bert.

'Noisy lot,' put in Gladys.

'Laughing and joking all the time and all over one cup of coffee,' moaned Bert.

'They made that cup last hours,' said Gladys.

'We don't want their custom,' added Bert. 'Do we, Gladys?'

'Certainly not,' agreed Gladys.

66

'But we can't turn them away. By law. As you know, Mr Rossiter,' said Bert, with a laugh.

'Did they fit in with the lorry drivers?' Asked John.

'No. The drivers resented them. Thought they were sending them up, trying to copy their accent when they were talking.'

'The kids adopted the drivers' way of talking, you mean?'

'As a gag, yes.'

'When were they last in, all of them?'

'We never saw them after the story in the paper about the death of that tramp.'

'They brought the paper in and sat at one of the tables in there,' explained Gladys.

'It was about the only time they were quiet,' said Bert. 'They all sat crouched over the paper and whispering together. You'd think the tramp was a friend of theirs. The big chap, Harvey they called him, seemed to be reading bits out to them. We never saw them again after that. Not all together. Except when the police came and took Tom Parker and one of the girls away.'

'That girl was my niece,' said John.

'Oh!' exclaimed Gladys. 'That's why you're interested, is it?'

'They've been squatting in an empty house of mine,' John went on.

'The devils!' said Gladys.

Bert's news only confirmed John's conviction that there was more than a passing acquaintance between the gang and the tramp.

'It's a funny thing,' mused Gladys. 'One minute they were full of beans and the next they were quite glum. Bert said perhaps one of the girls was pregnant, but it wasn't that. I know the signs. It was as if a cloud had come over them. And it was something in the paper.'

'The reason I thought one of the girls was pregnant,' explained Bert, 'was because they started taking food away. Pies and sandwiches. Something they'd never done before. They didn't eat them here. They took them away. For a picnic, I suppose.'

'I served them,' said Gladys. 'And one of the girls said a strange thing. She pointed to a pie and said "D'you think he'd like that?" and the other one said, "Yes and I hope it chokes him." What do you make of that, Mr Rossiter?'

'Perhaps one of the girls had fallen out with her boyfriend and wasn't feeling very generous towards him,' he suggested.

John was aware that even his own explanation was bogus. They were obviously taking food back to Falcon House for Old Bill whom they'd met in spite of Karen's earlier contradictions. As for choking him, although he was actually strangled, the girl's malicious wish that the food should choke him indicates that Old Bill was making something of a nuisance of himself. Would that suggest a motive for murder?' he wondered. He hoped not.

He left Bert's Caff as a line of hungry and thirsty lorry drivers arrived and Bert and Gladys hurried away to attend to them.

Driving home he could picture the scene at Falcon House, the little gang of six suddenly invaded by an inter- loper in the shape of Old Bill, the tramp. And why should the kids provide him with food? The food wasn't for them- selves for some midnight dormy feast. Judging by the com- ments of the girls the food was supplied grudgingly. So there was no love lost between the gang and the tramp. Was he in the way? He remembered Karen telling him that the boys had persuaded him to leave Falcon House. Did that mean feet first? How could he be in the way? He was on the top floor, the gang was on the ground floor. And there were two staircases. It was no use questioning Karen any more, he decided. He had an idea that she had told him all she knew except for the vital piece of information connected with the murder, which she was not prepared to reveal, even if she knew it, which he was inclined to doubt.

John thought he would try to tackle Harvey, who seemed

to be the boss man. He'd call at the off-licence that the boy's father owned and order some wine.

'Hello, John.'

He was greeted by Harvey's father, Henry Winter.

'Hello, Henry,' said John. 'I need some more Blanquette de Limoix.'

'I haven't got any in stock. But I can get it for you. How much do you want?'

'A couple of cases. I find that ladies prefer it to the usual champagne.'

'Yes. I've heard that.'

'How's Harvey?' John asked, innocently.

'Fine. Bored with the long holiday, of course.'

'I'd like the chance.'

'Me too.'

'When do they go back?'

'September.'

'Where is he now?'

'Out somewhere. I never know.'

'Ask him to give me a ring, will you?'

'Ring you?' asked Henry, in surprise.

'Yes.'

'What about, for Heaven's sake?' asked Henry again, somewhat offended. John laughed.

'We have something in common.'

'What's that?'

'Falcon House.'

'Your place?'

'Yes.'

'How come?'

'There've been strange goings on there with some students. I wanted to ask him about them. He may know them.'

'Well, I'll tell him,' said Henry, sullenly. 'But I doubt if he can help you.'

'Thank you,' said John. 'You'll deliver the wine, will you?'

'Of course.'

What started as an affable conversation ended rather

coldly and John left the shop convinced that his friendship with the wine merchant, though confined to purchasing, had taken a retrograde step. He doubted if the son would call him in spite of the tantalising part of the mention of Falcon House. He imagined Harvey ringing round to the rest of the gang to find out if they had been approached by the owner of the house. He wondered what Karen would tell him. She would probably be evasive. She would make the excuse that as the owner of the house was her uncle he had a right to contact her and question her. Would she admit to giving her uncle Harvey's name? She could always say that Norah, the housekeeper, had seen them all together and obviously knew the locals and where they lived. If Harvey did ring the rest of the gang, as John suspected, it would point to a sense of guilt rather than curiosity and John could only continue to ask questions. He had no official capacity for doing so but it was tacitly understood with Inspector Waller that he would pursue his own line of inquiry concerning the squatting and pass on to him any aspect pertaining to the murder of Old Bill.

At home John waited for the call, doubting that it would ever come. Harvey was more likely to tell him to go to Hell than offer to cooperate. He was, John knew, a swaggering bully, more at home in rugger clothes with a glass of beer in his hand. No wonder he was the leader of the gang. He probably had the others running round after him, his own contribution being the bottles of wine pilfered from his father's stock. No doubt, too, he thought up some of the dares that the gang pulled off. John held out little hope of getting any honest answers to his questions from Harvey. His girlfriend, Eva Thomsett, who helped out at Angela's dress shop, would be no more forthcoming than Karen, he felt sure. She'd run to Harvey as soon as he tried to contact her. In any case, it was becoming increasingly apparent that the girls were adjuncts, they weren't the prime movers in the gang, they couldn't steal cars and they certainly couldn't strangle a big chap like

Old Bill. That would be the responsibility of the boys: Harvey, Tom and Little Fred. Either one or all of them. If that is what happened.

Quite late that night John's phone rang. It was after midnight and no doubt Harvey hoped that he was disturbing him for it was Harvey himself on the telephone.

'Harvey Winter,' he said, abruptly. 'You wanted me to ring.'

'Yes, that's right, Harvey,' said John, amiably.

'What for?'

'I'd like to talk to you, Harvey.'

'What about?'

John suspected that the boy's arrogance was the result of too much beer.

'About Falcon House,' John explained.

'What about it?'

'Well, you know what's been going on there, don't you?'

'No. I don't.'

'Your little gang seems to have made themselves at home there.'

'What little gang?'

'You, Tom, Karen, Eva, Gillian and Little Fred.'

'Don't know what you're talking about.'

'I think you do, Harvey.'

'Either you tell me what you want or I ring off.'

'I want to meet you and have a little chat.'

'Well, I don't want to meet you.'

With that the telephone was put down at Harvey's end. With a bang, John presumed, wryly. He wasn't surprised. Harvey was a boastful bully and deserved what was coming to him which, in this instances, was being picked up and being questioned by the police. John had no compunction in passing on certain information to Inspector Waller that would precipitate such action.

The local newspaper ran the headline: 'Mayor's son arrested'. Henry Winter, who owned the off-licence, was

71

Mayor of Ambleford. But Harvey was not actually arrested. The newspaper assumed that it was an arrest and made the most of the story when, in fact, Harvey had merely been taken to the station in a police car for questioning. Unfortunately the two leading figures in the gang of six, Tom and Harvey, were both intransigent when it came to cooperation so little progress was made. As a result of their intransigence the police decided to detain them to the full extent of their privilege for further questioning.

The Mayor himself was on the telephone to John as soon as his son had been picked up.

'John, I need your help,' he said, urgently.

'Oh?' John answered.

'My son's been arrested.'

'Not arrested, Henry. Taken in for questioning.'

'Is it anything to do with you wanting him to ring you?'

'Yes. In a way.'

'In what way, for God's sake?'

'It's the Falcon House affair,' said John. 'The kids have been squatting there during their vacation but on top of that it's where Old Bill, the tramp, also used it for his dossing down.'

'The fellow they fished out of the river?' prompted Henry.

'That's right. Except that he didn't drown. He was strangled before he went in the river.'

'What!'

'Complicates it a bit, doesn't it?'

'But...'

Henry began to splutter in his anxiety.

'The police are hoping that the kids may be able to give them some information about the poor chap. They were all there at the same time.'

'But why my Harvey?'

'He's the leader of the gang. With Tom Parker.'

'Gang? What gang?'

'That's how they saw themselves. My niece, Karen, your son and a few others.'

72

'How do you know all this?'

'Falcon House is my property and I've been conducting my own little investigation in league with the police.'

'Did you tell the police about my Harvey?'

'I gave them his name, yes. As I'll give them the names of the rest of the gang as I come to them.'

'You mean you shopped my son.'

'He refused to answer any of my questions so I had no alternative but to let the police question him.'

'Thank you very much. I thought you were a friend of mine.'

'The boy's only being invited to help the police with their inquiries as he refused to help me with mine. He told me to go to Hell.'

'You know this can hurt me as Mayor.'

'Oh, I don't think so. If the kids are innocent it will soon blow over.'

'Of course they're innocent. At least, I know my Harvey is.'

'I hope you're right.'

'Who else is in the gang, as you call it?'

'Well, now. There's Millers Garage.'

'Millers?'

'Yes. His boy's one of them. Little Fred, they call him. Then there's Eva Thomsett.'

'The bank manager's daughter?'

'Yes. And Gillian Curran.'

'Curran, the grocer?'

'That's right.'

'But he's a magistrate.'

'I know.'

'Will they all be questioned by the police?'

'In time. You can't blame the police. They've got to question anybody and everybody who may have seen the tramp either on his own or with someone else. They may be able to describe the other person, for instance.'

'Is that all the police want them for?'

'Apart from some of their little pranks. Like stealing cars, shoplifting.'

'My Harvey never stole a car.'

'They don't steal them. They borrow them and return them after they've finished with them, which may be only a couple of hours.'

'And this has been going on under our noses?'

'Apparently.'

'What can we do? The scandal.'

'There won't be any scandal if you don't talk about it. I advise you to sit tight and await events.'

'You think so?'

The conversation had oscillated between animosity and petulant pleading and as John returned to his favourite wing chair he decided that it was the old, old story: what will people think? The mayor, the vicar, the magistrate, his own sister-in-law all worried about the same thing: their own personal reputations. Nobody gave a thought to the poor old tramp.

He decided to call on Detective Inspector Waller and compare notes.

As soon as he entered the station he met the Inspector himself who was on his way from one interview room to another.

'You sent me a right one this time,' the Inspector complained.

'Is he giving you trouble?' John asked.

'Like the other one. Won't say a word.'

'Let me see him.'

'You're welcome.'

John had not realised how big and burly Harvey Winter was. Even sitting down he looked enormous.

'Good evening, Harvey,' said John, politely.

Harvey didn't get up, he merely turned his head to look contemptuously in John's direction and then turned back again to stare ahead.

'Your father asked me to represent you.'

'No need.'

'You'll conduct your own defence, will you?'

'If necessary. If I'm charged with anything, which is unlikely.'

'I'll convey the message to your father.'

As there was no reaction from the boy John turned and left him. He'd done his duty by his father and that was that. He hadn't expected much else. Both Tom and Harvey, by their refusal to cooperate with the police, only emphasised their possible guilt. Guilt about what? Surely not the murder of Old Bill. There must be something they wanted to hide, apart from their vacation dares, for their refusal to cooperate was not bravado, it was fear. And that told John something.

John returned home, went to bed, and for the first time in many months slept soundly. In the morning, while he was dressing, he wondered how he could question Little Fred's girlfriend, Gillian Curran. He was particularly anxious to hear the reaction of one of the non-university types. For that reason, too, he dismissed Harvey's girlfriend, Eva. As a student she would know little more than Karen. And he was sure that the university types would stick together whereas the outsiders, who had a living to earn, would probably have a different attitude towards the behaviour of the students, even possibly mild disapproval. But how to reach Gillian? Could he ask Karen to fix a meeting? He knew where she worked but he hesitated to invade that territory. Would Karen bring her to the house? On what pretext? Gillian would already know about Tom and Harvey being questioned and could now be expecting to be questioned herself. In that case perhaps he could approach her himself.

Gillian was a blonde girl of about 18 or 19, tall, almost statuesque with her hair arranged rather like the Renoir painting of the girl at the *Folies Bergère*. She didn't have a figure as attractive as Karen's but at least it was not hidden in the uniform shirt and jeans.

She was the supervisor who walked up and down beside the checkouts at the local supermarket. She was the one who went to any of the girls who pressed the bell on their tills when an enquiry occurred. John stood watching her and admiring her efficiency. He decided to approach her.

'Gillian Curran?' he asked.

'Yes.'

'My name's John Rossiter.'

'Yes. I know. What do you want with me?'

'I'd like to talk to you.'

'Talk away.'

'Not here.'

'Why not?'

'It's rather important and personal,' suggested John.

'Then I'm afraid I can't help you, Mr Rossiter. As you can see I'm busy at the moment.'

John produced his business card and handed it to Gillian, who took it and read it.

'I'd like to talk to you about recent events at Falcon House,' said John.

At the mention of the name of the house the girl looked startled.

John went on, 'Do you think you could come to this address some time at your convenience?'

'You want me to come to your house?'

'If you wouldn't mind.'

'Why there? Why not somewhere else?'

'The questions I would like to ask you should not be overheard in public.'

'What questions?'

'Questions relating to Falcon House and an old tramp. I think you know what I mean?'

'I might.'

'You'll be quite safe at my house. I have a housekeeper who could act as chaperone. Or I could ask Karen to sit-in on our little talk.'

Still studying the card, Gillian replied, 'I'll think about it.'

'You can check with Karen if you like. Just give me a ring.'

Any further conversation was impossible because a bell rang calling Gillian to one of the checkouts where a cashier had a query.

'Excuse me,' said Gillian, hurrying away.

There was nothing more that John could do. Out of curiosity he watched Gillian deal with her problem and then he walked away. Once home he had high hopes of his talk with Gillian. She seemed a sensible girl and the only puzzle to his mind was how she ever became involved with the student pranksters. It was out of character. No doubt she would check with Karen before attempting to phone him but he imagined that his niece would give him a good reference as an understanding investigator. She could have no reason to suggest otherwise, he decided, perhaps a little too complacently. Gillian certainly couldn't contact Tom or Harvey because they were still in custody. So he waited that evening with his fingers crossed. The call came before his evening meal.

'Mr Rossiter?'

'Speaking.'

'Gillian Curran.'

'Ah. Thank you for ringing.'

'You wanted to talk to me.'

'That's right. Can you come round?'

'To your house?'

'Yes.'

'When?'

'Whenever you like.'

'Can I come now? I've just finished.'

'Yes. Of course.'

No thought, surmised John, of going home to freshen up, change her clothes or whatever it is women do. He admired her down-to-earth attitude. When she rang the doorbell he went himself to let her in and led her to the drawing room, not his study. He thought it was more relaxing.

'Sit down and make yourself comfortable,' he encouraged.

'Thank you,' she muttered.

'Would you like a drink?'

'No, thank you.'

'Coffee?'

'No, thank you.'

'You probably know what I want to talk to you about?'

'No. Not really.'

'Then why did you agree to come?'

'I spoke to Karen. She said I should come.'

'You didn't seem very surprised when I approached you.'

'No. I was half-expecting it.'

'It's this Falcon House business.'

'I thought as much.'

'You know that your friends Tom and Harvey are in custody, don't you?'

'Who doesn't?' scoffed Gillian. 'I don't know what the university bosses will say when they get back.'

'If they get back.'

'If?' cried Gillian. 'Karen said you would get them off.'

'I'm trying. They're not helping.'

'I'm not surprised.'

'You know your friends well, evidently.'

'They're no friends of mine,' said Gillian, defiantly.

'Oh?'

John was temporarily nonplussed but decided not to pursue that aspect of the relationship at the moment.

'Well now,' he began. 'We know about the car borrowing and the petty pilfering. What I'm trying to do, Miss Curran, is narrow down my line of enquiries so that I can eliminate certain people and concentrate on the main perpetrators.'

'How can I help you do that?' asked Gillian.

'In several ways,' said John. 'For one thing, what attracted you personally to join the gang?'

'I didn't join.'

The girl's directness again appealed to John. It was a change from Karen's evasive attitude.

'You were part of the gang,' John insisted. 'You were one of the six.'

'That's right.'

'I suppose you knew them all before they became such a thing as a self-styled gang.'

'Yes.'

'You knew them as residents of Ambleford. You recognised them in the street, probably nodded to them or waved or signalled somehow.'

'Yes.'

'Was that as far as it went?'

'Oh, yes.'

'You didn't go to university?'

'No.'

'Why not?'

'I've never wanted to. I don't see the point.'

'But you could have gone.'

'I suppose so. I don't know. I never thought of it.'

'Your parents didn't prevent you.'

'Oh, no.'

'So you have no grudge against parents as such as people like Tom and Harvey seem to have.'

'No. Not at all. I love my parents.'

'Do you think not going to university made a division between you and the others?'

'What others?'

'Public school versus grammar school. They don't always mix, do they?'

'Perhaps not always.'

'Karen, Harvey, Tom, Eva. They were all at university when you waved across the road or smiled or nodded or perhaps even said hello. Did they ever invite you for a drink?'

'Good Heavens, no!' laughed Gillian.

'Yet you became a member of their gang and took part in their exploits.'

'Yes.'

'That's beyond just having a drink,' commented John.

'I know.'

'You were invited to join, were you?'

'No. I wasn't. Little Fred was.'

'Ah!' sighed John, with some satisfaction. 'You call him Little Fred, too, do you?'

'Everybody does,' explained Gillian. 'He does himself.'

'So you went along as Little Fred's partner,' suggested John.

'That's it.'

'Why did they invite Little Fred?'

Gillian suddenly became embarrassed. She uncrossed her legs and crossed them again. She looked down at her feet. She was silent for some moments.

'You don't have to answer,' John assured her.

'Little Fred always admired Tom Parker,' Gillian declared, at last. 'Both Tom and Harvey.'

'What did he admire about them?' asked John.

'I think he envied them more than admired them. They were his "heroes".'

'He told you this?'

'Oh, yes. He was always talking about them, what they said, what they were wearing, what they were doing.'

John suddenly felt that the breakthrough that he was hoping for was about to happen. He knew that there would be a weak link in the chain somewhere and he had the idea now that it was Little Fred.

'He idolised them,' Gillian went on, as if relieved to talk about it to someone. 'Their accent, the way they talked, their careless, nonchalant manner. They talk so posh, he used to say. He'd do anything for them, given the chance. I think he was flattered into joining them.'

'Into joining?'

'Yes.'

'You mean he had a choice?'

'Yes, of course.'

'And he chose to join.'

'Anything to be with them.'

'And you went along with him as part of a pair.'

'Yes. There were other girls in pairs.'

'I don't understand this choice business. What choice? Joining or not joining. Need he have joined them?'

'No. I suppose not. At one time I would have said it was impossible.'

'Then how did it happen?'

Gillian hesitated some time before answering.

'It was a shop-lifting incident where I work.'

'In the supermarket.'

'Yes. Little Fred came in for a chat as he often did. While we were talking I saw this man put something in his pocket. The man was Tom Parker and Karen was with him.'

'Did she take anything?'

'No.'

'Go on.'

'Instead of calling Security I told Little Fred. Did you see that? I said. Yes, I did, he said, and went after him, his hero.'

'And?'

'Wouldn't you know? Tom put his arm round Little Fred's shoulder and said, in his posh way, you must be mistaken, old boy. Come and have a drink.'

'That's how the friendship started?'

'I wouldn't call it friendship.'

'Relationship.'

'Yes. He came back to me and said I must have been mistaken.'

'He must have been mistaken, too, because he told you he saw it.'

'I know. You can imagine Little Fred going off with Tom Parker, his hero. He could only splutter his apologies and string along. That easy charm did the trick.'

'But Tom was, in fact, shoplifting.'

'Oh, yes. Shoplifting was a kind of entrance exam to the gang. If you didn't do it you might as well leave.'

'Did you do it?'

'Me and Karen and Eva, yes. In a very small way. It never

81

amounted to much. It was only to show willing really. We didn't compare with the boys.'

'Like borrowing cars.'

'We contented ourselves with little things like screws and nails.'

'Didn't they want you to go on to bigger things?'

'No. But they got Little Fred to pinch things from his father's garage.'

'That wasn't very daring, was it? Not for an initiation.'

'Where Little Fred was useful, of course, was in borrowing cars from the garage.'

'Yes. I can see that.'

'It saved the others from stealing the cars. Borrowing, as they called it.'

'But they only did that for the thrill, didn't they?'

'Yes. In a way. But if they wanted to run out to Bert's Caff, for instance, there was always a car in the garage either for repair or new.'

'They didn't know what they'd been missing without Little Fred, did they?'

'No.'

'Once they'd let him join the gang did they exclude him from anything because he wasn't university?'

'No. Little Fred tried hard to curry favour, of course. We quarrelled about it sometimes.'

'You and Little Fred?'

'Yes.'

'Why?'

'I thought he was crawling.'

'I see.'

John decided to spring the shock question.

'Do you think Little Fred could have strangled Old Bill?'

Shock was right. The questions came as such a shock to Gillian that she just stared at John in a startled fashion.

'Little Fred?' she repeated, in a quiet voice.

'Yes,' urged John. 'You know the story.'

'Yes. But Little Fred. He wouldn't do such a thing. Not Little Fred.'

'Not even to please his hero, Tom?'

'Oh, no. He'd draw the line at that. I'm sure.'

'You know the man was strangled and not drowned?'

'I've heard, yes.'

'Do you think Tom or Harvey could have done it?'

'I couldn't say.'

'You can't say because you don't know or because you're afraid to, like Karen?'

John had asked Karen the same question and he expected the same answer from Gillian. The girls were quite prepared to discuss elementary rudiments of the gang's behaviour, the apparently harmless antics such as shoplifting and joyriding. But when it came to the real question, the murder of the tramp, there was a complete silence.

'I don't think fear comes into it,' Gillian said in answer to John's question. 'The six was not that kind of gang. There was no oath of allegiance and all that rot.'

'But it's just not done to tell tales.'

'No.'

'You've just been telling tales.'

'Harmless tales.'

'It's a pity we can't get Tom or Harvey to talk,' admitted John.

'I don't know what else I can do to help you,' concluded Gillian.

'My dear girl,' said John. 'There is a lot you can do, just as there is a lot that Karen could have done but neither of you is prepared to, any more than I anticipate Harvey's partner, Eva, would be prepared to.'

'She's beside herself with worry, I can tell you that.'

'And I can tell you that I tried to help Harvey, at his father's request, but he turned his back on me.'

'I'm not surprised.'

'He and Tom are sitting in he police station refusing to talk.'

'That's like them.'

'They've obviously brainwashed you girls.'

'No. That's not true.'

'Either that or you didn't always know what was going on.'

'I don't think we did. There were times when the boys shut themselves up in a room with a few beers leaving us girls to gossip among ourselves.'

'Why did they do that?'

'I don't know. Men's talk, I suppose.'

'Interesting,' mused John.'

'There's not much more I can tell you, Mr Rossiter.'

'No?'

'Is there?'

'Unless you can tell me who strangled Old Bill.'

'I'm afraid I can't do that.'

'Never mind. I'll keep probing.'

'Can I go now, then?'

'Yes. Yes. Of course,' said John. 'I'll see you out. And thank you for coming.' John shook hands with the girl as she left.

What could he make of all that? John asked himself. It was obvious that the girls didn't know everything that went on in Falcon House. While the boys were closeted on their own they could have been planning a way to get rid of Old Bill. But why should they want to get rid of him? He wasn't doing them any harm. He was a permanent resident, so to speak, whereas they were down from university. Yet one of the girls had said I hope it chokes him when they were buying food for him. That is, according to Bert's wife, Gladys, at Bert's Caff.

There was a spectacular ram-raid at the jewellers a little while ago, John remembered. He wondered if the boys had anything to do with that. The culprits were never found and there was nothing missing from the shop. Would the boys have done it for a dare? Little Fred could have supplied a Range Rover or even his own recovery lorry with the name of the garage masked out. There were no witnesses. It was done at three o'clock in the morning. They wouldn't have wanted the girls involved in that. That could have been what they were planning when they shut themselves away on their own. The girls might even have objected to such a plan. That wouldn't have stopped them, of course. It would if they had threatened to give the boys away. But would they dare? He didn't think the girls were afraid of the boys. Gillian certainly wasn't. They weren't what you might call gangsters' molls. They were equals. The university training made sure of that. So the girls were in no way inferior. So why are the girls protecting the boys at the moment? He was convinced that they were. Yet he had never considered the possibility of a third party being involved. That is, someone outside the gang, someone who knew Old Bill. It had never occurred to him. Even now he could hardly credit such a possibility.

There was a lot to admire about Gillian Curran, John decided. In spite of tagging along as Little Fred's partner she had a mind of her own. In calling her working class he in no way denigrated her in his mind. On the other hand it enhanced her value in his eyes.

With the exception of Eva, from whom he did not expect much help in his investigation, the only person who remained to be questioned was Little Fred, the son of the proprietor of the Cross Roads Garage. After what Gillian Curran had told him of the man's idolatry of Tom and Harvey it should be an interesting encounter.

There were two Freds. That was Big Fred and Little Fred. Big Fred owned the Cross Roads Petrol & Service Station which did a thriving business in the sale of petrol, new cars and repairs. Big Fred was exactly what he sounded like. He was large, loud and full of life. His son, Little Fred, was the exact opposite and probably took after his mother. He was small, quick, bespectacled and, as was said about him, frightened of his own shadow. He was just the kind of person you'd expect to be bullied at school. But

85

he was an excellent mechanic and everybody went to him with the least of their car troubles.

John stopped at the garage for petrol on the morning following his meeting with Gillian. It was a self-service station so he did not see anyone until he went into the office to pay.

He asked the girl there, 'Is Little Fred about?'

'He's in the workshop,' she said.

'Can I go through?'

'Yes. You'll find him in there somewhere.'

'Thank you.'

John pushed open a dirty door on a spiral spring and stepped into a world of clutter and noise and an over-powering aroma of oil. To the accompaniment of loud pop music issuing from a greasy, paint splattered portable radio on the floor beside one of the cars in for repair, two young men were either bent over it or under it, the one under-neath lying on what looked like a door on castors.

John went up to the one leaning over the engine of the car and tapped him on the shoulder. The man straightened up. It was Little Fred himself, grease on his face, hands covered in oil.

'Fred!'

John had to shout above the din.

'Hello, Mr Rossiter,' said Little Fred, looking frightened.

'I'd like to talk to you.'

'Something wrong with the car?'

'No. The car's fine. It's personal.'

'Oh.'

'Can we meet after work?'

'I suppose so. Where?'

'Can you come to my house?'

'Your house?'

'Yes. Where else?'

'I don't know. What about the King's Head?'

'I said it's personal, Fred. You can't talk personal in a pub. Or, if you like, I'll come out to the garage.'

'That would be better.'

'All right. What time?'

'Six?'

'Six it is.'

'Once I've cleaned up I'll be here. We can talk in Dad's office.'

'See you then, Fred,' said John and left, stepping carefully over cables and pools of oil.

Little Fred watched John leave the workshop. He was surprised that the man didn't fall over on the greasy floor. Once John was out of the way his first thought was to talk to Gillian. She would be at work so he couldn't phone her. The only thing to do was leave the garage and go to see her.

He was so anxious and worried that he told his companions, 'I've got to go out for a bit. Won't be long.'

He made his way to the washroom to tidy himself before taking a car and visiting Gillian.

She was walking up and down beside the line of checkouts supervising the operation when Little Fred approached her.

'Got a moment?' He whispered.

'You can see I'm busy,' Gillian protested.

'Mr Rossiter came to the garage.'

'I thought he might.'

'Did he ask a lot of questions?'

'No.'

'He wants to talk to me.'

'What about?'

'You can guess what about.'

'Yes. I can. I've been through it.'

'What do I do?'

'Tell him the truth. Tell him all you know. If you know anything. You haven't told me everything. I don't know what you know and what you don't know.'

'What about the others?'

'What others?'

87

'Tom. And Harvey.'

'Ask yourself what they would do for you apart from making use of you.'

'Is that what you think?'

'It certainly is.'

'I can't let them down.'

'Why not? Don't think they wouldn't let you down, the selfish, self-centred lot.'

'Why have you taken against them suddenly?'

'It's not all that sudden. I've put up with them for your sake but if you want to know what I think of them I think they're a spoilt lot of show-offs and if it weren't for them I wouldn't have to go through the humiliation of being questioned by a bloody lawyer.'

'I thought you liked Karen.'

'She's all right.'

'What about Eva?'

'She'll come to her senses one day. When Harvey's parents reject her.'

'Reject her?'

'Yes. They won't let him marry her.'

'Why not?'

'Too common.'

'You can't believe that.'

'I don't have to believe it. I can see it. It's a pity you can't. You're blinded by people out of your own class.'

'No, I'm not.'

'You're easily led.'

'No, I'm not.'

'You're impressed by their class. Their posh accents, as you call it. Lot of swank, if you ask me. What class are they, anyway? A vicar's son and the son of an off-licence keeper. The only one with any class is Karen, daughter of a stockbroker and niece of a famous lawyer. I tell you, there's something we don't know about that lot. You might. I don't. I don't think Karen and Eva know either.'

'What do you think I should do?'

'Tell Mr Rossiter all you know. Make a clean breast of

it. We have more to lose than they do. Our jobs. Now go away and let me get on with mine.'

When John Rossiter left Little Fred at the garage he wondered if he would, in fact, be there at six o'clock. He certainly appeared frightened. He lacked the arrogance of the other two, Tom and Harvey. He was the weak link in the chain that John had been seeking. After Little Fred there was no one who could throw any light on the Falcon House affair. It would be the end of the line and John knew it so he hoped that Little Fred was more forthcoming than the girls who, in fairness, may be ignorant of what was really going on up there.

When Little Fred left Gillian he felt both shocked and ashamed. He had no idea that she felt as she did about the gang. Come to think of it, she wasn't all that keen in the first place. It was true, as she said. Tom was shoplifting in the supermarket that day when he went after him and he did, in fact, allow himself to be sweet-talked out of doing anything about it. Now he would do anything to please Gillian who was more important to him than any of the gang. He didn't even include her in the gang in his own mind. An unwilling member, perhaps, to please him. Well, he would repay her by pleasing her.

He sat in his father's office at the garage waiting for Mr Rossiter. He was nervous and worried and his stomach was churning away with anxiety. At last he saw through the large showroom window John Rossiter arrive in his car. He went outside to meet him.

'Good evening, Mr Rossiter.'
'Hello, Fred. On your own?'
'Yes. We're shut.'
They went inside.
'Sit down, Mr Rossiter.'

Once John was sitting down he said, 'You're the last of the six, Fred. You know that, don't you?'

'The last to be questioned, you mean?'

'Yes. I haven't talked to Eva Thompsett because I don't think the girls know as much about Falcon House as you boys.'

Little Fred made no comment but recalled that Gillian had voiced a similar conclusion.

'You know, of course, that your friends, Tom and Harvey, are still helping the police with their inquiries?' John reminded him.

'Yes.'

'You know, too, that I've talked to my niece Karen and your girlfriend Gillian.'

'Yes.'

'Eventually you will all be called as witnesses when the police have solved the mystery of the murder of the tramp. So they needn't think it's all over.'

'I'm sure they don't,' admitted Little Fred.

The mention of the word murder, though, caused him to shuffle in the chair behind his father's desk, a reaction not lost on John Rossiter.

'You're not like the others, Fred. I can see that,' observed John.

'I don't come from the same kind of family,' agreed Little Fred. 'I didn't go to a public school.'

'But your father isn't exactly poor,' John pointed out.

'I'm a worker,' Little John persisted. 'They're not.'

'Don't use the word worker as a distinction,' protested John. 'When your friends finish university they'll be lucky to get a job. They'll probably be too over-qualified to be employed.'

'Perhaps the university will finish with them if...'

Little Fred checked himself thinking he'd gone too far. John picked him up.

'If what?' he asked, innocently.

'Well,' confessed Little Fred, hesitantly. 'If all this comes out.'

John Rossiter chuckled.

'It's bound to come out, isn't it?' he declared. 'It's already out as far as Tom and Harvey are concerned. The local paper splashed the stories on the front page. It only needs someone to tip off the national press and the story of the gang of six will be in every household in the country as well as every university. Once the murder is solved it will be a national story, anyway. A national scandal.'

'What do you mean?' asked Little Fred, vaguely.

'Fred,' insisted John, 'a murder has been committed.'

Little Fred became silent again. His resolve to justify himself in Gillian's eyes faltered when it came to giving people away. But a murder was a murder and Gillian would want him to tell John Rossiter all that he knew. And he knew quite a lot.

'Harvey was the leader, of course,' he said, tentatively.

'So I understand,' admitted John. 'Self-appointed?'

'Oh, yes. He's not as nice as Tom, though.'

'In what way?'

'Tom's more gentle.'

'A smoothie, you mean,' prompted John.

'Yes. Tom wouldn't tick you off in front of other people.'

'Did Harvey do that?'

'Sometimes.'

'To you?'

'No. To Eva. I don't know how she put up with it. He'd make fun of her, too. He'd make fun of her size. Yet he said he liked plump girls. I watched her. She was often near to tears.'

'How was he with Tom?'

'He never fell out with Tom. Nobody could. He's a real charmer, that one.'

'That's how you got in with them, I believe. You tackled Tom in the supermarket and he charmed you out of it.'

'Oh, that. Yes. I expect Gillian told you. But I don't see why Tom should take the rap for all of us.'

Little Fred was suddenly indignant.

'Rap?' echoed John. 'Rap for what?'

'Old Bill, the tramp,' explained Little Fred. 'We were all in it.'

'You didn't strangle him, did you?' laughed John.

'Good Lord, no,' cried Little Fred. 'Whatever gave you that idea?'

'The girls couldn't have done it,' John went on. 'So that leaves you, Tom and Harvey.'

'I'd better tell you what happened,' Little John decided.

'That's an idea. Get it off your chest.'

'That's what Gillian said,' admitted Little Fred, with some relief.

There was a prolonged silence. John Rossiter sat patiently waiting while Little Fred got his heart up high enough to take the plunge, as he later put it.

'It was done with a rope,' said Little Fred, in a quiet voice.

'I gathered that much from forensic,' said John.

'Tom held one end and Harvey the other,' Little Fred explained. 'The girls weren't there.'

'Where were they?'

'In another room. They didn't really know what was going on. Harvey would have sent them home but we only had one car.'

'Which you had borrowed from the garage.'

'Yes.'

'You could have taken them home and come back,' suggested John.

'There wasn't time. Everything had to be done quickly, according to Harvey.'

'All right,' urged John, a little impatiently. 'Tom held one end of the rope and Harvey the other. Was the tramp standing up?'

'Oh, no. Lying down. In a drunken stupor. Asleep.'

'What part did you play?'

'I supplied the rope.'

'From the garage.'

'Yes. One of those nylon tow ropes.'

'Is that all you did?'

'Yes. I had to stay and watch, of course.'

'Had to?'

'Yes. Harvey made me.'

'Made you? You have a will of your own, surely?'

'I was on my way to see how the girls were when Harvey said stay in case the man struggles and they needed help.'

'But he was in a stupor, you say. He was helpless. You didn't have to do anything.'

'As it happened, no. They were afraid he might wake up and start shouting. Tom and Harvey pulled and pulled until it was over. They were standing up, you see, so the tramp's head was off the ground. He was kind of sitting up because of the strain of the rope. I stepped back out of the way.'

'Then what?'

'I was sick.'

John decided to let the matter rest for a moment. Little Fred was visibly upset after recounting what was a macabre incident. He had heard what amounted to a confession but some vital details were still missing. The pieces of the jigsaw were only just falling into place.

John attempted to fill in the gaps between the depositions of Karen and Gillian.

'When did all this car borrowing and shoplifting start, Fred?' he asked.

'One summer holiday when they were all down, as they call it,' Little Fred replied.

'Who's they?'

'Tom, Harvey, Karen, Eva. They were all down from Cambridge.'

'You've adopted the jargon, I see. Down.'

'It's the way I heard them talking.'

'Do you envy them?'

'I did. I don't now. They've had many more chances and privileges than I or Gillian have had.'

'Yet they behave like lager louts.'

'Not all the time,' protested Little Fred, who couldn't resist the occasional flash of support for his fallen heroes.

93

'They don't hurt people or damage property.'

'They haven't exactly improved the decoration of Falcon House or improved Old Bill's health,' John pointed out.

'Well, yes,' admitted Little Fred. 'It got a bit out of hand.'

'These exploits only took place during the holidays. So when they went back you and Gillian behaved normally, I take it,' ventured John.

'Oh, yes. Gillian never played their games, anyway. She didn't approve in the first place.'

'Didn't you find it boring after they'd gone back? Didn't you miss them?'

'I did, yes. Gillian didn't.'

'So while they were away there was no undue influence over you.'

'I wouldn't call it influence.'

'Encouragement, then. Enticement.'

'When they came down again they asked what we'd been up to. When we said nothing much, they thought us very dull.'

'And then it all started again.'

'Yes.'

'Much to your relief, I suppose.'

'I don't know. There suddenly seemed something to live for again.'

'You can't mean that, surely?'

'Suddenly there was excitement.'

'A spurious excitement. Did you really want to get involved in their antics again?'

'They were good company,' admitted Little Fred, grudgingly. 'We had a lot of laughs.'

John realised that he was dealing with someone who was easily led, someone who was overawed by people like Tom whom he considered to be his superiors. It was obvious that his girlfriend, Gillian, tried to keep his feet on the ground.

'Gillian didn't think they were such good company, did she?' John pointed out.

'No,' agreed Little Fred. 'Gillian wasn't all that keen. She used to say, "Oh God, they're back again".'

'Did you join in with their pranks again because you thought you had to keep up with them, that you might lose face otherwise? Or did you really enjoy creating mayhem?'

'I don't really know, now that you ask me.'

'You admit that you were seduced by their ways because otherwise you would have reported Tom when you saw him shoplifting.'

'That's how it all started, yes.'

'Because you were grammar school and they were public school. Because you were working in a garage and they were doing nothing you were conscious of that famous gap known as class distinction.'

'I don't know about that.'

'It does exist, I'm afraid. Still.'

'Does it?'

'I don't suppose the girls would notice it. It's different for them. They're much more on one level. They talk about boys and clothes. Did you do any shoplifting, Fred?'

Little Fred had not expected the question and looked frightened. John Rossiter had a sudden vision of the boy being bullied at school, probably by the grammar school equivalent of Tom or Harvey.

'No. No. Not me,' answered Little Fred, fearfully.

'You only borrowed cars from your father's garage. So it was easy for you. You could take a car and put trade plates on it if necessary.'

'Harvey always said that was cheating.'

'What did he want you to do?'

'Take one from a public car park.'

'That would be your initiation.'

'Yes.'

'Did you?'

'No.'

'Did Harvey really accept you as part of the gang? I

95

mean Tom brought you in out of necessity to save his own skin. He didn't ask Harvey's permission and you said Harvey was the boss. When Tom explained his reason for inviting you, which I suppose he did, then Harvey had no alternative but to accept you. Do you think that could have been Harvey's reason for trying to bully you into attempting bigger things?'

'Probably. He was always on about it.'

'Now, Fred,' commanded John. 'To business.'

Little Fred sat up with a start.

'What business?' he asked, fearfully.

'Up to now we've been round the bushes. It's time to get down to brass tacks. How did Old Bill come into the picture?'

'I don't really know. He just appeared one day. We'd been meeting there for some time.'

'What do you call some time?'

'The whole of one summer holiday. We sat around and played tapes. We had to be careful not to make too much noise in case we attracted attention. We were there one evening chatting and laughing when one of the girls suddenly screamed.'

'Which one?'

'Eva. She was sitting on the floor facing the door. We all turned to look and there was this tramp.'

'What did he look like?'

'Tall, piercing blue eyes, dirty matted hair, very long and a drooping moustache.'

'How was he dressed?'

'You couldn't really tell. He had a long fawn overcoat, all grubby. Held together with a leather strap. And brown corduroy trousers.'

'What did you do?'

'We all kind of stood up. We didn't know what to do. We felt rather guilty as if we shouldn't have been there.'

'As you shouldn't.'

'Neither should he.'

'What happened then?'

'The tramp grinned and said, "Anything left in the bottle?" We'd got a bottle of wine, you see.'

'Stolen by Harvey from his father.'

'We let him have the bottle and he took a great big swig. Then he said, "Got any food going begging?" There was a pork pie nobody wanted so we gave him that.'

'Who handed it to him?'

'I did.'

'Were the others afraid of him?'

'I don't think so. They just held back.'

'Go on.'

'He came into the room and stood over by the fireplace. He put his arm on it and grinned at us. "My name's Bill," he said. "They call me Old Bill because of my droopy tash." Nobody said anything. Then he said, "I've been listening to your stories. Very interesting," he said.'

'What did that mean?'

'I don't know. But I didn't like the sound of it. It sounded kind of menacing. We didn't say anything, though. None of us.'

'You just stood there. Silent.'

'Yes. There was an embarrassed silence until he said, "Do your folks know you come here?" He meant our parents.'

'Did anyone answer?'

'Yes. Harvey. He said, "Yes, of course they do." Old Bill said, "I wonder". Then he gave a nasty little laugh.'

'Why do you call it nasty?'

'I don't know. But one idea suddenly came to me.'

'What was that?'

'Blackmail.'

'Ah!'

John thought he now had the key to the motive for the murder.

'Interesting,' he mused.

'He then said something peculiar,' Little Fred went on. 'He said, "When it gets dark you kids leave here to go home." Which, of course, we did. "But I can't," he said.

"I don't have anywhere to go. So could you let me have a few of those candles you've got there?"'

'Candles,' repeated John. 'Karen and the candles from Harcourt's shop. It's beginning to fit in.'

'You see,' agreed Little Fred. 'Harvey said, "All right. We'll bring you some candles", hoping that would be the last of it but the tramp wasn't satisfied. "I was here first" he kept saying. Harvey asked him how he got in. He said he picked the lock. That's why we found it open.'

'So he broke in. I thought it was you lot,' said John.

'No. Then he said, with that nasty little laugh, "Let's come to a little arrangement, shall we? You bring me some food and something to drink and I'll keep my mouth shut."'

'Blackmail, in other words,' noted John. 'As you said.'

'Yes. The others didn't think so at first. They all thought he was trying to be friendly. Very soon they were laughing and joking with him, going up to his room and all that. It was all a jolly jape according to them.'

'Not all that jolly now, is it?' John pointed out.

'No,' admitted Little Fred. 'I couldn't see what he had to keep his mouth shut about. Petty pilfering. The odd car. It didn't add up to much. There was no real harm done. The pilfered goods went to Oxfam. The cars were returned unharmed. There was the ram-raid, of course, at the jewellers.'

'So that was your doing, was it? I wondered. Nothing was missing, according to the jeweller, so it was assumed the villains were disturbed.'

'No,' explained Little Fred. 'I supplied the Range-Rover but Tom and Harvey drove it. They thought it would be great fun. But nobody wanted to go with them. I didn't and none of the girls wanted to. They thought it was too dangerous, someone might get hurt. The boys covered up the number plates and when they came back they were full of it. They were so excited you'd think they'd robbed a bank.'

'All for a lark,' muttered John. 'Some lark. I suppose they even looked on Old Bill as a bit of a novelty.'

'Something like that,' agreed Little Fred. 'He told us his life story and showed us pictures of his wife and family.'

'He had those in a wallet.'

'That's right.'

'The wallet that fell out of his pocket when he was carried out of the house.'

'Oh,' exclaimed Little Fred, in surprise. 'I didn't know that.'

'I picked it up and took it to the police.'

'He was a bit of a jailbird, you know,' said Little Fred. 'He used to say prison meant nothing to him. I wondered if he said that in case Tom or Harvey threatened him with the police.'

'As a matter of fact,' John pointed out, 'he made a habit of getting put inside for the winter months.'

'I think he told us that,' remembered Little Fred. 'We all thought it rather funny.'

'Did the sudden appearance of Old Bill put an end to your parties at the house?' John asked.

'Oh, no,' replied Little Fred. 'We still went there. He was upstairs. He didn't always come down. We took food and stuff up to him.'

'So it didn't stop what you might call your pairing off.'

'Oh, no. We paired off in different rooms.'

'I noticed that. Wasn't it uncomfortable on bare boards?'

'Grass isn't all that soft,' Little Fred pointed out.

'No. I suppose not.'

'We eventually went in for sleeping bags.'

'Stolen?'

'No. Too big for that. We kept them in a cupboard there.'

'Why did Old Bill have to be killed?'

'He started to blackmail outright.'

'What do you mean by outright?'

'Well,' Little Fed replied, hesitantly, 'it was only hinted before. I told you. I tried to warn them but they wouldn't listen. I didn't trust the man but they thought he was rather cute, as they called it.'

'What form did this new kind of blackmail take?'

'Oh, he became very awkward. He started making impossible demands. Bottles of whisky. Harvey couldn't keep up the supply. Even from his father's off-licence.'

'Why should that worry Harvey? He was the boss. He'd expect you or any of the others to do it.'

'Nobody stole anything big or important. Little things, perhaps. But two or three bottles a day from the shelves or the cellar was becoming difficult.'

'Did Old Bill drink that much?'

'That and more. He used to get legless. He'd pass out. Unconscious. We'd have to carry him back upstairs.'

'Poor devil. What were his blackmail terms exactly?'

'He threatened to go to the police and tell them everything. You can imagine the scandal that would have caused for that lot.'

'Hardly disastrous,' commented John.

'Perhaps not to you or to me but it worried them. It would ruin our bloody lives, they said. Then he wanted one of the girls.'

'What!' exclaimed John.

'Yes. He was down with us one evening, drinking as usual, all of us, when he went up to Karen and said, "Come on, girlie, show us your knickers".'

'What did Karen do?' asked John, concerned for his niece.

'She said, "Get out of it. You stink." '

'Oh dear,' sighed John.

'He didn't like that.'

'I'm not surprised.'

'He said, "So I'm not good enough for you." Then he started on Gillian. "What about you, dear?" he said. "You don't mind Old Bill, do you?" Gillian backed away from him. That did it. He took the bottle and went back upstairs shouting he'd go to the police tomorrow and turn us all in.'

'Do you think he meant it?'

'Oh, yes. So did the others. When he'd gone we talked

it over. Tom and Harvey were worried. So were the girls. At least, Karen and Eva. Gillian and I weren't so worried. We didn't think that kind of exposure could do much harm to our careers.'

'So you decided to kill him,' John prompted.

'No,' refuted Little Fred. 'Oh, no. We decided to parley. We all went upstairs. That is, the three men. We left the girls downstairs. Tom did the talking. We thought he'd be more tactful. Harvey was too much bull at a gate.'

'Did it do any good?'

'No. Tom said the girls didn't mean to offend. It came as a shock and they didn't know what to say. But it didn't work. He said he knew what the girls meant and no mistake. "They let you fuck 'em," he said, "but not me because I stink. You'd stink if you had to live as I do." Tom said didn't Old Bill think he was a bit old for them? They were young and didn't understand. "I'm only forty-five," he said. "I'm in me prime. Just right for them." You couldn't help wanting to laugh, really, but we daren't. Tom tried to placate him but it was no use. He told us to get out and leave him alone. He knew when he wasn't wanted and all that. I remember his words well because he was quite a colourful character. "Just you wait till tomorrow, my fine feathered friends. You'll find yourselves well and truly plucked. And what will Mummy and Daddy say then? What will the papers say? Mummy and Daddy's spoilt little children arrested for stealing, ram-raiding and drugs."'

'Were drugs involved?' asked John.

'No,' replied Little Fred. 'He was guessing. I think Tom and Harvey smoked something. I don't know what. Certainly not the girls. But what he said decided the boys.'

'What do you mean, decided them?'

'We came away and told the girls about Old Bill's threat. They got very frightened and worried. There was a lot of discussion and quarrels even.'

'Quarrels?'

'Yes. Harvey said we've got to get rid of him somehow. The problem was how. He wouldn't go of his own accord and we didn't have enough money between us to pay him off. In any case, he'd only come again and ask for more. Harvey said if we didn't get rid of him he'd give us away and that would mean goodbye to university, family scandals and some of us in gaol.'

'Harvey actually meant to kill him, you mean?' John asked, in disbelief.

'Oh, yes,' Little Fred confirmed. 'Tom agreed.'

'It's hard to believe,' mused John.

'They wanted to suffocate him. He was in a drunken stupor, anyway, when we left him.'

'Did the girls agree to that?'

'No. They were dead against anything. But Harvey and Tom were determined. They were thoroughly frightened of being given away. I think they were more frightened of the university and their families than the police.'

'Local pride,' muttered John.

'We all went over it a hundred times. What can he do? He can ruin us. That doesn't justify murder. It's not murder. It's getting rid of him. What use is he, anyway? He won't be missed. An old tramp. My father's the mayor. My father's the vicar. My father's a magistrate. And so it went on. To and fro. The boys decided to have a conference on their own without the girls. I was there, of course. Harvey said let's tell the girls we've managed to persuade him to leave and deal with him ourselves. The girls thought we'd been up to see him again but we hadn't, of course. So while the girls were chatting away in one room we went upstairs. The trouble was, we didn't have anything to suffocate him with.'

'You had the sleeping bags,' John suggested.

'We thought of that. But they were too big and clumsy. Tom asked me if I had a tow rope in the car. I hadn't so he said go back to the garage and get one, quick. Which I did.'

'That was a mistake,' John pointed out.

'Why?'

'Aiding and abetting,' said John, simply.

'I said I didn't mind going for the rope but I wasn't going to use it.'

'I bet you went down in their estimation then,' chided John.

'I did,' admitted Little Fred. 'They called me all sorts of shit. Tom and Harvey said they'd do it on their own.'

'Strangle him.'

'Yes.'

'I find it hard to accept that intelligent students would contemplate a cruel murder.'

'Anything to save their reputations, their good names, their careers. They kept saying they had a lot to lose and no dirty bloody tramp was going to stand in their way.'

Little Fred gave a nervous little laugh and went on, 'There was nothing that my Mum and Dad could get upset about. Or Gillian's. Dad would say I had his permission to take any car on the premises and Mum would say it serves me right for mixing with a lot of toffs.'

'I wouldn't call them toffs exactly. Snobs more like it.'

'Anyway, I went for the tow rope. When I got back the three girls were huddled in one room and Tom and Harvey were upstairs feeding Old Bill with all the whisky they could lay their hands on. He was already pretty drowsy. When they heard me Harvey came to the top of the stairs and put his finger to his lips. You know. Not to make a noise. So I crept up and handed him the rope. He put it outside the door and went in and sat with Tom and Old Bill.'

'Was Old Bill still belligerent?'

'Oh, yes. Very. But woozy with it. You couldn't say he was aggressive. He just kept muttering threats in his sleep.'

'Was he really asleep?'

'You couldn't tell. I thought he was but suddenly he'd stir himself.'

'Why did Harvey hide the rope outside the door?'

'He didn't want Old Bill to see it.'

'Well, naturally. But do you mean to tell me the three of you were waiting for him to fall asleep so that you could put a rope round his neck and pull it?'

'That was their idea.'

'Did they discuss it with you?'

'No. But what else could they do? They couldn't knock him out and strangle him.'

'That's how a professional would have done it. He wouldn't have gone through all that business with a rope. Not everybody carries a rope. A tie, a belt, a cord, anything like that would have done.'

'Well,' shrugged Little Fred, 'there you go. Harvey and Tom weren't professionals. They were just a couple of frightened kids.'

'How long did you have to wait?' John asked.

'Oh, I don't know. It seemed ages. We were all sweating and shaking. And then suddenly Harvey said, "Now!"'

'Now?'

'That's right. Harvey grabbed the rope, threw one end to Tom, slipped it round Old Bill's neck and pulled.'

'And that was it?'

'Yes,' muttered Little Fred. 'Horrible. Tom sat down with his head in his hands. Harvey leaned against the wall, shaking like a leaf.'

'And you were sick,' John reminded Little Fred.

'Yes.'

'You're prepared to repeat all that in court, are you?'

'If I have to, yes.'

'All that time the girls stayed in another room?'

'Yes.'

'Didn't they come out to see what was happening?'

'No.'

'Now, of course,' declared John. 'You had a problem. What to do with the body.'

'Yes,' admitted Little Fred. 'We couldn't leave him there. Even if we never went near the place again ourselves, even if we removed every scrap of evidence.'

'Including the candles,' prompted John.

'The candles, yes,' mused Little Fred. 'That's what put you on to us, isn't it?'

'Put me on to Karen,' corrected John. 'The rest stemmed from there. So whose idea was it to throw the body into the river?' asked John.

'Tom and Harvey between them,' answered Little Fred. 'I was told to go down to tell the girls to stay where they were because Tom and Harvey had persuaded Old Bill to leave. That's what I was to tell them. They didn't have to worry any more. Meanwhile Tom and Harvey carried him down to the car.'

'What did the girls say?' asked John.

'Nothing. They were crying.'

'What were they crying for?'

'Their little dream world had come apart. Nothing could be the same any more. No more escaping to the land of make-believe. Something like that.'

'That language doesn't sound like you, Fred.'

'No. It's what Gillian said the other two were wailing about.'

'In carrying the man downstairs his wallet fell out of his pocket,' John pointed out. 'The wallet that I kicked against in the dark. Tom and Harvey should have noticed it but in their panic they didn't.'

'That was it, I expect.'

'Who drove the car with the body in it?'

'I did,' confessed Little Fred. 'When we got to the river we had to find a quiet spot. Then there was more humping and heaving to get the body out of the car.'

'Did you do any of that?'

'No. Tom held one end of it and Harvey the other.'

'You dumped him in the river and then what?'

'We got in the car and raced back to the house.'

'To pick up the girls.'

'Pick up the girls, collect our belongings and get out of the place.'

'What belongings?'

'Sleeping bags. And the rope. I had to take that back.'

'It's still in the garage, is it?'

'Yes.'

'You'd better take it to the police,' suggested John. 'Forensic will want to look at it.'

'I'll do that,' promised Little Fred.

'Didn't you realise,' asked John, 'that killing the man was the worst thing you could have done? I mean, apart from the fact that killing is wrong, anyway.'

'We didn't stop to think.'

'You say "we" but the decision wasn't yours.'

'Nobody had time to think.'

'All that panic because an old tramp threatened to tell on you. Wouldn't it have been wiser to let him expose your little games?'

'You try telling that to the others. At first they thought of dropping him miles away when he was drunk and just dumping him. But they were afraid he would turn up again in time.'

'What made you so sure that the police would believe a dirty old tramp with a criminal record?'

'It's all very well to say that now. At the time they daren't take the risk.'

'Well, thank you, Fred,' concluded John. 'You've been a great help. You've filled in all the gaps.'

'I'm glad to get it off my chest,' confessed Little Fred.

'Is there anything you'd like to add?'

'No. No. I don't think so.'

'I'll leave you then,' said John, getting up from his chair. 'And thank you for all your help.'

'OK. Thanks,' said Little Fred, inadequately, shaking hands.

As John left the garage and got into his car he felt rather pleased with himself. His slight incursion into the realm of the private eye had proved productive and he could now send his report to Inspector Waller.

As a result of John Rossiter's report, which was a summation of his interviews, the remainder of the gang of six were rounded up by the police and encouraged to make statements, including Tom and Harvey who realised they now had no alternative but to conform. As a result they were all allowed to go home.

That afternoon John's peace was disturbed by the arrival of Susan, his sister-in-law, his *bête noire*. He had just settled in his study after dinner. Full of indignation and wrath, she arrived on the doorstep. She didn't ring the bell, she chose instead to bang the ornamental brass knocker as loud as possible as it was in keeping with her mood. She hammered it with great force and she herself could hear it echoing through the house like thunder. John even heard it in his study but took no notice of it, thinking some unversed stranger was calling and Norah, the housekeeper, would deal with it.

Norah went to open the door. Susan wasted no time on courtesies. She pushed past the housekeeper and stood in the middle of the hall.

'Where is he?' she demanded.

'In the study, I think, madam,' replied Norah, meekly.

She watched Susan stride towards John's study and virtually crash into the room. John was reading and sat up with a start as Susan barged in. She stood in front of him, threateningly.

'Now what have you done?' she accused.

'Oh, hello, Susan,' said John, casually.

She looked as if she could devour him and spit him out.

'Don't you hello-Susan-me. Karen's been taken to the police station again.'

'Yes, I know.'

'You know? And you've done nothing about it?'

'She wasn't taken to the station. She was invited to call in and make a statement, as the rest of the gang were. After that, she goes home. It's for the records. That's all.'

Slightly mollified, Susan sat in the nearest armchair, took out a handkerchief and dabbed her eyes.

'You don't care,' she moaned. 'You never did.'

'You don't know whether I care or not so don't make ridiculous statements.'

'Those boys,' Susan went on, regardless. 'I never did like them. If you hadn't started probing everything would have been all right and Karen would never have been arrested.'

'She hasn't been arrested, you daft ha'porth! Can't you get that into your noddle?'

'What good has it done her? In and out of police stations.'

'Susan,' said John, patiently. 'A man has been murdered.'

'Karen had nothing to do with it,' Susan almost spat out.

'The police know that now.'

'The scandal. We'll have to move.'

'Nonsense.'

'If you'd moved into Falcon House yourself none of this would have happened.'

'You prefer the killers to go free, do you? And a murdered man's family to mourn in vain.'

'He didn't have a family,' muttered Susan, grudgingly. 'He was a tramp.'

'He had a wife and a son and daughter.'

'Karen can't go back to Cambridge now.'

'That's up to Cambridge. Once the papers get hold of the story...'

'The papers!' wailed Susan. 'What will it do to Frank's business?'

'Nothing.'

'He'll be ruined.'

'I wouldn't be surprised if one of the national dailies doesn't offer Karen a fat fee for her story of life with the Gang of Six.'

'How can you be so cynical?'

'Dry your eyes that aren't wet, go home and collect Karen from the police station, if she's not already home and then you and Frank come round to dinner tonight and I'll give you a run-down on the whole situation.'

'Why don't you come to us?' Susan asked, suddenly conscious of her social status.

'Because I don't want to.'

He stood up and helped Susan out of her chair.

'Cheer up, Susan,' he chided. 'It's all over bar the shouting.'

'It's the shouting I'm worried about.'

He led her by the arm out of his study towards the front door. The black and white tiles in the hall had never looked so bright. If only everything was so cut and dried, he thought.

Susan didn't even say goodbye or turn round at the door, but she went down the path with less determination than she had approached it earlier. John stood at the door expecting to have to wave but it was not necessary. Susan never turned her head.

John returned to his study while Norah prepared dinner for John, his brother and his sister-in-law. Norah was no more enamoured of Susan Rossiter than was her employer but she had to keep such feelings to herself. She was grateful that she was not called upon to serve at table otherwise she might be tempted to pour the soup in the lady's lap.

During the meal, for which Frank later congratulated John's housekeeper, John recited the facts of the case against the Gang of Six, as he saw it.

'It's a case of student pranks going wrong with disastrous results,' he declared. 'A case of car stealing, shoplifting, ram-raiding and eventual murder all perpetrated, with the exception of murder, to relieve the tedium of a too-long summer vacation. It had been going on during previous breaks from university, of course. They originally called themselves the Gang of Four but they were supplemented later, as a result of a shoplifting incident, by two local non-students, namely Gillian Curran, who works in the supermarket, and Little Fred Miller, son of the proprietor of the Crossroads Garage. The leader of the gang was Harvey Winter, son of our present mayor and owner of the local off-licence. Second in command was Tom Parker, son of our vicar. The rest of the gang was made up of what you might call camp followers, not innovators of any kind. They were Eva Thompsett, daughter of one of our bank managers, and Karen Rossiter, daughter of a well-known local resident and commodities broker.'

'Oh, get on with it, John,' complained Susan. 'You're not in court now.'

'A collection of little beauties, you might say,' John went on. 'In the old days they might have been called Bright Young Things but they didn't steal or murder then. Personally, I think they all deserve what they might get. They've abused their own privileges and ridden roughshod and unfeelingly over other people's property and interests.'

'That's none of your business,' interrupted Susan. 'It's not up to you to tell people how to behave.'

'The whole affair is my business, Susan, if I am to return to the Bar to represent the culprits.'

He went on to recite the story from the beginning as he pieced it together from interviews with individual members of the gang. Some of it Susan and Frank knew, most of it they did not. But they listened. He told them how Gillian and Little Fred were co-opted into the gang, how the girls were really only ornaments, how their little world of pranks and japes was shattered by the emergence of Old Bill, how he tried to make up to the girls and then tried blackmail when he was rebuffed.

When John had finished his recital he said, 'Now let me tell you what is likely to happen.'

'About time,' muttered Susan.

'Tom and Harvey have been charged with murder and, if found guilty, could go to gaol for anything up to fifteen years or life. Little Fred could be charged with being an accessory before and after the fact and with aiding and abetting but I doubt if he would get more than a couple of years and that probably suspended.'

'What about the girls?' Frank asked.

'The girls will be sentenced, of course.'

'Oh, no!' cried Susan.

'But it will only apply to their pathetic attempts at shoplifting and whatever the sentence it's bound to be suspended. Tom and Harvey, of course, will also face the charge of ram-raiding and that sentence will run concurrently so they may end up doing more than we think. And there you have it,' he concluded.

'Will you be able to represent Karen in court?' asked Fred.

'Oh, yes,' replied John.

'I still say it would have been better if you hadn't interfered,' moaned Susan. 'If you'd gone and lived in that bloody house instead of moping about here wallowing in Dot's memorabilia.'

'You live your life, Susan, and I'll live mine,' said John.

After the dinner-table conference the whole subject was gone over again with no further conclusions achieved. John waited with ill-concealed impatience until it was time for his guests to leave but Susan insisted on going over and over the facts until Frank had to intervene.

'We can talk about it until the cows come home,' he said, 'but nothing can change it. We're in John's hands and I suggest we leave it there.'

'All right, dear,' sighed Susan, extraordinarily submissive for once. 'If you say so.'

To John's relief they got up to go and he escorted them dutifully to the front door. He retired to his study and sank into an armchair.

He looked at the photograph of Dot and said, 'And I'm supposed to be retired.'

His self-satisfaction was somewhat punctured when, one morning a few days later, he received a telephone call from Detective Inspector Waller.

'That you, John?'

'Yes.'

'Can you come down to the station sometime?'

111

'Of course. What's it about?'

'I'd rather not say over the phone.'

'All right. I'll call in this afternoon.'

'See you.'

As John replaced the receiver he presumed that the Inspector had unearthed some new evidence concerning the Gang of Six that would obviously interest him. It must be related to Falcon House because it was the only aspect of the case in which they had a mutual interest. No good guessing. Better wait and see. There was lunch to enjoy first.

During the afternoon John made his leisurely way to the police station. He was shown into Inspector Waller's office.

After the usual preliminary courtesies, John asked, 'What's happened?'

For answer, Inspector Waller passed over to John an official looking paper.

'Forensic report,' mused John. 'We've already had one.'

'That's a new one,' said the Inspector.

As John read the report the Inspector explained, 'As you probably know, Doctor Evans was on holiday when we fished Old Bill out of the river and his place was taken by his assistant, Doctor Green. He did the work on Old Bill.'

'Doctor Green's the young fellow with the red hair,' commented John.

'That's right.'

'New to the game.'

'Exactly.'

'Nice chap.'

'He is.'

As John continued to read the report the Inspector went on, 'When Doctor Evans came back he went over Doctor Green's notes and came on something that puzzled him.'

'Like the old boy being strangled instead of drowning, you mean?'

'No. Haven't you come to it yet?'

As he read on, John exclaimed, 'Oh, my God! Yes!'

'He died of a heart attack before he was strangled,' the Inspector pointed out.

'So, I see,' mused John. 'Well, I'm buggered.'

He handed back the report to the Inspector.

'They murdered him after he was dead. So it wasn't murder at all.'

'I've had to let the boys go,' admitted the Inspector.

'Naturally. All you can charge them with is the ram-raid.'

'The only evidence there is Little Fred's deposition, which they could easily deny, and it wouldn't be difficult to prove that Little Fred an unreliable witness.'

'You'll drop all the charges, then?' questioned John.

'Have to.'

'It's probably taught the little fools a lesson.'

'Let's hope so.'

John Rossiter and Inspector Waller parted in an aura of anti-climax. Neither had ever wished to charge the young students. The object of the exercise was not purely and simply to charge them. The evidence pointed to them and the leads had to be pursued. The students themselves had every right now to accuse the police of wrongful arrest and claim damages. It would put them right in the eyes of their university and the local residents and the irony of the situation was that John could possibly represent them in their claims. That would be a laugh, he thought, as he made his way back home. He didn't anticipate much of a laugh when his sister-in-law heard the latest news.

He wasn't wrong about that. He had not been in the house five minutes before the telephone rang and Susan's harsh voice called out, 'John?'

'Yes.'

There was a pause while Susan obviously drew breath before the verbal onslaught.

'Aren't you ashamed of yourself?'

'Not particularly, why?'

113

'After all the anguish and worry you've put us through? After the sleepless nights? I should have known better than to trust you. Call yourself a lawyer? I could have done better with *Pears' Encyclopaedia*.'

John held the telephone away from his ear and he could still hear her shrill voice.

'There's poor Karen scared stiff she might go to prison,' Susan went on. 'To say nothing of the agony and stigma of being arrested in the first place. And the humiliation of the newspaper stories. What you've put us through with your interfering!'

Susan paused suddenly in the middle of her tirade.

'Hello, John? Are you still there?' she asked.

'No,' replied John, quietly.

'The best thing you can do,' Susan continued. 'Is retire properly and give it all up before it gives you up. If that's an example of your legal brain I don't think much of it...'

John didn't need to listen to any more. He'd heard it all before. She would go on for ages, non-stop. If he put the telephone down she would hear the click at her end and be offended. Not that that would worry him very much. He decided, instead, to put the phone down on the table and leave it. He got up from his chair and went into the hall.

He called out, 'Norah!'

From somewhere upstairs a voice answered.

'Yes, sir?'

'I'm going for a walk.'

'All right, sir. I'll take any phone messages.'

'I don't think there'll be any,' he muttered to himself with gleeful satisfaction as he selected a walking stick from the collection by the front door.

Now for some fresh air, he thought. A walk by the river and a talk with Dot. He had so much to tell her.

114

I'LL DIE IF IT KILLS ME

When John Suter decided to kill himself he thought it would be easy. It wasn't. He found it very difficult and every time he thought he'd succeed something or somebody got in the way and spoilt his plans. He'd curse and swear and have another go. He could have committed suicide. That would have been easy. He could have sat in the car in the garage with the engine running and all that sort of thing or he could have shot himself or cut an artery. He didn't want to do it that way. He wanted it to look like an accident. In that way the insurance money would go to his wife. That was the object and he didn't want to prejudice the outcome. He realised that you had to be very careful in staging an accident. There were people called special investigators whose duty it was to make sure that it was an accident and not contrived. He had to anticipate their antics. It was not his intention to cheat the insurance company. He knew that they didn't pay out on suicides but they weren't to know that he was planning his own accidental death. He kept his plans to himself so that, by rights, no one, once the accident had taken place, could accuse him of having planned it. He wanted to be able to leave his wife comfortably off. That was the object. He was determined that she should want for nothing after he'd gone. He knew that for quite reasonable premiums the insurance companies paid out large sums of money, out of all proportion to other monies, when it came to accidents. To his wife, Julie, it would be like winning the lottery. He had to make sure, of course, that there were no small print loopholes. With the help of his insurance agent, a trusted friend, he could make sure of that. He didn't want to die only to find that she didn't get the money after all. He couldn't come back and alter anything but he'd make bloody sure he'd haunt the guts out of anybody who stood in his way.

All married couples and, these days, couples who weren't married, argue about who should go first. There's something selfish about wanting to go first. 'I hope I go before you,' Julie used to say. John never told her he thought it was a selfish idea, he simply thought how awful life would be without her, how much he'd miss her, how lonely he would be to see her bed empty. He wouldn't be able to see her sitting in the armchair that they called hers. He'd be eating alone, driving the car without her sitting beside him. Yet if he went first how would she cope with the central heating, the fuses, the water softener, the refuse bins? Did she know where the stopcock was? If he died in bed there might be time to dictate instructions but in the case of the kind of accident he planned that would not be possible. What an ordeal it was going to be for her. He felt a pang of guilt when he thought of it. Floods of tears would obscure her concentration and she'd spend her time looking up people in the *Yellow Pages*. Neighbours might help, of course, and certain relatives but, knowing Julie as he did, she would hesitate to enlist their aid. Lovely lady that she was, still only in her early thirties, a lot of men would be only too willing to help, including that cultured vulture Dr Tony Bradley who was really responsible for this whole business of getting rid of himself. She may even marry again. He wouldn't like that but he wouldn't be able to do anything about it. He shouldn't begrudge her the chance. He didn't like the idea of someone else stroking her, making love to her. Most of all he wouldn't like her submitting. But, of course, she'd be lonely and that could be terrible. He'd know how terrible because he could compare it to his own anticipated feelings. He himself wouldn't have married again. He was certain of that. The odd dalliance, perhaps, but nothing permanent. He'd even feel like wanting to apologise to Julie afterwards though she wouldn't be there.

He wouldn't be worrying about it at all if it were not for the fact that he had been told he only had so long to live. For that reason he couldn't insure his own life. Besides, he didn't want Julie to know.

John's plans, however, went awry. There's an old country saying that if you pluck a chicken against the wind the feathers will fly in your face. And that's what happened to John. He couldn't kill himself no matter how hard he tried. Something always happened. He got so used to it in the end that he thought it funny. The one close shave he had wasn't funny, though. It happened when he'd given up trying. And that, too, was funny in itself.

John Suter, a good-looking man of medium height who was in his middle thirties, had a very good job. He was one of the directors of Seymour Beauty Products so he always smelt nice. His wife, Julie, however, preferred not to use it. Seymour's scents and lotions and so on were well known. A household name, in fact. You couldn't get away from the name or the products. They were advertised in all the glossy magazines. The name was as well known as Shell, BP, Heinz or Rolls-Royce. It was a multi-million pound conglomerate that occupied the whole of a glass and steel skyscraper in the centre of London known as Seymour House. John's office was on the top floor where all the important executives were accommodated and he had his own fast lift that went from the ground floor to the top without stopping.

John's particular speciality was European Sales. It was he who was responsible for the colossal turnover of Seymour goods on the continent, including France. To compete against French perfumes, as he did, was considered quite an achievement. He would visit the Seymour agents in the various capitals of Europe and make sure that they were getting all they could out of the area.

On such jaunts he would take his wife with him and she

would amuse herself shopping or sightseeing, joining him in the evening when she acted as hostess to his more important clients.

They lived in a house with a couple of acres of garden in Newbury Cross, a popular and affluent dormitory of London. It was only 20 miles from the office. John didn't drive into London. There was a very comfortable train that got him there in half an hour.

Julie was a very attractive young woman and was popular in the village. She had her own interests, her own little circle of friends, playing tennis and golf regularly. The young men of the community enjoyed her company because, they said, she had lovely long, slim legs that went right up to her armpits and a bottom and bosom to write home about if you could find the words. Her blonde hair was worn long to her shoulders.

They had met when John was visiting one of Seymour's West Country agencies and Julie was acting as demonstrator at the local Debenhams.

From John's office window you could see for miles across London to the green fields beyond. The view was so vast that you never really knew what to look at so you ended up just looking without taking anything in. John often stood there just looking as he did now, at the end of the day, coughing every now and then, an irritable cough that had been with him for some weeks and disturbed other people rather than himself. He didn't hear his secretary come into the room.

'When are you going to do something about that cough, Mr Suter?' she asked, casually, as she put the letter book on the desk and waited for him to sign his letters.

'I don't know, Jane. It's not really a cough. Just an irritation,' he replied as he moved away from the window to sit at his desk.

He opened the leather bound book and began signing the letters.

'Don't you think you should see Doctor Watson?' Jane suggested.

'No. I'll give old Tony a ring and ask him for some anti-biotics.'

Even as he spoke he was interrupted by spasms of coughing. Doctor Watson was the company doctor, more used to anti-flu injections and broken limbs than internal complaints. The Tony that he referred to was Tony Bradley, a Harley Street doctor who had been a friend of the family for years. They had been at school together and the relationship between them was not one of doctor and patient but as long-standing friends. Tony was a bachelor which always surprised everybody because he was such a handsome, elegant character.

The cough that seemed to be bothering John did not sound dangerous. It wasn't a deep cough. It didn't come from the stomach or the chest. It sounded more like a throat irritation. Both his secretary and his wife had been urging him to do something about it, not only because they thought it was in any way worrying but because it was becoming a social irritant. He sucked some kind of sweet occasionally but it had no lasting affect. With his annual European trip coming up soon he thought he'd try and get rid of it before meeting his overseas' clients. Julie called it a nervous cough and said he could stop it if he tried. She didn't say it unkindly but she'd noticed that some days he didn't cough at all.

He didn't cough as he carried the tea tray from the kitchen to the bedroom early this morning. Even in his dressing gown and slippers; with his dark hair combed only with his fingers he was a good-looking man. He stood between the twin beds holding the tray and looking down at Julie, still asleep, fair hair spread on the pillow, one bare arm on the coverlet, half a breast exposed. As he put the tray down on the table between the beds the rattle of the cups woke her. She roused herself and struggled into a sitting position.

The bedroom was roomy and light and Julie had furnished it not fashionably but to her own taste so that it was as comfortable as it was attractive.

'It was my turn to make the tea,' she yawned.

'Couldn't wait,' said John. 'But you can pour.'

He sat on the side of his own bed while Julie poured for both of them.

'You're about early this morning,' said Julie.

'I want to call on Tony on my way in.'

'You haven't coughed this morning yet.'

'Haven't I?'

'You see?' said Julie. 'You don't know when you're doing it.'

'I haven't got a definite appointment. He said call in and he'd fit me in.'

'Get him to do an X-ray.'

'I will.'

As Julie drank her tea she asked, casually, 'Is he still having an affair with that radiologist?'

'Oh, she left.'

'Pregnant?'

'Poor Tony. He can't help it.'

'I don't think he wants to.'

Having finished his tea, John got off the bed and moved to go into the bathroom to run his bath.

'What are your plans for today?' he asked.

'I thought I'd go up to Town and do some shopping for our trip.'

'We can go up together,' he suggested.

'No. I don't want to go up as early as that. I can't go until Martha gets here, anyway.'

Martha was the name of the woman who came and 'did'. Although Julie would do some shopping in Paris and Rome there were some things she wanted to get in London before she went. If questioned she would not be able to itemise anything, but once she got inside a shop she would know.

'Would you like me to give you lunch while you're in London?' John asked.

'No, dear. I won't stop for lunch. Very kind of you.'

John went into the bathroom and Julie soon heard the hum of his electric razor.

*　*　*

Doctor Antony Bradley did not believe in getting to his rooms in Harley Street too early. Although he only lived a short distance away in Regent's Park he thought that ten o'clock in the morning was early enough for a first appointment since most of his patients came from London or within a 25-mile radius. Sometimes, of course, he would visit a patient in hospital, nothing less than The London Clinic, before arriving at his rooms; though he preferred leaving that chore until the end of the day. His rooms occupied the whole of the ground floor of the elegant old house that boasted some of the most ornate ceilings in London. As he entered the building the large waiting room was on his left, facing the street. In his splendidly furnished consulting room Miss Denny, his white-coated secretary-receptionist, was putting his appointments book on his desk. She was a middle-aged, sour-looking woman with jet-black hair pulled back tightly in a bun. She adored the doctor. She thought he was the most handsome, elegant creature that existed. He was tall, always wore a dark suit with pin-stripe trousers and a red carnation in his buttonhole. He had black, wavy hair. At 40 years of age he was most impressive and his patients were devoted to him. He was a fashionable doctor but he was also a good doctor.

'Good morning, Miss Denny,' the doctor greeted her, jovially.

'Good morning, doctor.'

'What mischief have you lined up for me today?'

'They're all in the book. Mr Dukes confirmed his appointment.'

'Oh, good,' said Tony, as he sat at his desk and opened the book. 'He should be good for a nice fat fee even if it's only a check-up. Pity he doesn't get ill sometimes. He doesn't deserve good health as well as all his millions.'

Miss Denny listened to Tony's comments stoically, inwardly disapproving of his attitude.

123

'Your new radiographer hasn't arrived yet,' she said with some satisfaction.

'No?'

Tony Bradley looked at the marble clock on the mantelpiece and frowned. It wasn't a good sign, the girl being so late on her first day.

'When she came for the interview she struck me as unreliable,' said Miss Denny.

'Oh. She struck me as rather attractive,' admitted Tony, with a grin, aware of Miss Denny's prejudice.

'I wouldn't know about that,' pouted Miss Denny.

'Mr Suter will be calling in sometime,' said Tony. 'I said I'd fit him in between appointments.'

'Yes, doctor.'

Later that morning John Suter's taxi pulled up outside the Harley Street house and he pressed the electric bell push and entered.

'Good morning, Miss Denny,' said John.

'Good morning, Mr Suter.'

John Suter was one of the very few patients that Miss Denny honoured with a smile.

'Doctor Bradley said he'd fit me in.'

'That's right. If you go into the waiting room I'll tell him you're here.'

'Thank you.'

John went into the waiting room where he found himself alone. Poor old Tony didn't seem to be very busy, he thought. He sat at the large mahogany table that stood in the middle of the room on which an assortment of magazines was spread out. He chose an out-of-date copy of *The Tatler* and turned the pages idly. What could he tell Tony? He had a silly cough that didn't hurt but was a nuisance. Well as he knew Tony and could confide in him, he felt embarrassed to be taking up his time on such a trivial matter, though the man didn't seem to be all that busy at the moment. He didn't feel that he could ask for an X-ray, in spite of Julie's insistence. That would be going too far. He hadn't coughed at all today so far. He certainly couldn't do it to order.

His ruminations were interrupted by Miss Denny coming to the door and telling him that the doctor would see him now. He put the ancient magazine aside and stood up. He followed Miss Denny to the door of Tony's consulting room.

She opened the door and announced, 'Mr Suter.'

Tony got up from his desk to shake hands.

'John!' he declared. 'Nice to see you.'

'Hello, Tony,' said John, somewhat demurely.

'Sit down and tell me all about it.'

John sat on the chair facing the doctor's desk.

'Well,' he began. 'I've got this bit of a cough. It's not on the chest. It's more a tickling in the throat.'

'Let's have a look at you.'

Tony led his friend to a curtained-off corner of the room where there was an examination couch and various medical instruments.

After a brief examination, Tony said, 'Let's go along to the X-ray room.'

Tony Bradley was one of the few doctors in Harley Street who owned a fully operative X-ray machine.

As they made their way down the corridor Tony called out to Miss Denny, 'Has that girl turned up yet?'

'I'm afraid not, doctor.'

'Never mind. I'll do the X-ray myself.'

Once in the darkened X-ray room the usual routine took place. Tony put on the heavy protective apron and John simply took his jacket off. After two or three exposures they were interrupted by an agitated Miss Denny.

'Excuse me, doctor,' she begged.

'What is it?'

'Mr Dukes has arrived.'

'Oh, my God,' exclaimed Tony as he hastily removed his apron. 'I'll have to chase you off, John,' he said. 'Sorry.'

'That's all right,' admitted John.

'Dukes is too rich to be real. He's come for his annual check-up and he hates to be kept waiting.'

'Thanks for your time,' said John as they went down the corridor again towards the front door.

'Call back at the end of the day,' said Tony, hurriedly. 'I'll have had a chance to study your X-rays.'

'I'll do that.'

Tony put his hand on John's shoulder.

'For all his money, John, I can tell you the great Ashley Dukes is impotent.'

'Bad luck.'

'See yourself out.'

John did not catch sight of the famous Mr Dukes as he passed the waiting room. He was too important for Miss Denny to show him in there. He would be shown directly to the doctor's consulting room even if he'd had a patient with him. Tony had told them at dinner about some of his famous patients, particularly Mr Dukes, supposedly the richest man in the world. How Tony, a playboy general practitioner, managed to afford such patients they never understood for, apart from such people as Mr Dukes, he could count stars of stage and screen and television and even highly-priced call-girls among his regular patients. Julie was the one who was always intrigued to hear about the call-girls for Tony did not consider telling tales to his old friends as anything like disclosing a confidence. He never mentioned the actual names. To John and Julie he was an amusing friend and quite useful because he was a very clever doctor. Added to which, he never sent them a bill.

John hummed a happy little tune as he travelled in the executive lift to the top floor of Seymour House.

'Someone's in a good mood this morning,' muttered Jane as John passed through her office on the way to his own.

She followed him into the office with her notebook. The bright sunlight streamed through the window onto his desk.

'Shall I draw the curtains?' she asked.

The curtains were vertical venetian blinds that could be adjusted by slanting the slats without losing light.

'No,' said John. 'We have so little sun it's a shame to shut it out.'

'I expect it's going to be an Indian Summer again.'

'September is always good. So is October. After that, once the clock's change, it's goodbye till spring. I think we should all hibernate.'

'Together?' asked Jane.

'That would be interesting.'

'Shall I start booking your tickets and hotels?' asked Jane.

'Oh, yes,' enthused John. 'The grand tour is coming up, isn't it?'

'For two?'

'Of course. My wife's looking forward to it. She's gone shopping today in preparation. The usual hotel in Paris, remember.'

'Yes,' laughed Jane.

'I know,' said John. 'Everybody expects us to stay at the Georges Cinq or the Plaza Athenée but the wife and I still prefer the little family hotel in the Boulevard Raspail.'

'Where you spent your honeymoon.'

'That's right. I'll do my entertaining at the other hotels, of course.'

'It saves the company money,' commented Jane.

'Don't worry. I'll make up for it in Rome or somewhere.'

'When I've got the dates shall I advise the agents?'

'Yes. The usual routine.'

While John and his secretary were discussing the European trip, Tony Bradley was fawning over his richest patient, assuring him that he was in perfect health and seeing him off the premises. By the time he had returned to his consulting room, rubbing his hands together, adjusting his Old Etonian tie in the mirror and smoothing his hair, a very attractive, provocative, nubile girl entered the building. This was Helen, the new radiologist, recommended by one of Tony's doctor friends.

'Good morning,' she greeted Miss Denny, brightly.

'You're late,' grunted Miss Denny.

'Am I?' asked Helen, innocently.

'The doctor's been asking for you.'

'Oh, good.'

'He's not very pleased.'

'Pity.'

She knocked on the Consulting Room door and entered without being told to.

'Good morning, doctor,' she said.

'And what time do you call this?' asked Tony, looking up from the papers on his desk.

'Greenwich Mean Time, actually,' replied Helen.

'How kind of you to come at last.'

'I am a little late, I must admit.'

'I shall be fascinated to learn why.'

'Do you want an excuse or the truth?'

'Don't they tally?'

''Fraid not.'

'Well?'

'I overslept.'

'Alone?'

'I never sleep alone, doctor. It's bad for me.'

Tony was far from put out by the girl's provocative remark. After all, she was the daughter of a fellow member of one of his exclusive clubs.

'You realise, Miss Woodhouse...' he began.

'Oh, call me Helen, please. And I'll call you Doctor.'

Tony admired the girl's self-assurance. In fact, he rather enjoyed the exchanges.

'You realise, don't you,' he suggested, 'that if you want to keep this job you'll have to adjust your sleeping habits.'

'Someone will have to,' admitted Helen.

Tony got up from his desk.

'Well, let me show you where everything is,' he said, leading the way out of the room.

He was conscious of the girl's expensive perfume.

'Don't bother, doctor,' said Helen. 'You showed me when I came for the interview. I haven't forgotten.'

'Oh,' exclaimed Tony, halted in his tracks. He returned

slowly to his desk. 'In that case,' he went on, 'if you go into the dark room you'll see the two X-rays I did before you arrived. The one on the left is Ashley Dukes, the one on the right is John Suter. Got that?'

'Yes, doctor.'

'Mark them up and bring them to me.'

'Yes, doctor.

The girl lingered provocatively.

'Go on, then,' urged Tony.

'Yes, doctor.'

The girl almost waggled her bottom as she went out of the room.

In spite of the girl's behaviour Tony was not displeased. He was confirmed in his opinion later in the day when she sat opposite to him, notebook on her knee, skirt hitched high enough to show an expanse of thigh. He was dictating notes on the day's X-rays.

'Ashley Dukes,' he intoned. 'Cardiac shadow normal. Lung fields normal. Send a letter to his office. Dear Mr Dukes, as usual your chest X-rays are notably interesting for their complete lack of abnormality. Yours sincerely.' Tony put the X-ray film aside and picked up another. He continued to dictate:

'John Suter.'

Realising that the X-ray film that he held in his hand was that of a particular friend of his he pondered at length before dictating to Helen.

'Poor devil,' he muttered to himself. 'Mediastinal growth.'

'What was that?' asked Helen, uncertain of what he said.

'I don't know what to do about this one,' admitted Tony. 'He's a great friend of mine and he's got a cancer that will kill him in a matter of weeks.'

'Oh, Lord.'

'Yes. It is oh Lord. He's calling back later in the day for the result of these. I shall have to tell him.'

'Shouldn't I put something down for the record?'

'Yes. Of course.'

Tony began to dictate the medical details relating to John Suter's condition. In the process he was secretly surprised how easily the girl, to all outward appearances a bit of a bimbo, tackled the unusual and tricky medical euphemisms. She didn't query his dictation even once, which impressed him.

While Tony Bradley was busy with Helen, in more ways than one, his long-standing friend, John Suter, was similarly engaged with his own attractive black secretary, Jane. The letters that he was dictating, however, were less dramatic, being what could be regarded as warning notices to the European agents that the Boss was on his way.

At the end of the session Jane closed her notebook and said, 'Do you know, Mr Suter, you haven't coughed at all this morning yet.'

'Really?'

'Didn't you notice?'

'Now you come to mention it, no.'

Jane laughed.

'You needn't have gone to the doctor,' she said.

'Oh, Tony's all right,' confessed John. 'He doesn't even charge me.'

'That's useful.'

'I've told you before. We were at school together.'

'Well, he's cured your cough just by looking at you.'

'Oh, he took pictures. I'll call back later and he'll show me. Not that I'll understand any of it.'

'I know the feeling.'

Jane went out of the room. John was surprised that he didn't cough even then. It was obviously a nervous thing. And yet when he did cough he did so because of an irritation at the back of his throat. Julie always told him that he coughed unnecessarily but he could not accept that. It would be wonderful if he could go for 24 hours without coughing. It was such a silly cough, anyway, not the sort of cough you get with the common cold or with influenza. It had been nothing but an irritation to himself and other people. In the middle of a speech in the boardroom he would start coughing and he could read the impatience on the faces of other board members.

At the end of the working day John always left his office before his secretary.

'Goodnight, Jane,' he called out as he walked through her office.

'Goodnight, Mr Suter,' she answered.

In his consulting room Tony was instructing Helen.

'I'm off on my hospital rounds now. When John Suter calls keep him here until I get back. I must speak to him.'

'How do I do that?' asked Helen.

'Do what?'

'Keep him here.'

'I don't know. Use your wiles.'

'My what?'

'Your wiles. You must know what they are. They seem pretty obvious to me. In fact, if you keep him here, I'll take you out to dinner.'

'Oh, I don't think that would be a good idea, doctor.'

'Why not?'

'It would be a waste of time.'

'Oh.'

There was an awkward pause until Helen went on:

'You're bound to want to take me back to your flat afterwards, aren't you?'

'Well...' Tony hesitated.

'So I suggest we go there first and have dinner afterwards,' Helen concluded. 'If necessary,' she added.

'Good girl,' enthused Tony.

'I hope you don't mean that,' said Helen.

Giving the girl a pat on her pert little bottom, Tony went out of the room.

'See you later,' he cried, happily.

Both Helen and Tony were pleased with themselves. Tony was convinced that the delectable Helen would keep him amused for some time. Helen, for her part, was pleased with herself because it was only her first day at work and she seemed to have made a good impression. She had expected to be invited to dinner at some time in the future, as usually happened with her, but not so soon. She was aware of Doctor Bradley's reputation. Who wasn't? Her uncle, who had recommended her for the job, had warned her that Doctor Bradley had what he naively called 'a reputation'. She had a reputation of her own of which she was rather proud. She was quite sure that she would be able to twist Doctor Bradley round her little finger.

She felt the same way about John Suter whom she first met when he called at six o'clock that evening. He rang the bell and was puzzled when there was no answering voice from the front door intercom. He was aware that it was late for consultations but this was a personal call and he knew that Tony invariably worked late. Suddenly the heavy door was opened not by Tony, as John had anticipated, but by a very attractive girl wearing a white coat that somehow suited her and enhanced her sexuality.

'Oh,' said John, taken aback.

'Yes?' said Helen with a smile, head on one side.

'Er ... Doctor Bradley. I've called to see Doctor Bradley.'

'Are you Mr Suter?' asked Helen, eyeing him up and down speculatively.

'That's right.'

'Come in.'

She stood back, opening the big, black door wider. John stepped inside. Helen closed the door and led the way to the consulting room, talking over her shoulder:

'I'm afraid the doctor hasn't got back from his hospital rounds yet,' she said.

As soon as they entered the consulting room Helen closed the door, which John thought surprising. He thought she'd keep it open for when Tony got back.

'Sit down, Mr Suter,' said Helen.

John looked about the room. A doctor's consulting room is rarely furnished to provide opportunities for lounging so John decided to sit in the chair facing the desk. Helen decided to sit on the edge of the desk facing him. She crossed her legs to reveal an expanse of thigh once more, a habit she seemed to enjoy. Her idea was to arrest his attention.

'I'm to entertain you until Tony gets back,' she explained, smiling invitingly.

So she calls him Tony, thought John.

'What would you like?' asked Helen. 'Strip tease, song and dance, a recitation or a drink?'

John was embarrassed by the girl's attitude. Did Tony really engage such outrageous people to work for him? His secretary, Miss Denny, was a prim and proper character and he and Tony had always made fun of the poor old dear, but this girl was the other extreme. John was no prude and no doubt this new girl satisfied some of Tony's requirements but he didn't relish her qualifications being directed at himself.

'I – I think I'll just wait,' said John.

Helen realised that she was being a bit outrageous but how did you entertain a man who was just about to learn that he had only a few months to live?

'Not a drink?' she asked.

'No. Thank you.'

'I think I will.'

Helen knew where Tony kept his drinks, not in a cabinet but in the bottom drawer of his desk which was deeper than the others and ideal for the purpose. She took out a bottle of scotch and a glass.

'Sure you won't?' she offered.

'Quite sure. Thanks.'

She poured herself a glass of whisky and proceeded to sip it neat.

'Mmm...' she exclaimed. 'Tony certainly has good taste.'

John had never before experienced such a bizarre reception in a doctor's consulting room. He knew that Tony had a certain reputation and the staid Miss Denny was circumspect in the extreme, but he would never have believed that he would let his radiographer, no matter how out-going or how attractive, behave in such a way. She was virtually flaunting herself. Any minute he expected her to do a strip tease, as she had suggested. She was either very sure of herself or not sure enough. He sat hoping that Tony would come as soon as possible. He kept looking at his watch.

At length he said, 'I don't think I can wait much longer.'

'Oh, don't go,' cried Helen, in alarm. 'He won't be long. He's taking me to dinner. Not bad on my first day.'

'No. I suppose not.'

'I used to work for a doctor, who shall be nameless, in Wimpole Street. I couldn't stand it. A succession of Indians, Asians, Arabs. A convoy of Liquorice Allsorts. I never saw a white patient from one day to the next. I had to give it up. At least here you meet civilised, cultured people like yourself.'

'You shouldn't talk like that, you know,' admonished John.

'I know. Nobody should. But a hell of a lot of people want to. I wouldn't say it outside this room.'

'Have you seen the report of my X-ray?' John asked, suddenly.

Helen was suddenly cautious.

'I'm sorry,' she said. 'What did you say?'

'Have you seen the report of my X-ray?' John repeated.

'Oh, yes,' Helen replied.

'Funny,' mused John, 'I haven't coughed since I saw Tony this morning.'

'That's good.'

'Can I see the report? As he's not here.'

'Well...'

Helen hesitated.

'A patient is allowed to see his report, isn't he?'

'Well, yes, but I don't know about seeing it before the doctor.'

'The doctor's already seen it.'

'I mean, without the doctor's permission.'

'He can't withhold it.'

'No, that's true.'

'Then where is it?'

Helen hesitated. She hadn't anticipated the encounter developing in such a way. She thought that all she had to do was entertain John Suter until the doctor arrived. Knowing the content of the report she was loath to let the man read that he had an inoperable cancer.

'I really think you should wait until Tony gets here. He can explain...'

'I can't come back tomorrow or any other time this week and I can't wait here forever, so you might as well show it to me.'

'Well...'

Helen still hesitated.

'Do you know where the report is?' asked John.

'Yes. It's there on the desk.'

John reached over and took up the manila folder that was resting on Tony's desk pad. Helen made a quick move to intercept him but failed.

'Mr Suter, I don't think you should. Not without the doctor.'

'Don't worry. I'll fix it with Tony. You won't get into trouble.'

Pleased with himself, John leaned back in his chair and opened the file. Helen watched him anxiously, all coquetry abandoned. Her hand shook as she put her drink down on the desk.

John read the report. He did not react in any way except for a slight frown. He turned the file back and read the report again. He looked at the front of the file where his name was written.

'Are you sure this is mine?' he asked.

'Yes.'

John just looked at her, steadily.

'Cancer of the lung,' he said.

Helen merely nodded, dumbly.

'I haven't coughed all day.'

135

'It's nothing to do with the cough,' said Helen.

John returned his attention to the report.

'A few months,' he muttered. 'At most.'

He looked up and gazed into space.

'That takes us to Christmas,' he said to himself.

He's taking it pretty well, thought Helen, relaxing and feeling less anxious. She took up her drink again.

'Would you like a drink now?' she asked.

John had closed the folder and was simply gazing into space.

'No. No,' he said, distractedly. And then, 'Thank you.'

There was a long silence while John sat still, tapping his hand on the file.

'What did the doctor say?' he asked.

'He wanted to talk to you. That's why he wanted you to wait. He wanted to explain to you about treatment.'

'Treatment?' echoed John, showing some animation for the first time. 'I've heard about some of the treatments. They're worse than the illness. No thank you.'

He threw the file back on the desk and stood up.

'You're not going?' pleaded Helen, also on her feet.

'Yes,' said John 'There's no point in waiting.'

'But he won't be long, I'm sure.'

'If he's held up wouldn't he phone?' asked John.

'No,' said Helen. 'He was quite sure you'd wait. That's why he asked me to entertain you.'

'I'll leave him a note,' said John.

He wrote on Tony's pad, tore it off, folded it and handed it to Helen.

'Give him that,' he said.

He turned and made his way to the door. Helen hurried after him.

'Please, Mr Suter,' she begged. 'Don't go.'

John ignored the girl's entreaties. He strode across the hall to the front door, heaved it open and went on his way down the steps to the street. Helen stood at the open door watching him. She saw him step out into the road and flag down a passing taxi.

136

Helen closed the door and walked slowly back to the consulting room. She'd failed. She felt sorry for the man. She was close to tears as she poured herself another drink. She sat in Tony's chair and read again the report on John Suter. She wondered if she should have let him see it. But how could she have avoided it. It was a pity that the file should have been on the desk. She wondered at John's reaction as he read it. He seemed to take it in his stride. But he must have been shocked and frightened. He didn't show anything. He seemed to be in a daze. Perhaps the real reaction would come later. How would she herself have reacted? She felt quite sure that she would have been devastated and in floods of tears. The mere idea of a life ending was frightening. It wasn't as if John Suter was an old man. He was hardly in his prime. What would he do now? She felt sure that the doctor could persuade him to submit to treatment. Not that any treatment would save his life. She knew that.

Her musings were interrupted by the banging of the front door. That would be the doctor, she decided, and vacated her seat at the desk. She crossed the room to open the door.

Tony strode into the room carrying his black leather medical bag which he dumped on his desk. He turned to Helen.

'No John Suter yet?' he asked.

'Been and gone,' said Helen.

'What!'

'He said he couldn't wait any longer. You are rather late, you know.'

The barb was not lost on Tony when, earlier in the day, he'd chastised Helen for lack of punctuality.

'I felt sure he'd wait. As a friend. Not as a patient.'

'Not after he'd read the report,' said Helen.

'What!' Tony exclaimed again.

Tony sounded and looked shocked and alarmed.

'You showed it to him?' he accused.

'It was on your desk. He helped himself. I said he should

wait and let you explain but he said something about a patient having the right to his report.'

'That's all very well,' said Tony.

'He went off quite calmly. No hysterics.'

'No. There wouldn't be with him.'

'He left you a message,' said Helen, handing him the note that John had written.

Tony took the note and read it.

'If you say a word to his wife he'll kill you,' said Helen. 'I read it.'

'I see,' said John.

He sat down at his desk and tried to compose himself. The cat was well and truly out of the bag. On the other hand, John had only learned for himself what he, the doctor, would have told him. He must try to speak to John and talk about the possible treatments for his condition, none of which, unfortunately, he had much faith in. It was only a matter of prolonging the agony. He couldn't ring him at home in case Julie became suspicious. He would phone him at the office in the morning.

In the meantime he had rather an intimate appointment with Helen and as he poured himself a drink, he said, 'How about a top-up?'

'Oh. I always like the top-up,' replied Helen, suggestively.

'No comment,' said Tony as he replenished Helen's glass.

Sitting in the taxi on his way to Marylebone Station John felt as if he was in a vacuum. His ears felt as if he had gone deaf. He was looking without seeing. He couldn't believe his own thoughts. Would he see these London streets again? He had a few months left so, of course, he would see them again just as he would sit in a taxi again. The realisation that there was a limit to how often made him look at things with more interest. The back of the taxi driver's head. Did he have a wife and family? Would he live to an old age? What would he do if he were told he only had a few months to live? Break down and cry? Get drunk? No doubt he'd still be driving his taxi after John was dead and gone. To all outward appearance people would assume that John was unaffected by his news, but inside he felt numb, as if under the effect of some kind of anaesthetic. He had come to the end of the line yet he was on his way home as if nothing had happened. In fact, nothing had happened. He simply knew that his time was coming to an end. Otherwise everything was as it used to be. He felt no pain. He hadn't coughed all day. Something had cured that.

In the train he found an empty carriage and sat down hoping that no one else would get in. Because of the delay at Tony's the usual crush of regulars had gone on their way.

He wouldn't tell Julie. She wouldn't be on the train as she sometimes was when they have been to London together. She would have used her car because of her shopping. He would have to act normally when he got home, behave as if nothing had happened. He wondered what happened Afterwards. Would he be able to see things? Would he be able to watch Julie, keep an eye on her? He'd want to. He'd want to see her with her friends. And there was Tony, of course. He should be able to help her. They'd done so many things together, the three of them. Dinner parties, theatres, holidays. Tony always with a different girl. Could Tony be mistaken about the cancer business? Should he ask for another opinion? What's the point? Tony's no fool. In spite of his philandering he was a bloody good doctor. Whenever he or Julie had been ill he had got them right in no time. He was also very well thought of by other doctors. On top of that, you can't get away from the X-ray. There it was, so to speak, in black and white. What a bloody nuisance. Just as he was about to embark on the European tour with Julie. It would be a lovely break for her. Give her something to remember. One last fling. He'd make sure she had a good time. That's it. That's what he'll do. She needn't know. She wouldn't notice anything. He wasn't likely to turn into a skeleton overnight. Behave as if nothing had happened. He kept telling himself that. Perhaps he'd take her out to dinner tonight. She'll be tired after her shopping. No need to cook tonight. What about Marlow? The Compleat Angler. She likes it there.

When he arrived at Newbury Cross he made his way across the car park to his car. The registration number of his car was reproduced on the boundary fence for which he paid a certain sum of money every year for the privilege. His home was only a couple of miles from the station and as he turned into the driveway he was pleased to see Julie's car standing there. That's another thing. Would she sell her own car and use his or vice versa? She didn't like driving big cars. She said they were difficult to park.

As he opened the front door he called out as usual, 'I'm home.'

The echo came from upstairs, 'Coming down.'

He went into the garden room, a long room with huge sliding windows that gave access to the terrace and the garden. They used the room as a general sitting room during the summer months so that they could enjoy the flowers and shrubs and watch the birds feeding on the food they put out for them.

He stood looking out at the garden. Julie wouldn't have to worry about that. Contract gardeners came once a week to keep it tidy. He wondered if he would see the daffodils next spring. And the snowdrops. There was the winter to get through first, though. He should still be around then. Christmas? Would he last that long? He would try to get Julie to deal with the central heating. He would slyly teach her how to adjust it. The fuses in the house were simple. She knew how to deal with those because it had been necessary on occasions last winter before he got home. She also knew how to replace light bulbs. In an emergency, of course, there were certain telephone numbers to call.

Julie came into the room looking happy and youthful. She was wearing a dark blue dress with white cuffs and collar.

'Hello, darling,' she cried.

They kissed briefly, habitually.

'You're later than usual,' she remarked.

'I know,' said John. 'I had to wait for Tony to finish his hospital rounds.'

'Oh, what did he say?'

'Nothing. He said it's habit. And I haven't coughed all day.'

'What did I tell you?'

They laughed together.

'What about you?' John asked, anxious to keep away from anything medical.

'Oh, quite successful,' Julie replied.

As they were ensconced in their normal armchairs Julie said, 'I still think Selfridges is a good bet. Harrods was impossible.'

'Prices, you mean?'

'No. People. And the assistants. I got out of there as soon as I could.'

'You know what I was thinking in the train?' said John.

'What?'

'Why don't we go to Marlow for dinner tonight?'

'Oh, I don't know, dear,' said Julie in a tired voice. 'Do you really want to?'

'I was thinking of saving you the trouble of cooking anything.'

'There's nothing to cook, really.'

'Don't you want to go out?'

'Not really. I'm a bit tired from shopping.'

'All right,' concluded John. 'Tomorrow then.'

'See how you feel,' said Julie.

Julie wanted to relax but John couldn't. He wanted to do something. Keep himself occupied. He had to be careful, though. He was usually as relaxed as Julie in the evening and he didn't want to give her the impression that anything was wrong. As a rule they had a glass of wine with their evening meal and he decided to wait for that. If he went to the drinks cabinet straight away that might arouse suspicion. In any case, he didn't think that drink was the answer to his problem.

'I bought one or two nice things for going away,' said Julie.

'Good.'

'I'll show them to you later.'

'Good.'

'I think you'll like them.'

'I'm sure I will.'

Even with the television and the meal over John could not forget his problem. When would he begin to feel anything? What form would it take? Would Julie notice anything? Was there any medication he could take? These, of course, were questions he would have asked Tony if he'd stayed on in his consulting room. He would ring him in the morning from the office and go and see him again. Perhaps he should have waited. But that would have made him later still getting home and what could he have told Julie? Drinking and chatting? She knew he was meticulous about getting home in the evening. He would also have a word with his accountant, he decided. He wanted to make sure that Julie would be well provided for. His bank balance was pretty healthy, he knew that. But it wouldn't be added to once he was no longer part of the Seymour conglomerate. There would be a company pension, of course. He had a life insurance policy. From memory he didn't think it was an awful lot. He couldn't increase that now because he wouldn't pass the medical. Julie could sell the house, of course, and move into something smaller. That would give her extra money. But he still felt it wasn't enough. Money. Money. Money. It wouldn't cure a broken heart or alleviate any grief but for his own selfish peace of mind he would like to know that she was safe. Money was the problem that nagged at him more than the actual cancer.

He discovered that his sense of application was in no way impaired. He managed to eat his meal without any difficulty. Also, surprisingly, he slept well. He started working out a plan of directions which he would get his secretary to type out setting out detailed instructions on how to operate such things as the water softener, the central heating, the hot water, electrical fuses, intruder lights. To him, as he lay in bed, it was the equivalent of counting sheep for half-way through his catalogue he fell asleep. It was one of the best night's sleep that he had had for a long time. The irony of the situation struck him in the morning when Julie told him that she had had a bad night. He didn't feel any different in the morning. He didn't notice any difference in himself when he looked in the mirror and examined himself in the bath. The only difference he noticed was that he hadn't coughed since he called on Tony the previous morning. He weighed himself. He hadn't lost anything. He ate his breakfast and enjoyed it. He kissed Julie goodbye at the door. Instead of the perfunctory farewell peck he gave her a real kiss, a warm, affectionate embrace which rather surprised her and caused her to chuckle, as if to say what on earth is the matter with you? He felt a slight pricking behind the eyes as he left her but he told himself he must be careful not to show any undue emotion for that could give the game away. He drove to the station, parked his car and waited for the train. It was a beautiful morning and a blackbird was singing his heart out somewhere along the line. He tried to locate it but couldn't see it.

As soon as he arrived at the office he asked Jane to put a call through to Tony Bradley. Jane noticed that John was not his usual smiling self. He was stern and businesslike as if he was preparing to quarrel with someone.

'Tony,' said John when the call came through. 'We've got to talk.'

'Certainly, old boy,' replied Tony. 'When?'

'This morning.'

'Lunch?'

'No. Your rooms.'

'What time?'

'Twelve o'clock.'

'I'll make time for you.'

'Thanks.'

That was the extent of the conversation, brief, to the point, friendly and perfectly understood.

When Jane came into the office with the morning's mail and her notebook, John said, 'I've got an appointment with Doctor Bradley at twelve.'

Jane made a note in her book and was prompted to ask, 'I hope everything's all right, sir.'

'Quite all right. Thank you.'

'You haven't coughed since you saw him yesterday. I hope this appointment doesn't start it up again.'

'I don't think it will.'

'I expect Mrs Suter is looking forward to her trip.'

'Yes. She is.'

As John said it he wondered if it would be wise to take Julie with him. If anything happened while they were away what would she do? She may even have to find her way back alone. Would she notice any deterioration in him as time went on? What form would that deterioration take?

'Shall I arrange the usual accident policies?' asked Jane.

John wasn't paying attention.

'I'm sorry. What did you say?'

'Should I arrange the usual accident insurance for flying?' Jane repeated.

'Yes. Yes. Of course,' said John.

Then, as an afterthought, he asked, 'How much is it?'

'I don't know exactly,' admitted Jane. 'But it's very little. I know that. Accident policies usually are.'

'Are they?'

John was suddenly interested.

'Oh, yes,' Jane enthused. 'I used to do a lot of it for my previous boss. Apart from flying it can cover being run over, falling off a cliff, anything.'

'Really.'

Insurance was something that John had never thought about seriously apart from the usual life policies and household risks such as fire and burglary.

144

'How much do you cover us for when we travel?' he asked.

'As much as you like. Half a million?'

'As much as that?'

'Would that be enough?' Jane asked.

'Oh, I think so,' admitted John. And then added, 'Each?'

'Oh, yes,' agreed Jane.

When the girl had left the office John got up from his desk and went to the window. He looked at the fantastic panoramic view without really seeing it. There were green hills in the distance but he'd forgotten where they were supposed to be. While he was gazing into space an idea began simmering in his brain, an idea emanating from Jane's chance remark about insurance. What if he took out an accident insurance on himself only? Not just while flying. He could then leave Julie a large lump sum. He thought he could manage an accident somehow. He looked down into the street below. He didn't fancy falling out of the window. Apart from the pain, he'd occupied the office for so many years that such an accident would be viewed with suspicion. Such an action would be regarded as suicide and he knew that insurance companies did not pay out on suicides.

He returned to his desk and busied himself with his work until it was time to visit Tony Bradley.

They sat across from each other in Tony's consulting room.

'I must say, John, you're taking it very well,' said Tony.

'How else can you take it?' replied John, somewhat aggressively. 'Tearing your hair out won't help. I'll be losing that, anyway, I expect.'

'Not necessarily,' said Tony.

'I'm not going in for all that fancy treatment. I've seen what happens to other people. We had a poor sod in the office who went through all that. He said he'd rather be dead. And he was. Very soon.'

'I can't help agreeing with you to some extent. But as a doctor...'

145

'As a doctor, bollocks!' John burst out. 'I want you to promise me one thing.'

'What's that?'

'Not a word to Julie. Not a hint. Not a whisper.'

'If you say so.'

'Let me deal with this in my own way.'

'Fine.'

'If you say anything to her I'd kill you and have nothing to lose.'

'Dramatic but understood,' noted Tony, calmly.

There was a silence between them.

'What do you plan to do?' asked Tony at last. 'Just go on as usual?'

'Yes,' admitted John. 'Why not?'

'Julie is bound to notice some time.'

'Not necessarily.'

'But she's bound to nearer...'

Tony hesitated.

'Nearer the end, you mean?'

'Well, yes.'

'We'll deal with that when we come to it.'

'Up to you,' said Tony. 'What about painkillers? You're not anti those, are you?'

'I'm not in pain.'

'You will be.'

'Then I'll have your painkillers as a stand-by.'

'I'll give you a prescription. You can cash it when you like so long as you don't take them all at once.'

'That would leave Julie in a fine mess. I wouldn't do that.'

Tony began scribbling on his prescription pad.

'No,' he said. 'I think you're more sensible than that.'

'I know someone who used to take sleeping pills,' said John. 'Instead of pills he used suppositories but still the doctor would only give him a few at a time. As if he was likely to stuff the bottle full up his bottom.'

John laughed at his pathetic attempt at humour.

'The way they smuggle drugs these days you never know,' said Tony.

146

He handed John his prescription.

'Thanks.'

John put the piece of paper in his wallet so that it would not easily be discovered, not that Julie would ever think of such a thing. He and Tony parted amicably murmuring about having dinner or Sunday lunch or a golfing day sometime.

It was near lunch time but John did not fancy any of the fashionable restaurants where he had an account. It was too much like being on parade, a curtain-up kind of feeling. There would be people he knew and he would have to engage in small talk if only to the waiters and staff with all of whom he was quite friendly. He chose instead a cosy pub in one of the mews in the Harley Street area where he could sit quietly and enjoy his bread and cheese and pickles and a glass of wine. He was doing a lot of thinking lately, not about himself but about Julie. He wanted her to be safe, secure. He kept thinking about it so much that it became an obsession. He wished that he knew someone who could move in with her and look after her. She had a sister who lived down in Sussex but he wasn't sure that they got on all that well together. Occasional meetings were happy enough but anything permanent could, he was sure, spell trouble. There was Tony, of course. In spite of his philandering and womanising he was a steady and reliable character and he was fond of Julie in as much as he was happy in her company and John was well aware of his friend's boredom threshold. When he had a chance he would ask Tony to keep an eye on Julie if and when anything happened to him. He could tell him that on the telephone. He should have thought of it when he was with him just now.

Returning to his office he at once called Jane and gave her instructions.

'First of all,' he declared, 'change that accident insurance to one person. One.'

'Still for half a million?'

'Three quarters.'

147

He decided that if he increased it to a full million it might cause suspicion.

'Does that mean your wife's not going with you?' asked Jane.

'Yes,' said John.

'She'll be disappointed.'

'Unfortunately,' John said. 'I called her at lunch and her sister's not very well. She doesn't think she can leave her.'

'Oh. What a pity.'

'Yes.'

John hoped that his lie was convincing. He only hoped that he could be as convincing when he broke the news to Julie. He knew that Jane and Julie were friendly. Sometimes when Julie was in London she would call in the office and they would chat together.

'Is that all?' asked Jane.

'Yes. I think so.'

'The same hotels?'

'Oh, yes.'

'Including your old favourite in Paris?'

'Of course.'

He chuckled at the idea but it was something of a poignant chuckle as it would be the first time that he had stayed there on his own since he and Julie stayed there on their honeymoon. Whenever he went on business trips with her to Paris they always stayed there and in the same little suite where they spent their romantic first night. It amused the Seymour accountant who was always anticipating massive Ritz-style expenses. He made up for it, though, in all the other cities on his route.

All through the afternoon he was worrying about explaining to Julie that she would not be joining him on his trip. He could hardly explain it to himself. All he knew was that once he was away on his own he would contrive to bring about an accident of some sort that did not look like suicide. He didn't quite know how he would bring it about but he knew that the presence of Julie would hamper his efforts. He would need to be completely alone. He

148

wasn't planning to throw himself off the Eiffel Tower or anything so spectacular. He would simply keep his eyes open for a natural hazard that he could turn to his advantage.

Such an occasion occurred on his way to Marylebone station that evening. It was such a lovely evening that he decided to walk instead of taking a taxi. On his way he had to pass an area where some houses were being demolished to make way for a high-rise office block similar to the Seymour building. A man on a crane was operating one of those heavy balls used to knock down buildings. There was a sign which said 'No Admittance' which John either did not notice or chose to ignore. He saw the opportunity of a short cut and took it. He was walking beside a high brick wall when the heavy ball operated by the crane driver crashed into it a few yards in front of him. He stopped. He found himself enveloped in a cloud of brick dust. While he was coughing and spluttering the foreman of the works in his white hard hat came running across the site to John.

'What the 'ell are you up to?' he shouted, angrily.

'I was taking a short cut,' explained John, shaking the brick dust from his clothes.

'Short cut to 'eaven,' accused the foreman.

John smiled to himself at the appropriate remark.

'Can't you see the notice? It says Danger. Keep Out. That wall could have come down on top of you and killed you.'

'I'm sorry,' John apologised. 'I didn't see it.'

'Get out as quick as you can,' urged the foreman. 'Unless you want to commit suicide. We're working overtime and the boys are in a hurry. They haven't got time to look out for jaywalkers.'

The man turned away in disgust and returned to his little shed which served as the site office.

'Spoil sport,' muttered John as he picked his way out of the rubble.

That was just the type of accident he was trying to create but, in this instance, his hopes were thwarted. Of course he saw the sign. He purposely walked into the path of the demolition ball.

He tried again later as he was walking along the pavement. He heard a bus coming along behind him. He decided to cross the road but just as he was about to step off the pavement a man walking beside him grabbed his arm and pulled him back.

'Look out,' he cried.

'Oh,' said John. 'Thanks.'

'Nearly copped it there, old chap,' said the man. 'You'd have been a gonner.'

The man walked on and John followed slowly feeling dejected and chastened.

'Why can't you mind your own business,' he moaned, scowling at his rescuer's back.

After that he gave up the idea of trying to devise a spontaneous accident. He would have to make sure there could be no outside interference. He remembered the items which were excluded from an accident policy. Jane had read them out to him for amusement. They included war, invasion, hunting, polo, racing, hazardous adventures, fits, pregnancy, venereal disease. The only item that worried him was hazardous adventure. Could his trespassing on the building site be classified as hazardous adventure? Or stepping off the pavement? He felt sure that the term applied more to mountaineering or some such pastime. Potholing, scuba diving, bungee jumping and so on. None of which John had any intention of attempting.

His problem now was to convince Julie that it was not possible for her to accompany him on his European trip. He hadn't finalised his story yet or decided when would be the right time to tell her. He didn't want to fudge the issue by making excuses or organising some anaesthetising function such as dinner or the theatre to soften the blow. He decided that the best course of action was a straightforward lie. He would say that the chairman of the company, known among the staff as Auntie Annie because of his founding of the Ann Seymour company, called him

150

into his office and explained that he was introducing certain economies, not because of any falling off of business but as a safeguard. The same stricture, he would say, applied to the other directors who were planning on taking their wives with them to New York, South America and the Far East. That should sound convincing. She wouldn't know about the other wives. It was not anticipated that the restriction would be permanent but was intended as an experiment. He would say that he himself doubted that the experiment would create anything but a deterioration of good will among the agents abroad who always looked forward to introducing their wives into the Seymour circle. It sounded a plausible enough story.

In the train he went over the dialogue in his mind. Tell her at once. That was the thing to do. Before he put the car in the garage. She would be disappointed, of course. But how would she react? She could only accept the situation. She was unlikely to contact any of the other wives in the company to exchange commiserations. It wouldn't matter if she did once he himself was abroad and out of the way.

At Newbury Cross Station, as he was crossing the metal footbridge that spanned the track and gave access to the car park, he wondered how safe the side rails were. He took hold of one and shook it. It was rigid. No luck there if he fancied falling against it and onto the track below. He couldn't even throw himself under a train from the platform. That would be too obvious. He must find a way of disposing of himself that was natural or as a result of someone else's negligence.

He made his way to the car park and drove home giving the traditional toot on the horn as he entered the driveway. That meant that Julie would open the front door for him if she wasn't busy. It was something they always did.

'Hello, darling,' she cried, in greeting.

'Hello, dear.'

After a brief kiss he moved into the hall with her.

151

'Bad news, I'm afraid,' he announced at once.

She shut the front door and followed him into the garden room.

'What's happened?' she asked, fearfully.

John turned to face her as she came into the room. They were both standing up.

'Aunt Annie called me into his office this afternoon. He's starting an economy drive. God knows why. The company is rolling in money. Anyway, he says no wives on foreign trips.'

'Oh, no,' exclaimed Julie as she collapsed into one of the armchairs.

'Sorry, dear,' said John, sitting down.

'But why so sudden?' asked Julie.

'Search me,' said John. 'All the other wives are probably asking the same question.'

'The company's not in trouble, is it?' Julie asked.

'Far from it.'

'Then why?'

'He's got a bee in his bonnet. Perhaps he thinks the wives detract from our concentration. Which is ridiculous because the whole thing is only a PR exercise anyway.'

'What do the others say?'

'Who?'

The conversation was going well so far, he decided. He hoped that Julie was not thinking of involving the other wives in some kind of communal commiseration.

'Why, the others who take their wives,' explained Julie.

'It's the same for all of us,' said John. 'Mike Somerfield is furious. His wife loves New York.'

'What a shame,' murmured Julie.

'Sorry,' said John again, feeling inadequate.

'If it's a matter of economy,' suggested Julie, 'I could pay for myself. That wouldn't concern Aunt Annie.'

John hadn't anticipated that argument and was somewhat nonplussed. He didn't know what to say.

'I don't think he'd like that,' he said, lamely.

'He needn't know.'

'He'll find out.'

'How?'

'I don't know. He's bound to. It would be going behind his back.'

'Would that matter? He wouldn't fire you, surely.'

'I don't know what's in his mind. He says it's not a permanent thing, just an experiment.'

There was a silence between them. John felt that he had got away with his ruse.

'Of course,' said Julie eventually. 'I could go to Paris ahead of you and we could meet accidentally.'

John laughed.

'And in Rome and Athens?' he asked.

'Yes. Why not?'

'It's a thought but it won't work.'

'I don't see why not.'

'I'd be worrying about you all the time. Travelling on your own like that.'

'That's ridiculous. I'm quite capable of...'

John cut her short.

'Ridiculous or not, I'd worry,' he declared.

The remark silenced Julie until she muttered, 'Why the sudden economy drive?'

'I don't know,' confessed John. 'Aunt Annie's just got it into his head. You know how unpredictable he is.'

'He's not cutting down on other things, is he? Advertising, for instance.'

'It's just a phase. It'll pass over.'

'Not in time for us.'

John could feel himself losing ground in the argument.

'I particularly wanted to be with you on this trip,' said Julie, sadly.

John wondered, fearfully, if his wife had some kind of premonition in which case he decided to laugh it off.

'What's different about this trip? I've been away before. Often. Unless you don't trust me, of course.'

'No. It's not that. I can't explain. It's just that I'd like to be with you.'

153

'I'd like it, too,' said John, mollified. 'But it's just not on. Sorry.'

'Oh, it's not your fault.'

'I'll hurry the trip up a bit. Get back sooner.'

'I don't want you to neglect anything on my account. Aunt Annie wouldn't like that.'

'What will you do?' asked John, anxious to change the subject.

'I don't know,' mused Julie. 'I'll have to think. I could go and visit Isobel, I suppose.'

Isobel was Julie's sister who lived in Sussex where her husband farmed several hundred acres.

'Would you like that?' asked John.

'No.'

Julie was inclined to be suddenly tearful.

'Darling,' cried John, solicitously, 'I'd love you to come with me. You know that.'

'Yes. I know. Don't worry.'

'But I do. I don't want to go without you.'

He started pacing about the room.

'Hell!' he exploded. 'Why don't I tell Aunt Annie to go to hell?'

John felt his resolve deserting him. Seeing Julie so upset he wanted to abandon his plans and stay with her. He wanted to confide in her, tell her about his consultation with Tony. And then what would happen? She would worry herself sick and watch him gradually deteriorate. He couldn't inflict that on her.

'Nobody tells Aunt Annie to go to hell, darling. You know that,' said Julie, resignedly.

'I love you, darling,' said John, simply.

Julie looked up at him in surprise. Why should he say that out of the blue? She knew that he loved her. She loved him, too, but they didn't mention it except perhaps when they were actually making physical love and even then it seemed obligatory. John sat beside her on the sofa and put his arm round her. He kissed her on the cheek.

'John!' she exclaimed. 'Don't be silly.'

154

'Sorry. I just felt sorry that you wouldn't be coming with me.'

'If I didn't know you I'd think you'd been drinking,' she laughed.

John felt guilty, wary.

'Either that,' she continued,' or you're putting me off going because you're meeting someone else over there.'

'You'd still be able to come.'

'Would I?'

'Why, yes. I'd make out I had a business date and nip off and see whoever it might be. And you'd be none the wiser.'

'You think.'

They laughed together and John gave Julie another quick kiss. Their lovemaking that night was as tender and peaceful as ever. They had their exciting moments but John always thought the enjoining was something comforting. He remembered, way back in his early days of lovemaking, how reassuring and friendly it felt to contact someone else's feet at the bottom of the bed. And the actual insertion, as he called it, was a real fusion of spirits. He even considered that the exciting climax rather spoilt the peace. For her part, Julie appreciated the tenderness which was obviously unique to John. She blessed him for it for she judged it an expression of his sincerity. John could never be a rapist, she decided.

At the office next morning John entered whistling quietly to himself.

'Someone's in a good mood this morning,' remarked Jane, getting up from her desk and following him into his office.

'Good morning, Jane.'

'Good morning, sir.'

'Do you know what you are, Jane?' John asked, standing and looking her up and down.

'No, sir,' she answered.

'Beautiful.'

'Oh dear.'

John suddenly put his arms round her and kissed her. 'There,' he said, standing back from her. 'Put that in your filing cabinet.'

'Thank you, sir,' said a smiling Jane. 'I will.'

The man wasn't drunk, she was sure of that. It was too early in the morning for one thing. Perhaps he was excited about the European trip. In any case, she wouldn't object to such a greeting every morning. John was a very handsome man and no one could object to his attentions no matter what form they took.

'Your mail, sir.'

She put a small pile of letters on his desk.

'Thank you.'

She went out of the room. John sat at his desk and began reading his letters. As he read his mind wandered. He thought of Julie having to put up with her sister while he was away. After a couple of days they would be fighting as usual. They were so different from each other. He felt guilty about inflicting it on her. He could hear Isobel's voice as she greeted her sister and her critical remarks. 'I don't like that colour on you, dear.' 'Are you sure that fits properly?' 'There was a button off one of those blouses you sent me.' She just didn't know how to be gracious. Fortunately Julie was used to it and took no notice. But it registered nevertheless.

John couldn't wait for his European tour to start. He was convinced that at some time during the tour he would find a way of manoeuvring a fatal accident. Until then he was virtually marking time, treading water. He didn't consider it a matter of facing Death with a capital D. It was more a way of looking after Julie. He was suffering no pain organically and he hadn't coughed since calling on Tony. No doubt that part would come eventually. He hoped to be able to end it all by the time that happened.

At the end of the day, five o'clock, John was in no hurry to leave the office. He looked out of the window and could see, many floors below, men and women pouring out of the building like ants. He was too high up to be able to identify anybody. He opened the window and leaned out to get a better look, something he'd never done before. He wondered if, for safety reasons, the windows shouldn't be locked. It was obviously presumed that executives on the top floor were responsible characters of a sound mind. The window sill, such as it was, was hip high so you couldn't fall out. John measured the height against himself. It was a possibility, he thought. He couldn't lose his balance but if he eased his bottom onto the metal frame that made up the lower part of the window, the secure part that didn't open, and rocked himself to and fro would it be possible to fall out? He tried it. No. It didn't work. He sat there, half of his bottom in the office and half out of the window, wondering what he could do to make his fall look like an accident. He could make out that he'd fallen backwards out of the window. He would have to do it in front of someone else, though, to make it authentic. For instance, he would have to be stepping back, laughing at something, say, and fall back against the window frame. Even then he would need some kind of propulsion to precipitate a fall. He tried sitting astride the bottom half of the window, one leg outside and one in just as if he were sitting in a saddle. He wasn't frightened. He was just about to swing the office-side leg over when the door opened and Jane came in. She stopped and stood aghast.

'Mr Suter!' she cried. 'Are you trying to kill yourself?'

She hurried to him and helped him back into the room. How did she guess, he wondered, pleased with himself, amused. He returned to his desk.

'No, dear. There's no value in it,' he explained.

Jane went to the open window and looked down into the street.

'Ugh!' she shuddered. 'Shall I close it?' she asked.

'Yes, please.'

Jane closed the window while John signed the letters that she had put on his desk.

'Everybody's gone home,' she said.

'Why haven't you?' John asked, accusingly.

'I rather like the place when it's empty,' she replied.

He finished signing his letters and handed them to her.

'Will you want me for anything?' she asked.

'Such as?'

Jane shrugged her shoulders.

'Not tonight, thanks,' John told her.

'Then I'll say goodnight.'

'Goodnight.'

He watched her go out of the room and shut the door. He took a sheet of paper from his desk drawer and began to write:

My dearest love. By the time you read this I hope to be out of your life, not because I wish it but because I think it is for the best. Tony will tell you...

He stopped, put his pen down and went over to the window again. Without opening it he looked down. He didn't think he could do it that way. He returned to his desk. He screwed up the message that he had written and threw it into the wastepaper basket. He sat quietly for a moment then he realised that what he had written could be interpreted as a prelude to suicide so he retrieved the paper, spread it out on his desk and tore it into very small pieces and put it in his pocket. He didn't want an inquisitive cleaner putting it together. He would throw it out of the railway carriage on the way home. Feeling rather frustrated he prepared to leave the office. He felt disappointed in himself. He wasn't frightened of the drop from the window. No doubt there'd be a sudden thud and he'd know no more about it. It was the difficulty of staging it that angered him. That bloody window. What a stupid design. Obviously designed for safety, dammit. In the fast executive lift he wondered idly if a falling body would travel any faster. It was certainly a fast lift and when he got out at the ground floor he felt as if he had made a parachute jump.

At home that evening Julie thought that he was particularly quiet. Not unhappy or worried. Just quiet.

158

'Are you all right?' she asked.

'Yes. I'm fine. Why?'

'You seem quiet.'

'I was thinking of the trip.'

'You're not worried about it, are you?'

'No. Just wish you were coming.'

'Oh, don't keep on about it,' urged Julie. 'I've resigned myself to a fortnight with Isobel so let's forget about it.'

John felt rebuffed but he realised that the sharpness in Julie's voice was probably due to disappointment and he shouldn't have reminded her.

The morning came when a hire car was waiting in the driveway ready to take John to the airport. The suitcase and the briefcase were put into the car while John and Julie held back in the hall to say goodbye. They didn't want to be seen kissing though the kiss was maritally perfunctory.

''Bye, darling,' said John, with a choke in his voice.

'Be careful,' said Julie, equally choked.

John sat in the back of the car. He blew a kiss to Julie and waved as he drove away. At the end of the driveway he turned and waved out of the back window. Julie stood in the doorway waving the car out of sight. John realised that it was the last time that he would see his wife waving to him. The picture of her standing in the doorway and waving would have to last him for what was left of his life. He had to admit that he felt rather tearful.

An equally tearful Julie made her way to the kitchen and began to pour herself some coffee. They hated being parted from each other. She looked at the kitchen clock. Eight fifteen. In a few hours he would be phoning her from the Paris hotel where they had spent their honeymoon. She wondered if it had changed very much. She remembered that it was privately owned and had been in the same family for years. It always looked as if it wanted a lick of paint but the family seemed loath to spend money on it. Perhaps they couldn't afford to. It was situated on the Left Bank in the Boulevard Raspail and it was a taxi drive or a good walk to the Champs-Elysées. John would obviously take a taxi to the George Cinq to meet his important clients.

On reaching the airport John found the usual upheaval. There can be no doubt that the best and most convenient part of air travel was from the moment you got in the plane to the moment you got out. The rest was bedlam, boredom and frustration. As John took his seat in the Paris plane he had no sooner settled himself in than an elegant gentleman chose to occupy the seat beside him.

'Do you mind?' the man asked.

'Not at all,' said John, hoping that the man didn't start talking to him.

John preferred to look out of the window and think.

There was the usual safety belt instruction at take-off which John always chose to ignore. He'd heard it so often. The man beside him fastened his seat belt dutifully. John studiously looked out of the window. The seat belt creased his jacket so he didn't bother with it. If there was an emergency he would use it, of course. Once the plane was airborne and the man next to John had unfastened his seat belt, he turned to John and said:

'You know, you're the sort of person who makes my life interesting.'

'Oh?' said John.

'I noticed that you didn't fix your seat belt.'

'Oh,' said John. 'Didn't I?'

'I don't think you were paying attention.'

'Probably not. Sorry if it alarmed you.'

He hoped that it was the end of the conversation. Another interfering bastard like the foreman on the building site, John decided.

'It didn't alarm me,' the man went on. 'It's part of my job.'

'What is?'

'Noticing things like that.'

'Oh.'

Once again John hoped that the conversation was over. But it wasn't.

'I'm in insurance,' said the man. 'I'm a claims assessor. I investigate the cause of so-called accidents.'

John was inclined to ignore the remark and then thought better of it.

'That's funny,' he said.

'Is it?' the man asked.

'A coincidence, anyway,' John explained. 'I insured myself before coming on this trip.'

'You and everybody else on the plane. Myself included. But if the plane did crash and it was discovered that you hadn't fastened your seat belt your claim would be invalid.'

'Really? I'll make sure next time. Thank you for telling me.'

'You're welcome.'

John resumed his survey of the clouds but wondered if he could question his neighbour to his own advantage. He turned to him and remarked:

'As an assessor I suppose you're a kind of detective.'

'Something like that,' the man agreed.

'It's up to you to find out if an accident is phoney.'

'That's right. You'd be surprised, for instance, the different ways people try to kill themselves.'

'Really?'

'Earthquakes, floods, hurricanes, lightning. They're easy,' the man went on, warming to his subject. 'No mystery about them, except a scientific one, of course. It's the murder that looks like an accident and the accident that's really a suicide that fascinates me.'

'Surely it's difficult to prove that sort of thing,' suggested John, tentatively.

'Difficult? No. A challenge, yes. You develop a nose for it. The unexpected explosion, the gun that just went off, electrocution in the bath, swallowing something by accident and no witnesses. No witnesses, that's the suspicious bit. Catch a lot of people out there.'

'Yes,' agreed John. 'I can imagine.'

Witnesses, he thought. How was he going to manage that?

'It's very interesting work,' the man concluded.

'I'm sure,' said John.

Bore that the man was, John decided that the information was useful. It didn't deter him from his intention but it made him mindful of possible snags. He wasn't sure that he could provide witnesses to any accident he might devise. On the building site that interfering foreman would have been a witness. When he tried to step off the pavement the bus driver would have been a witness. Provided he made sure that his accident took place in public there was bound to be a witness. He didn't intend to hang himself. Although there have been incidents of accidental hangings. He had read about them in the newspaper.

The sight of Paris from the air always excited John. If Julie had been with him she would have been sitting by the window and she would have given his hand a squeeze at the sight.

'Paris!' exclaimed the man beside him. 'Fantastic, isn't it? What do you think when you look down there?'

'As a matter of fact,' said John, 'I was thinking how much my wife would have enjoyed it.'

'What!' the man laughed. 'That's taking a sandwich to a banquet and no mistake.'

One of those, thought John, dismissively.

'Don't forget your safety belt this time,' prompted the man.

'I won't,' said John and proceeded to struggle with the straps.

It took longer to get through the airport in Paris than it did to fly through the air to reach there. John eventually acquired a taxi to take him to Boulevard Raspail, a journey of something near an hour since the airport was far from the city centre and the roads were jam packed with traffic. There was no rush hour in the world like the Paris evening rush hour. It was an event, a spectacle. It was a performance and you got the impression that those taking part knew each other and were thoroughly enjoying themselves.

The Hotel Fleury in Boulevard Raspail was named after the Fleury family who had owned it since it was built many years ago. It was a building flush with the street, having a central doorway with revolving doors and two sets of windows either side. It was a tall building, six storeys high with narrow balconies to the upper floors. The suite at the very top of the building was known as the honeymoon suite and it was this accommodation that John and Julie always occupied when they stayed there. They always joked about the meanness of the Fleury family in not spending money on the property, though there was never anything lacking in comfort or service. In fact, the peeling paint had become quite familiar. Now, however, much to John's surprise, decoration was in progress. As soon as he got out of the taxi he was aware of ladders and scaffolding and when Madame Fleury herself greeted him she apologised for the disturbance.

'Welcome home, Mr Suter,' she beamed, her large, black-clad bosom heaving in her excitement. She was a short, dumpy soul with prematurely grey hair.

'Hello, Madame Fleury,' said John.

'No madame?' queried Madame Fleury.

'I'm afraid not this time. Her sister is not very well,' explained John.

'Oh, I'm so sorry. But I've booked you in your usual suite. I hope that is correct.'

'Yes. Thank you.'

He looked about himself, noticing the newly-decorated reception area.

'Not before time, eh?' commented Madame Fleury.

'Well...' John did not like to agree.

'Monsieur Fleury's mother died,' said Madame Fleury, conspiratorially, laughingly.

'Ah!' exclaimed John, understanding.

Franco, the ancient porter whose uniform, shiny with age, had not yet been replaced, carried John's suitcase as they entered the lift. Franco spoke no English and was determined never to try, such was the attitude of many of the residents and shopkeepers in the area. It was a kind of silent rebellion against the Americanisation of the Champs-Elysées district. They were determined that such infiltration should not enter the Left Bank.

The suite that John occupied was not exactly grand. It was more bijou. The twin-bedded bedroom – twin beds were installed for John and Julie much against Madame Fleury's instinct – was furnished in the typical heavy French style. The windows looked out over the boulevard as did the windows of the sitting room adjoining. Once Franco had put down the suitcase he left without lingering for a tip. That was also part of his resentment of foreigners. John wandered about the suite remembering the times he had stayed there with Julie. After loosening his tie and taking off his jacket he sat in one of the armchairs in the sitting room, picked up the telephone and dialled his home number. As he was waiting for the connection he noticed a sign hanging from the handle of the glass doors leading to the balcony. It was in English and French: 'Attention. The Management warns guests that it is dangerous to use the balcony whilst repairs are in progress'. He was so pre-occupied by the significance of the notice that he was not aware that Julie was saying hello at the other end of the telephone.

'Hello, darling,' said John, suddenly.

'Hello, sweetheart,' said Julie. 'It's very quiet here without you.'

'I'll soon be back, dear. I'll make it as short as possible.'

'Please. Was it a good flight?'

'Oh, I'm all in favour of flying but Heaven preserve me from airports.'

'I know,' Julie laughed.

'I hope you're sitting down, dear, because you're in for a shock.'

'Oh. What's that?'

'The hotel is being re-decorated inside and out.'

'No! I don't believe it.'

'Old man Fleury's mother died and obviously she was the one who put the brake on.'

'Not before time. What's our room like?'

'They haven't reached the top floor yet but they're doing some repairs to the balconies.'

'I never felt safe out there at the best of times.'

All the time they were talking John had his eyes fixed on the balcony. He couldn't wait to investigate the possibility of a convenient accident out there.

'What are you going to do now?' Julie asked.

'First of all I must ring Andre and ask him round. He's not a George Cinq fan. He's only round the corner from here which is convenient.'

'Give him my love.'

'I will. When are you going down to see Isobel?'

'Some time tomorrow, I think.'

'I'll ring you there about this time.'

'That'll be nice.'

'Must go now, dear.'

'Bless you.'

'And you.'

After John rang off he went at once to the balcony window. He looked out to see that the balcony itself was in a pretty dilapidated state. But for the slender support of a bracket loosely bolted to the wall on one side it would surely fall to the ground. He took out his pocket handkerchief, spread it in his hand and picked up the warning notice hanging on the door handle and dropped it on the ground near the central heating radiator. He made sure it was face to the carpet and kicked it aside so that it was out of the path to the window. He opened the double windows and knelt down to inspect the balcony. He was not prepared to step out onto it at the moment. It was obvious that the structure wouldn't stand the weight of a normal adult. He got to his feet and, leaving the glass doors open, went to the telephone and called a number.

He was calling Andre Rousseau, an old friend and agent for Seymour Products in Paris. He was a tall, elegant,

165

boulevardier interested in good food, good wine and willing ladies. He appreciated John's fondness for the Hotel Fleury, not only for its sentimental attachments but he knew that the food in the area was far superior to the grand, expensive establishments on the opposite bank. Andre was a middle-aged bachelor but was never without female company.

'Hello, Andre,'

'John!' boomed Andre as he recognised the voice of his friend.

'How are you, Andre?'

'I'm fine, as usual. And you?'

'I'm fine, too.'

'And the delightful Julie?'

'She's fine.'

'What does she think of the new Hotel Fleury? I see they're giving it a facelift.'

'She's not with me this trip,' said John.

'Oh,' said Andre, disappointed. 'That means we will not be so happy.'

'I'm afraid she had to stay with her sister who's not very well,' John persisted in the lie.

'Oh, what a pity. My new friend, Josette, was looking forward to meeting the oh-so-elegant English lady.'

'How is Josette?'

'Obedient,' said Andre, simply.

John laughed. He knew what Andre meant. This man was not a sadist by any means, which could be interpreted from his remark. He really meant that she conformed, fitted into his way of life.

'When can you come round?' asked John.

'When you like, dear sir,' countered Andre.

'Come round now,' suggested John. 'And share a bucket of champagne. Then we can talk business and discuss where we're going to eat.'

'Ah, yes!' exclaimed Andre. 'There is a new little place just opened at the end of your boulevard. I have been there and it's very good.'

'Good. Let's try it.'

'Unless, of course,' said Andre, somewhat meaningfully, 'you want Maxims and the Lido and all the trimmings.'

'I certainly do not,' John assured him.

'I shall put some clothes on and be with you in a few minutes.'

'Aren't you dressed?' asked John.

'My dear friend, it is matinée time. One does not keep one's clothes on during a matinée.'

'Of course,' conceded John. 'How stupid of me.'

John was always a little taken aback by Andre's sexual programme.

As soon as John had replaced the telephone he rang for a bottle of champagne and two glasses. Then he remembered the warning sign hidden on the floor by the central heating radiator. He'd better put it back in place before they came up with the champagne. Again using his pocket handkerchief to avoid finger prints he retrieved the sign, hung it on the door handle and closed the windows. Before Andre arrived he would again hide the sign and open the windows to the balcony. Remembering the words of the insurance man on the plane he intended Andre to be the witness to his planned accident.

He sat innocently on the sofa as the waiter struggled in with a bucket of champagne and glasses.

'Shall I open it, sir?' the waiter asked.

'Please.'

He watched the man open the bottle expertly, easing the cork out so that it made hardly any noise and fanning the neck with his towel to avoid it bubbling over.

As soon as the waiter had gone out of the room John was across the room hiding the warning sign once again and opening the doors to the balcony. It was a beautiful evening and Paris still looked sunny and green in spite of the time of year. Julie used to like standing on the balcony and looking down the endless expanse of Boulevard Raspail and across to the white dome of Sacré Cœur. Leaving the casement windows open, John returned to the

167

sofa and waited. He wouldn't step out onto the balcony himself until Andre arrived.

Andre, tall, handsome, dressed like an Englishman, entered the sitting room as if he'd been encored. There was always something theatrical about Andre. He could speak perfect English but affected an accent because he knew that it attracted the ladies. He was very knowledge-able about food and wine and never failed to air his views in company. In spite of all that he was very efficient at his job and John and the Seymour Company valued his services.

John stood up as Andre came into the room and there was much embracing and Gallic kissing.

'Ah!' exclaimed Andre as he caught sight of the champagne. 'How civilised.'

John began to pour the wine. They raised their glasses to each other as they sat together on the sofa.

'Your health,' proposed Andre.

'That's a laugh,' muttered John to himself.

'What did you say?'

'I said not 'arf,' John lied.

'Not 'arf? What is that?'

'An expression. It means very much. That sort of thing.'

'Does that mean I can say to a lady I love you not 'arf?'

'Of course you can.'

'I will try it.'

'Let me know what happens.'

The two men raised their glasses to each other and sipped their champagne. Either because he was anxious about his forthcoming balcony scene or out of sheer ner-vousness John started coughing and choking.

'Your champagne has gone the wrong way,' remarked Andre, idly. 'There is only one way for it. Down the throat.'

John was almost asphyxiating himself, struggling for breath. Andre hurried to him and slapped him on the back. John got up and hurried to the bathroom. Andre thought it best not to follow. He could hear John cough-ing and spluttering so he decided that the crisis was over.

'Sorry about that,' John called out. 'Won't be long.'

'Do not worry,' Andre answered. 'I am admiring the view.'

In the bathroom John straightened up in alarm.

'What did you say?' he called.

The answer was a horrified scream and the sound of a crash. John ran out of the bathroom and across the sitting room. The casement windows were open, the balcony was hanging precariously from only one unstable bracket and Andre was clinging to the edge of the floor with his finger tips and crying for help.

On the pavement below a small crowd had gathered attracted by the fall of masonry and the man clinging to the ledge of the building. John got down and flattened himself on the floor so that he could grab hold of Andre's wrists to prevent him from falling.

'I can't lift you,' cried John.

'Help me. Pull me up,' pleaded Andre.

'I can't.'

At that moment the sitting room door burst open and Mrs Fleury and a couple of porters rushed in. They ran to the window and hauled Andre inside where he collapsed on the sofa in a state of exhaustion.

John poured him a glass of champagne, which he brushed aside.

'Cognac,' he demanded.

John went to the mini-bar and found a miniature of brandy which he poured into a glass and took to Andre, who swallowed it in one gulp.

'Not a very good brandy,' he muttered.

Meanwhile a gabble of excited French was being exchanged among Mrs Fleury and the porters, who began searching for something on the floor, behind furniture and outside the window.

'What are they saying, Andre?' asked John, anxiously.

'They are looking for a notice which should be hanging on the window,' he explained.

'Ah!' said John, understanding.

169

'Don't worry,' chuckled Andre. 'I will sue them for heavy damages and you will be my witness.'

That's funny, thought John. Andre was supposed to be his witness.

'I could have falled to my death,' Andre complained, now fully recovered and rather enjoying himself.

With a triumphant cry one of the hotel porters found the warning notice that had fallen down behind the central heating radiator. He waved it in the air.

'*Voilà!*'

Mrs Fleury protested volubly. How did the notice get there? It should be hanging on the door handle. It couldn't have fallen there. Someone must have moved it. Who? One of the cleaners? She would investigate forthwith. She replaced the notice on the door handle, ushered the porters out of the room and turned to Andre.

'My apologies, monsieur,' she exclaimed. 'The notice, as you see, should have been on the window. Someone moved it. I will find out who. Have no fear.'

'Fear?' echoed Andre. 'I've never been so frightened in my life.'

'I apologise,' was all Mrs Fleury could say and went out of the room.'

'Idiot,' moaned Andre. 'Wait till I sue them.'

'I'm not coming all the way across to Paris to appear in court,' said John, pouring champagne for them both.

'No. Of course not,' agreed Andre, subdued now. 'I don't suppose I'll sue. But I'll threaten and they may make me an offer.'

'They're insured I suppose,' said John.

'Oh, yes. But that will mean investigation. Who moved the notice? Did you see it when you came in?'

'No,' John lied.

'If it had fallen it would have been on the floor at the bottom of the window. It couldn't fall sideways behind the radiator. Unless the vacuum cleaner pushed it there.'

'Proper little Inspector Maigret, aren't you?' commented John, anxious to change the subject.

'The porter showed you to the room when you arrived. Did he notice that the sign was missing?'

'I've no idea.'

'You'd think he'd call your attention to it as a warning.'

'You'd think so.'

'This was your honeymoon suite years ago, wasn't it?'

'That's right. Otherwise I'd have had one of the other rooms.'

'This is the only suite.'

'That's right.'

'I don't understand it,' concluded Andre. 'It's a very efficient hotel. They could have locked the windows and removed the key. Then they wouldn't have needed a notice. Or they could have warned you at the desk.'

'Oh, let's forget it,' urged John, whose sense of guilt was beginning to worry him.

There was a silence between the two men. It was almost a silence of embarrassment except that they were the best of friends. Out of friendship John felt that he should make some kind of explanation to Andre. So he said:

'Can you keep a secret, Andre?'

'Not if it's a good one,' Andre replied.

'I'm serious.'

'If you don't think I could keep a secret you wouldn't tell it to me.'

'I did it,' admitted John.

'You did what?' asked Andre.

'Hid the notice.'

After a shocked silence Andre asked, 'Why?'

'It's a long story.'

'There's plenty in the bottle.'

Andre's flippancy did not disguise his concern. John told him exactly why he moved the notice from the window. He told him about his little cough, which was nothing, and his visit to his doctor friend, the revelation of the X-ray. He told him that he had insured himself against an accident so that Julie should be well cared for. He explained why he hadn't brought Julie with him on this trip because it was not his intention to return to England alive. It had been his intention to step out onto the balcony and fall to his death while Andre was watching so that he could be a witness. But the whole thing had gone arse upp'ards, as he concluded.

Andre listened to his friend in serious silence.

'Of course it is a secret between us,' he assured John.

Then, after a reflective silence, Andre said, 'My dear man, you can't do it.'

'Why not?'

'There has been so much progress in medicine.'

'I've seen it,' John interrupted. 'I've seen what some of the poor buggers have to go through in the name of what they call a cure, which it isn't. It's only a postponement.'

'Isn't that something?'

'How long do you prefer to stay in God's waiting room?' asked John, lightly. 'A week? A month? It's going to happen in the end and I don't want Julie agonising and suffering as she watches me deteriorate.'

'What can I say?'

'Nothing. Forget I told you.'

'You have made me sad,' said Andre. 'I wanted to have a happy dinner with you but now...'

Andre was almost tearful.

'We can still have a happy dinner,' protested John. 'Come on. Drink up and let's get going.'

He pulled Andre to his feet and took his glass from him.

'Now then,' said John,' you're going to take me to this new restaurant you mentioned. Where is it?'

'Just down the road,' muttered Andre, not very happily.

'Can we walk it?'

'Oh, yes.'

'Good.'

While John and Andre were enjoying a gourmet dinner at L'Etoile in Boulevard Raspail Julie was sorting out the clothes she would pack in the morning to take down to Sussex where she would stay with her older sister, Mary.

When it came to choosing she was careful not to select her latest acquisitions. She could not bear to hear her sister bleat, 'I haven't seen that before. Is that new?' She wasn't looking forward to the visit. She didn't like her sister. They just didn't get on. She found her domineering and critical. She had even been like it at home. At meal times she would say, 'You don't pronounce it that way,' or 'Oh, that's out of date now.' She was forever putting Julie down. Mary was married with children and that was another bone of contention. 'Of course you've never had children,' Mary would say, as if childbirth carried with it some divine right, some universal accolade which relegated Julie to a tribe of untouchables. The children were in their early teens and very seldom at home so what pleasure Mary gleaned from their company Julie could never discover. They always turned up when Julie visited, however, and she got on very well with them, as she did with Mary's husband. Although he was a farmer he was a very go-ahead character who knew all about computers and any new-fangled gadget that came onto the market. He was a slim, slightly handsome man who obviously thought it his duty to have children, for he did not take much notice of them. Julie suspected that he was not altogether faithful to his wife, though not seriously. It was just something he took in his stride like everything else in his life.

The telephone in Mary's house was in the hall at the bottom of the stairs. There was an extension in Mary's bedroom but Julie couldn't expect to use that. John usually called her early each morning when he was abroad and when she was home it was simple because they could linger over their conversation and enjoy the long silences that people in love seem to enjoy. In Mary's hall, however, she could only say things like 'I love you' if the coast was clear.

John phoned the first morning that she was with her sister. He told her that Paris had not changed very much. Some of the streets were dirtier than he had remembered and at night you could see the odd vagrant in the street sleeping against the wall but otherwise it was the same gay city of food and laughter. He told her about the dinner with Andre but he said nothing about the collapsed balcony. He also told her that he was just leaving for a meeting at the Ritz with the Seymour representatives. It was known as a working lunch. The company hired a private room at the Ritz and the Seymour representatives from all over France, shepherded by the ubiquitous Andre, gathered at the Ritz to air grievances, if any, and listen to future plans expounded by John. For some of the representatives, of course, it was an excuse for a couple of nights in Paris with accompanying comforts, but nobody worried about that, least of all the Seymour Company. Good food; good company and good beds, as Charles Dickens may have asserted, was the Seymour slogan on such occasions.

When Julie later recited John's news to her sister the uncharitable comment was, 'You should have gone with him.'

Did this mean that Mary would rather not have her sister's company thrust upon her or that John had some ulterior motive in not taking her? You could never tell with Mary.

'He wanted to take me,' said Julie, lamely.

'You should have insisted.'

'I couldn't do that. It was a company decision.'

'Bit sudden, wasn't it? After all the years you've gone together.'

'It's an economy measure.'

'Economy?' Mary scoffed. 'Yet they spend a fortune entertaining at the Ritz. Pull the other one, dear.'

Julie certainly did wonder, Mary had that effect upon her. She trusted John. He wouldn't make excuses for not taking her.

'I expect if the truth were known,' Mary persisted, 'John didn't want you to go. I know what men are like when they get the chance to be off on their own.'

'John's not like that,' protested Julie, regretting the remark once she had said it, knowing that her sister would ridicule her apparent naivety.

174

Which she did, of course. When she laughed Julie wanted to hit her. She wondered how long she could stay with her sister, what excuse could she make to leave? She should never have agreed to visit in the first place. She would have been much happier in her own house, even on her own. Poor John thought she would be lonely. She couldn't feel more lonely than she did at this moment. At least at home she could go to London and call in have coffee with John's secretary. She was very fond of the dark-skinned Jane. She was a very attractive and friendly girl.

John, of course, would soon be on his way to Athens, the next stop. He would phone again tomorrow morning. She began to wish that he wouldn't if it became an embarrassment in front of Mary. She wondered if she could invent some ruse to get home. It would mean talking against John, talking over his conversation, but he would understand. She would make out to Mary that John was curtailing his trip and coming back. She was feeling that desperate. Her day was made up of accompanying Mary to the supermarket and pushing the trolley while Mary raided the shelves. Each purchase was an excuse to complain about the cost of living, the ever increasing spiral of prices. 'And they talk about no inflation,' chided Mary. Although not specifically aimed at Julie being an extra mouth to feed the inference was not lost on her.

Fortunately, when John phoned next morning there was no fear of being overheard on Mary's extension because Mary was in the kitchen preparing breakfast. It didn't matter if anyone heard her side of the conversation so long as they didn't hear John's. John himself was puzzled at first, but very soon understood Julie's motive.

'Oh, John, what a shame,' said Julie. 'Just as you were off to Rome, too.'

'Shame?' asked John, puzzled. 'What's a shame?'

'It must be a great disappointment to you.'

'Julie, are you all right?'

'That's taking economy too far, I'd say,' persisted Julie.

'Calling off a tour before it's even started. But don't worry. I'll get home and get everything ready for you.'

'Ah!' exclaimed John, realising that Julie wanted to get away from her sister.

'Have you fallen out with her already?' he asked.

'No,' said Julie. 'I'm not disappointed. I'll be glad to see you home. You're the one who should be disappointed.'

'All right, dear. I'll give you a ring at home when I get to Athens.'

'Good. I look forward to that. Goodbye, darling.'

Julie had to be careful not to appear too jubilant when she met Mary.

'Everything all right?' asked Mary as she poured coffee for her sister.

'Fraid not,' said Julie.

'Oh?'

Julie waited until she could speak without appearing too pleased with the news.

'I don't know what the company's coming to,' she said.

'You mean Seymour Products?'

'Yes.'

'Why?'

'First of all they economise by barring wives from travelling with their husbands, now they're recalling the husbands.'

'What do you mean?' asked Mary, puzzled.

'John's having to curtail his trip.'

'You mean he's coming home?'

'Yes.'

'When?'

'Now.'

'You mean he'll be home?'

'Before me if I don't get back.'

Julie looked blankly at her sister. Did she suspect anything, she wondered.

'The company's not collapsing, is it?' asked Mary.

'I hope not,' replied Julie.

'No,' continued Mary. 'John wouldn't want to go looking for another job at his age, would he?'

176

Julie could not help noticing a note of triumph in her sister's remark.

'Oh, that's nothing to worry about,' said Julie. 'Another company would snap him up.'

'It's worrying, though, isn't it?' Mary persisted.

'Not really. John's already been headhunted.'

'Oh, has he?' Mary was still not satisfied, so she went on. 'I've never understood what all this junketing is about. People are going to use the cosmetics of their choice no matter how often John goes prancing around Europe.'

'I suppose you're right,' admitted Julie, ready to agree to anything so long as it didn't stand in the way of her getting home.

'So you've got to get back?' concluded Mary.

'I'm afraid so.'

After a brief silence Mary said, rather sadly, 'I'll miss you.'

'I'll miss you,' said Julie.

'Hardly worth making the bed up, was it?' laughed Mary.

'Hardly.'

Julie laughed, too, but still felt guilty.

'Mind you,' said Mary. 'I've always thought John was a bit unreliable.'

'It's not his fault,' protested Julie, wondering if this departure would end in a fight as it usually did.

'Maybe not,' conceded Mary, grudgingly. 'But I can't think of jobs like John's as anything but precarious.'

'Why?' asked Julie, aggressively.

'Well, it's not serious or important, is it? Anything to do with leisure or entertainment is a bit iffy.'

'You don't consider cosmetics important?'

'No. Not like medicines.'

Julie decided not to continue with the argument. She would never be able to convince her sister that John did a proper day's work. She was always inclined to look down her nose when anything to do with Seymour Products was mentioned. She herself did not use the product, of course. Otherwise she would have been more sympathetic and would certainly expect to be fully supplied with cosmetics for the rest of her life.

Julie escaped to her bedroom as soon as she could in order to pack and get ready to leave.

Meanwhile John was preparing to leave Paris for Athens. The ever-faithful Andre met him at the hotel and accompanied him to the airport, staying with him as long as possible. That is, until passengers were isolated in the departure lounge. Andre tried to dissuade John from continuing with his campaign of creating a fatal accident to himself.

'Think of Julie,' Andre suggested.

'That's just what I am doing,' argued John.

'She's living in blissful ignorance.'

'That's better than living in perpetual anxiety.'

'No. She would want to help you.'

'She can't.'

'She would want to try. She would hate herself for not trying. She would be so full of remorse.'

'Nobody can help. They can only prolong, put off the evil day.'

'She will be very hurt. That's not the same as grief.'

'Andre, my mind is made up.'

'I don't like leaving you like this,' moaned Andre.

'Don't worry,' John assured him. 'I'll be all right. If I'm not it means I've succeeded.'

'How will I know?'

'How will you know what?'

'What happens to you. I mean it won't be on television, for instance.'

Andre chuckled at his own feeble little joke even though he felt a lump in his throat.

'I suppose you'll simply be told there's a new man assigned to Europe.'

'I don't like him already.'

'Andre, I repeat. My mind's made up.'

'That's the trouble with your mind. Once you've made it up you won't unmake it.'

At that moment the loud speaker system announced the departure of the plane for Athens.

'That's me,' said John.

He stood up. Andre would have lingered. He rose to his feet reluctantly. John held out his hand.

'Goodbye, Andre.'

Andre ignored the proffered hand, threw his arms round John and hugged him. There were tears in his eyes, his throat tightened and he was too choked to say anything. John released himself, patted Andre on the shoulder, turned and followed the rest of the passengers to the plane. At the last moment he turned and waved and could see that tears were pouring down Andre's cheeks. He managed a weak wave.

As John followed his fellow passengers through the corridors to the plane he became aware with a sudden cold realisation that he would never see his old friend Andre again. He had put the fact at the back of his mind all the time that he was with him and all the time they were discussing his sinister decision. No wonder Andre was tearful.

Once he was in flight, though, John forgot all about Andre and began to concentrate on how he would achieve his objective in Athens. The announcement over the speaker system told them that in a few moments the plane would be landing at Hellenkon Airport and that passengers should fasten their seat belts and extinguish cigarettes. This was lost on John, whose thoughts were elsewhere. Equally neglected was the wish expressed by Captain Matthews and his crew that passengers had enjoyed the flight.

John was met at the airport by a plump, energetic, smiling man names Colouris, the Athens equivalent of Andre in Paris. Although this was by no means John's first visit to the city he was determined to be a tourist this time, complete with camera, and send photographs back to

179

Julie. He told Colouris as much as they travelled in the car to the city. Colouris wasn't a man like Andre. John never called him by his Christian name. It was always Mr Colouris. He was not someone you could laugh and joke with or take to your heart in any way as you could dear old naughty Andre. With Mr Colouris it was purely business.

As they drove, John asked Colouris to drive slowly so that he could take some photographs. At Leoformus Amalias, for instance, the Arch of Adrianos and the Temple of Olympian Zeus.

'There are plenty of postcards of such places,' commented Colouris, 'but still everybody goes click, click, click. It seems such a waste of film.'

'Don't you believe it,' said John, an idea forming in his mind. He would emphasise the tourist bit on this trip, something he hadn't bothered with before.

At the top of the Avenue Venizelos was the King's Palace Hotel where John would be staying. They both got out of the car. Colouris could not resist a little sarcasm.

'Some people,' he said, 'think this is the best building in Athens.'

'Indeed,' remarked John.

'But I don't suppose you'll be photographing it. It is less than two thousand years old.'

John ignored the remark and made his way into the hotel, Colouris following. Once established in his suite of rooms he flopped down on the sofa, exhausted.

'What's tomorrow? Sunday?' he asked.

'All day,' added Colouris.

'It's strange how you lose track of time when you're travelling.'

'The conference is arranged for Monday,' Colouris told him.

'Good.'

'Everyone is looking forward to it.'

'Good.'

There was a silence between them.

180

'Better open the champagne,' suggested John at length.

Colouris took the bottle from the cooling bucket and began to unravel the wire from the cork.

'Why do you always drink French champagne?' he asked.

'Habit,' replied John, wearily.

'We have very good champagne here in Greece,' said Colouris.

'I'm sure you have.'

John was beginning to find Mr Colouris a bit of a bore. No doubt the man considered himself a wit and a sophisticate but John remembered that on his last visit he had found him getting tedious. He was good at his job and was respected by all the other agents in the country but John was missing Andre already.

'When you are refreshed, Mr Suter,' said Colouris, 'I would consider it an honour if you would dine with me and my wife in our apartment.'

John knew the invitation was coming. It happened every time. Dinner with the family. It was the last thing he wanted. He did it once. Never again. Pass the bread. Pass the potatoes. As John hesitated to reply Colouris went on in his somewhat sarcastic manner which he presumed was amusing.

'Or would you prefer somewhere livelier with belly dancing?'

John chuckled.

'No,' he replied. 'I find belly dancing neither amusing nor titillating. I find it rather tasteless and unnecessary. No, Mr Colouris, tonight I fancy resting here in my suite with something light and appetising from the hotel kitchen. At the same time I will telephone my wife.'

'Ah!' exclaimed Colouris, in appreciation.

John knew that he had to keep Colouris at arm's length. It was difficult. The man was such a pushing, insensitive, self-important individual, quite convinced that he was always welcome. He was forever wanting to impose his idea of Greek family life on John and despised hotel living. John fell for it once in the early days of his association with Colouris. Fortunately it was during the lunch period and he was able to get away after what seemed an interminable ordeal of family small talk and not particularly appetising food. He was determined not to fall into the trap again.

'As tomorrow is Sunday,' John suggested, 'I'll give you a little peace and become the inevitable tourist.'

'What does that mean?' asked Colouris.

'Well, I can't wait to photograph the Acropolis. I've seen it many times but never photographed it. So there's no need for you to turn out tomorrow.'

'Ah!' exclaimed Colouris once more. He often said Ah! as if some invisible doctor was telling him to open wide. 'That would suit my plan perfectly.'

'Good.'

That's settled, thought John.

'I will come with you to the Acropolis,' announced Colouris, 'and after that you can come to lunch with the family.'

John's face fell. Was there no limit to the man's insensitivity? He was trying to be kind and hospitable, that John knew, but it was not wanted. It was embarrassing.

'Mr Colouris,' began John, patiently. 'I don't want to appear ungracious...'

'You prefer your hotel,' Colouris cut in, bitterly.

'No, it's not that. I don't want to impose upon you.'

'You're not imposing. I'm offering.'

'You are too kind.'

'On the contrary, I am not kind enough to such a Hellenophile as yourself.'

John laughed.

'At least let me take you to the Acropolis and look after you. Then we can go our separate ways. I will apologise to my wife on your behalf.'

The man was impossible. He had a habit of making John feel guilty. But John was determined to resist the man's blandishments. He would find a way of giving him the slip when they got to the Acropolis.

As it turned out no such stratagem was necessary for on arrival at the parking lot for the Acropolis Colouris got out of the car in such a hurry that he tripped and sprained his ankle. He gave a loud yelp, stumbled and fell. John hurried to his side.

'What is it? What's happened?' he asked, anxiously.

Colouris sat on the ground holding his ankle and rocking to and fro in pain.

'My ankle,' he moaned.

'Have you broken it?' asked John.

'No. No. A sprain, I think.'

He struggled to get up but couldn't. John helped him to his feet and supported him as he hobbled back to the car.

'You stay in the car,' advised John. 'I'll join one of the guides.'

John collected his camera from the car.

'You stay there and rest,' he suggested.

'I'm so sorry,' wailed Colouris.

John had to admit to himself that he was not particularly interested in the Acropolis as such. He had seen it many times and it was so well known as a landmark and ancient monument that he never bothered even to describe it to anybody. It was the Acropolis, a pile of ancient stones and that was it. The same applied to the Parthenon which he automatically coupled with it. His idea of making use of the Acropolis was ulterior in the extreme.

As John joined the tail-end of a group of sightseers who were following one of the official guides he looked up at the high point of the statue of Kekops and Pandrosos whose decapitated figures stood out stark and challenging in the sunlight. Mr Colouris and his ankle had wasted so much time. His aim was to climb as high as he could and let himself fall. Butterflies were fluttering in his stomach.

He heard the man in front of him say to his lady companion, 'I want to take a panoramic shot from the highest point I can reach but the guide says no climbing's allowed.'

'I expect they're frightened of accidents,' said the woman. 'All the steps are crumbling. You can see.'

'Red tape,' scoffed the man. 'In the cradle of civilisation.'

The lady companion made no further comment.

No climbing, thought John. That's a blow. Everybody is standing in the way of his killing himself. But what does it matter? He would make out that he was deaf. He would climb to the top whether it was allowed or not. They couldn't prosecute him if he was dead. The group was now gathering round the guide, a young university student wearing an official armband proclaiming his position as an official guide. He began to address his followers:

'Before we go any further I must impress upon you that climbing the ruins is strictly forbidden. You follow me on the track that I take and there is to be no deviation from it. Is that understood?'

There was a murmur of acknowledgement from the crowd. The guide continued, 'In the twenty-four centuries since it was built, the Parthenon has suffered great sacrifice. The Turks, for instance, used much of the marble for making lime.'

The congregation laughed dutifully.

The guide was standing on the lower steps of Propylea with his followers a little below him at the base.

'On that bare rock,' he said, 'down there to your right, the rock called Aveioe Pagos, stood a man. He delivered a sermon to the Athenians, the people of Athens. His name was Paul. Saint Paul.'

The guide led his party up the final steps towards two particular statues. John was aware of a jumble of stones and slabs of marble. It was the western end of the Acropolis. John was entranced by columns rising sheer to the emblature and, above the cornice, the two high-point headless statues.

He heard the guide's voice intruding upon his own pre-meditations, 'These two figures are the supposed group of Kekrops and Pandrosos.'

While the sightseers were busy flashing with their cameras John was working out how he could get to the top. The lowest section of the wall was a good six feet drop. Going up, other sections of the broken wall ranged in depth from a few inches to a few feet. The first was the steepest. It was all crumbling stonework with, as far as John was concerned, possibilities of foot and hand holds. At the top it looked fairly easy to get out onto the pediment.

When the guide and his party moved on John made himself unobtrusive and stayed behind. The last human beings he thought he would ever see vanished into the distance, a shambling, shuffling clutch of humanity. The rays of the sun cast an eerie light on the scene.

John crept stealthily to the beginning of his climb. He jumped to reach the top of the six foot block and missed. At the second attempt his fingers managed to grip the top of the wall. Now his camera was in the way, dangling from his neck. Lashing out with his feet in the hope of getting some kind of foothold he was able to heave himself to the top of the wall where he sat breathless, aware that he was not as fit as he thought he was. Not surprising, he decided, considering that he only had a few months to live. He scrambled to his feet and continued to climb. It became more difficult and dangerous than he had anticipated and the camera lead kept tangling with protruding stones and impeding his progress. He began to wish he'd never embarked on the climb. At last he reached the top and was surprised to feel a wind that was quite strong. Only then did he realise how dangerously high he had climbed. Sweating as he was from the exertion he felt cold with fear as he looked down and saw how far he intended to fall. To steady himself he decided to try to take a photograph of the view from his eyrie.

Mr Colouris, sitting in his car with the door open and nursing his injured ankle, reacted to the flashlight of the camera. He looked up and saw John making his final steps to the very edge of the wall.

John closed his eyes, breathed out fully and let his body go limp. He swayed forward just as he heard the shout.

In spite of his painful ankle Colouris jumped to his feet and yelled at the top of his voice, 'John! Mr Suter! Come down!'

At the same time the guide, alerted by the flash, looked up and saw John in his precarious position.

'Hey!' he shouted. 'Come down from there! You're breaking the law!'

Trying to break my neck, more likely, thought John as he realised his plan was thwarted. He instinctively recovered his equilibrium. He opened his eyes and looked down. The shock of the realisation of how near he had come to his death caused him to stagger. He sat down on the stone wall to steady himself. He was frightened now. He saw the crowd of sightseers looking at him, aghast. Some of his old defiance returned.

'Interfering lot of bastards,' he muttered to himself.

He stood up shakily with the intention of climbing down but found he couldn't. He was frightened of falling. That's a laugh, he thought. He stood still, unable to move.

The people below were calling out to him, 'Come down! Come on!'

One witty gentleman with an American accent called out, 'Jump!'

John wondered how he'd had the nerve to climb up in the first place, let alone climb down, which was always worse. He sat down again, this time as far away from the edge as possible. The young guide summed up the situation and with the agility of a mountain goat began to climb the crumbling walls to rescue him. It did not take him long and his expertise earned him a round of applause from the sightseers. He helped John to his feet and guided him down the precipitous descent, going ahead of him and virtually handing him down step by step.

As they came down the guide told John, 'You have broken the law and you will be prosecuted.'

'I know. I know.'

John was prepared to face the consequences of his adventure.

'I will need your name and address.'

'John Suter. King's Palace Hotel.'

'When we get down, please.'

They continued the scary climb down where the group of watchers stood waiting. When they reached the bottom the little crowd applauded again. The guide protested.

'No. No,' he shouted. 'It is against the law!'

John gave the guide his card and scribbled his address on the back with a shaky hand.

'My card,' he said.

'Thank you.'

John turned and walked away, making his way to the starting point of the tour. He crossed over to the car where Colouris was sitting in the driving seat with the door open.

'That was a dangerous thing to do, Mr Suter,' he said.

John shaded his eyes with his hand against the sun and looked up at the ruins.

'It doesn't seem all that high, does it?' he remarked.

'It is very dangerous,' repeated Colouris as he struggled into the driving position.

'Can you drive?' John asked.

'Oh, yes. I think so.'

John walked round to get into the passenger seat.

As they drove away he said, 'The guide's going to report me but I'll be in Rome tomorrow.'

'I don't suppose he will do anything about it,' suggested Colouris. 'He may put in a report to cover himself, that's all.'

He laughed. It is unlikely that anyone would be bothered about the stupid antics of a tourist.

As they drove through the heavy traffic Colouris said, 'If you had fallen it wouldn't have helped your wife very much.'

'Why not?'

'You are insured against accidents?'

'Yes.'

'But not against breaking the law.'

'You mean...'

'They wouldn't have paid out.'

'Why not?'

'You were breaking the law.'

'I see.'

John was thoughtful for a moment. So all that could have been a waste of time, after frightening himself into the bargain.

'Where are we going?' asked Colouris.

'Back to the hotel,' said John. 'After that I need a drink.'

'Quite right,' agreed Colouris. 'And don't go doing anything dangerous in Rome like climbing to the top of the Colosseum.'

'Not me.'

True to his word, when John got back to his hotel he ordered a glass of champagne and sat at a table trying to think of some easier way of killing himself. So far he'd failed. Or, rather, his attempts had been frustrated. He wouldn't admit that he had failed. The collapsed balcony in Paris was meant for him, not Andre. The recent debacle was interrupted by Colouris shouting his head off. Why couldn't he be left in peace to kill himself? There was nothing else he could do in Athens. Could he electrocute himself in the bath? Drop his razor in the bath, for instance. The lead wasn't long enough. Besides, it was a walk-about razor. That wouldn't work. If he didn't think of something soon he'd arrive back in England intact and then the trouble would start. Julie would discover that she could have come on the trip anyway. How would he explain that? And could he rely on Andre to keep his mouth shut? And then there would be the gradual deterioration in his health and Tony Bradley would have to be brought in. Mr Colouris will say 'See you again next year' when they part in the morning, but John was determined that it wouldn't be John Suter who would be the Seymour Products executive because he had not given up hope that he would either be six feet underground or a pile of insignificant ash. Idly he wondered who, in the Seymour hierarchy, would take his place. He couldn't think of anyone. Poor Jane, the beautiful young black secretary, would have to get used to a new face.

The sustained introspection prompted him to wonder about Julie. He wanted to speak to her. It wasn't the usual time that they made contact. It was only lunch time. He would go upstairs and see if he could contact her. He just wanted to talk to her. He'd had a fright, self-inflicted as it was, and he wanted to hear her voice. He wouldn't tell her anything about his adventure at the Acropolis, though. It was early afternoon and he didn't feel like eating. He dialled the number. It rang for a long time. Julie wasn't expecting him to call so she had obviously gone out. He wondered where she could have gone. What did she do when he was away? Tony Bradley said he would keep an eye on her so perhaps he had taken her out to lunch. He hoped he wouldn't tell her anything about his condition. He thought idly, as the phone was still ringing, that it would not be a bad idea, after his own demise, if Tony looked after her. He put the phone down and fell onto the bed and was surprised, some time later, to realise that he had slept. He refreshed himself in the bathroom, changed his clothes and decided to go downstairs and have a high tea in the lounge. After that he would phone Julie at the accepted time. The hotel prided itself on its English teas and as John had had no lunch, he tucked into buttered scones with jam and fancy cakes. It was something he never did at home but remembered family teas with his mother and father. As he sat alone he decided that he really must make an effort to get rid of himself. His exasperation at the intervention of the guide at the Acropolis was tinctured with relief. He didn't think that jumping from a height was the answer. The nearest he'd got to it in Athens, apart from the aborted climb at the Acropolis, was when he nearly got run over outside the hotel and a policeman ticked him off for jaywalking. He wondered what Seymour Products would say if they could see him now. No one could say that he was very busy.

When he returned to his suite he managed to contact Julie and it was reassuring to hear her voice. She listened patiently to his plaint about Mr Colouris. She had heard it all before and had even met the gentleman herself so she could understand John's impatience. Fortunately she had not had to endure a family meal with the man. She told John that she had had lunch with Tony Bradley. So he had surmised correctly.

'What did he have to say for himself?' asked John, tentatively, hoping that his own secret was safe.

'Nothing much,' admitted Julie. 'He was his usual suave self. Why no woman has hooked him, I don't know.'

'He's probably waiting for you, dear,' said John, without thinking.

'He'll have to wait a long time.'

'Let's hope so,' agreed John, knowing that it would be sooner than anyone thought.

'I'm going to London to do some shopping one day next week,' announced Julie. 'I might call and have a coffee with Jane.'

'Good idea. I haven't spoken to her yet. No need.'

'You leaving for Rome in the morning?'

'Yes. I look forward to Rome. Do you remember lunch on the Hassler roof?'

'Don't remind me. If it wasn't for that skinflint Seymour I'd be with you and we could have dinner on the roof again.'

'I know. Next year perhaps.'

'Let's hope.'

John felt that he was getting into dangerous waters and tried to change the conversation.

He said, 'Must go now, dear. Bye-bye.'

'Bye, darling. Be careful.'

'I will.'

When John put the phone down he had a bad attack of conscience. He'd lied about the trip. But only because

190

of his plan, his decision to create an accident. Not to deceive her. He couldn't have her with him when it happened. That reminded him that he had not achieved anything yet. He must definitely bring it about in Rome.

He was met at Rome airport by the Rome agent for Seymour Products, Signor Emilio Lanbi, a handsome, middle-aged Italian, full of energy and ideas. In the past, when John travelled with Julie, Emilio brought along his attractive secretary and the four of them had a few days sightseeing, usually in expensive restaurants. It was always a happy affair. But this time there was no Julie so there was no need for Emilio's secretary. So Emilio was alone at the barrier. As soon as he saw John he started waving his arms about and jumping up and down.

'Signor Suter! Signor Suter!'

John saw him and waved back sedately. He remembered how excitable Emilio was. Emilio threw his arms round John and attempted to embrace him, Italian fashion. John submitted to the embrace patiently and urged Emilio towards his car. Emilio chatted excitedly all the way, John humouring him with his platitudinous replies.

They had not travelled far when John realised that he was on an unfamiliar road.

'This isn't the way to the hotel,' he said.

'No. It's not,' admitted Emilio, joyfully.

'Where are we going? I want the hotel,' John insisted.

'I have a surprise for you, Mr Suter,' said Emilio.

'What's that?'

'We not go to hotel,' Emilio explained. 'While you are in Rome you are guest at my apartment.'

Oh, God! thought John. Another one. How was he going to get out of this? He did not want to stay with any family, he wanted to be on his own, to feel free.

'The London office booked me at the Excelsior,' said John.

'The Rome office book you out again,' laughed Emilio. 'You?'

'Yes. My wife is a wonderful cook, as you can see by me.'

Emilio patted his corpulent stomach.

'You stay with us,' he added.

'I can't do that,' said John, simply.

'Why not?' asked Emilio, sternly.

John was trying to think of an excuse.

'I must have time to...' he began.

'Time?' echoed Emilio, interrupting. 'At my apartment you will save time. More convenient for you. More convenient for me. We work together.'

'But your wife...' John suggested.

'My wife has five children,' boasted Emilio. 'She will not mind one more.'

Emilio laughed happily. John began to panic. He could not think of a plausible excuse to avoid staying with the Lanbi family. He worried, too, about getting his room back at the Excelsior. It was never easy to get in there and if Emilio has upset them by cancelling his booking they may not be too happy to help him get it back. He may have to stay at the Hassler or the Hilton. He never found the Hilton convenient because it was on the hill out of the city and you needed a taxi to go anywhere. He was racking his brain to think of an excuse while Emilio was chattering on.

'I have mapped out a programme,' he was saying. 'Work and some sightseeing – The Vatican, Trevi, Villa Borgliesi, night clubs, cabarets. In Rome we have the most beautiful girls. I show you some special places.'

John suddenly had an idea. Girls. That's it. He'll make out he's got a girl at the hotel.

'I'm sorry, Emilio,' he said, firmly. 'There are reasons why I must stay at the Excelsior. Private reasons.'

'But surely...' Emilio began to protest.

'I will not be staying alone,' announced John, flatly.

'Ah!' exclaimed Emilio, his voice full of understanding, if not envy. He nodded wisely, rocking himself backwards and forwards as he drove. Then he burst out laughing.

'Well done! Congratulations,' he declared. 'I will change my plans.'

192

'Thank you,' sighed John, with relief.

'We must go out together. The four of us, eh?'

Another snag, thought John. The bloody man will want to see the girl.

'Your wife might not approve,' John suggested.

'Who said anything about my wife?' Emilio chuckled.

Another bloody obstacle, John decided. Why couldn't people leave him to kill himself on his own? He thought of the Colosseum. Could he achieve in those ruins the feat he failed to bring off at the Acropolis? The laws forbidding tourists access to certain parts of these old buildings was a bit of a handicap. Perhaps he should abandon the idea of throwing himself off old buildings and think of something else. In any case, he concluded, it would be very uncomfortable. He would prefer a method that was more instantaneous. He did not want to inflict unnecessary pain upon himself.

Luckily he was able to retrieve his suite at the Excelsior and Emilio helped him to move in. The man was determined to hang about in the hope of meeting 'the girl' who didn't exist.

After a glass of champagne, however, he had the grace to say, 'Well, I'll leave you to it.'

'We'll meet up in the morning.'

'What time?'

'Ten o'clock.'

'I'll be here.'

'Downstairs.'

'Of course,' Emilio grinned, knowingly.

At last John was on his own. He felt exhausted. He flopped down on the sofa and closed his eyes. When he opened them again he wondered where he was. He looked at his watch. He had been asleep for an hour. So much for the soporific effect of the threat of Emilio's family gathering. After a shower he felt refreshed but the niggling anxiety was still with him. After these few days in Rome he was expected back in London but he didn't intend to return even if he hadn't achieved his objective by then. The worry was affecting his sleep at night. He would toss and turn as he thought of one idea after another and rejected them all. It was easy enough to kill yourself, of course. There was the gun, pills, the usual overdose. That would be easy and pain free. But he didn't take pills, he'd never needed them. Julie had been known to take sleeping pills but she gave them up because they ruined the next day for her. She said she felt like a zombie. John worried about the insurance money, of course. He didn't want to prejudice Julie's claim by doing anything unlawful. The lesson at the Acropolis warned him of that. Besides, when it came to it he really did funk that fall. He had to admit it. Throwing himself in front of a bus or a train could hardly be called an accident unless he could get someone to push him. What about a car crash? He could hire a car and crash into a tree or something. That was definitely an idea. Death, in those circumstances, could be instantaneous. He felt better.

In the meantime each morning after his call to Julie there was enacted a comedy scene with Emilio.

He told Julie about it and although she laughed, she couldn't help asking, 'Are you sure you haven't got a girl there?'

'If I had, dear, I wouldn't tell you about it, would I?'

'I don't know. It could be a clever subterfuge.'

Soon after the call to Julie the telephone would ring and it would be Emilio announcing his arrival and offering to come up to the suite. He had done this for the last two days and this morning, being the last day of John's stay at the Excelsior, Emilio was inclined to be emotional. He always had a choke in his voice when he said goodbye and John would have to put his arms round him and tell him not to be foolish. It made no difference. He came into the sitting room of the suite this particular morning, looking round in the hope of seeing 'the girl'.

When he saw John he exclaimed, 'John! What have you been doing?'

'Why?' asked John, puzzled. 'What's the matter?'

'You look half dead.'

John couldn't agree more except that, in his case, it was no good being only half dead. He didn't think Emilio's sense of humour would go that far. John went to look at himself in the mirror, wondering if his illness was beginning to show.

'I never do anything by halves, Emilio,' he said. 'You know that.'

He turned to face Emilio and explained, 'I didn't sleep much last night.'

As soon as he said it he knew he'd made a mistake.

'When am I going to meet this girl of yours?' asked Emilio. 'She must be very good.'

He strode purposefully to the bedroom door, opened it and looked in. Only one bed had been slept in. Emilio shut the door and turned to John.

'Ah!' he declared. 'You go to her room I see. That is wrong. It is too tiring. She is the one who should travel then you can turn over and go to sleep. Where is she now?'

'Er... She's asleep,' John admitted.

'You see? She sleeps and you are worn out.'

'Not that much.'

'So,' concluded Emilio, 'our work is done and, against my will, I must drive you to the airport to a plane that will take you away from me for a whole year. Oh, John. Why? Why?'

Tears came into Emilio's eyes.

'Because there is work to do, Emilio, and if we don't work we don't live.'

'You work too hard.'

'As a matter of fact, Emilio,' said John, placatingly, 'I don't want you to take me to the airport.'

'Oh, but I must,' protested Emilio. 'I always do.'

'I want you to take me to a garage.'

'Oh?'

Emilio's curiosity overcame his exuberance.

'I'm going to take a little holiday before going back to London.'

'With the girl?'

'No.'

'Oh.'

'I want to hire a car.'

'Where will you go?'

'I don't know. I'll make for the sea.'

'That's not far away. Half an hour.'

'I'll drive and stop when I feel like it.'

'You want me to call the office in London and tell them?'

'No. I'll do that.'

He had no intention of doing any such thing. He was determined that during the next week he would find a solution to his problem and the office in London would know soon enough that a certain Briton living abroad had come to a sticky end. There was a sense of urgency now about John. He wouldn't even tell Julie about his so-called holiday. Not at the moment, anyway. He would only tell her that there was more work to do in Rome than he had anticipated and he would get home as soon as he could. He hated having to deceive her. He was due home within 24 hours and he didn't want her worrying when he didn't turn up.

Emilio drove John to a hire car garage, the owner of which happened to be a relative. As they drove into the forecourt they could see a badly smashed-up car.

'That's the sort of car I want,' said John.

'The man who drove that did not live,' Emilio told him.

'I'm not surprised.'

They got out of the car and Emilio led the way to the proprietor's office where voluble introductions were effected. John cast lingering eyes on the smashed car. It had given him an idea. In a smash like that death must have been instantaneous, surely. He would see what he could do.

The business of hiring a high-powered sports car was complicated even by Italian standards what with insurance, period of hire, guarantees and the rest. Fortunately the proprietor relied on Emilio's word and a lot of the complications were eased and John was soon driving back to the Excelsior to pick up his luggage in a beautiful red Ferrari. The sight of the car caused the doorman to whistle and the girls to turn their heads.

It was an easy drive from Rome to Vacchio, a small seaside resort a mere 30 or 40 miles from the capital. It was the end of the season and the little town looked empty and forgotten, yet one or two enterprising hoteliers were hanging on in the hope of attracting last-minute holidaymakers. Pedalloes and floats and similar beach pastimes were still available and the hotel on the front appeared to be open. John decided to stay a few days and try to work something out. It was still warm and sunny. He would buy a pair of shorts and a singlet. He might even try drowning himself. He couldn't swim so it should be easy. He had been told that the sensation of drowning was not unpleasant, though how anyone could know for certain was hard to believe. After all, you had to drown to know if you were drowning and if you drowned you were dead. So how could you tell anyone what it felt like? It was a thought, though. It had been impossible to crash the car as he'd hoped. As soon as a straight piece of road presented itself so that he could get some real speed up another car would appear on the horizon and, although the driver may have been a useful witness, there was no tree to drive into. But first, he realised, he should phone Julie. That meant finding a hotel.

The so-called Grand Hotel, or Hotel Grande as they preferred to call it, was a dilapidated building with plaster peeling off to reveal crumbling brickwork beneath. John pulled into the gravelled driveway and entered the hotel. The whole atmosphere smelt of end-of-season. The foyer was deserted. Stairs led up to the bedrooms. There did not appear to be a lift. The carpet may at some time have boasted a pattern but was so threadbare that it was impossible to discern it. John rang the bell on the desk that said 'Ring for attention'. There was no response. He rang it again. Still no response. He walked through the archway at the end of the foyer and found himself in the combined terrace and swimming pool area. There was a portable bar in the corner that was out of use. He could hear the splashing, yelping and laughter of swimmers. These came from three teenagers, two boys and a girl. They were shouting in English which, given the time of year, surprised him. As John stood watching their antics he was approached from behind by an ancient hall porter who looked as dilapidated as the hotel.

'*Buon giorno, signor.*'

John turned to face the old man.

'*Buon giorno,*' John repeated. 'Do you speak English?'

'*Si, signor.* Enough,' the old man smiled, revealing yellow teeth.

'Have you any rooms?'

'Plenty, signor. How many would you like?'

'Only one. Thank you.'

The two men made their way back into the hotel.

'Have you any luggage, signor?'

'Yes.'

'I'll get it if you would sign the register.'

'I would like to make a telephone call to England,' said John.

'No trouble, signor. You give me the number.'

While John signed the register the hall porter collected the luggage from the car. John wrote his telephone number on a piece of paper and handed it to the hall porter.

'Could you get that for me?' he asked.

'*Si, signor.*'

The old man took the paper and studied it.

'It will be in the box, signor,' he said, pointing to a telephone box on the other side of the foyer. He then retired to a room behind the counter and John heard him holding forth in a spiel of Italian, giving some important emphasis to the word England. In a surprisingly short time the call was through and John hurried to the telephone box. As he picked up the receiver he heard Julie's voice.

'Haven't you left yet?' she asked, anxiously.

'Well, no,' said John. 'I haven't quite finished here yet.'

'Anything wrong?'

'No. Far from it. I'm not in Rome, at the moment.'

'Where are you?'

'By the sea.'

'Very nice. What are you doing there?'

'I thought I'd take a little break.'

'Good idea. Are you all right?'

'Yes. I'm fine. A bit tired.'

'When do you think you'll be back?'

'You don't mind?'

'Of course not. So long as you're all right.'

'A couple of days, I'd say.'

'You'll ring me, won't you?'

'Yes. Each day. As usual.'

'Be careful, darling.'

'I will, dear. Don't worry.'

John hated himself as he left the phone box. His object was to save Julie expecting him. She wouldn't object to his taking a break. She wouldn't object to his doing anything, come to that. She was a wonderful person and he would never stop loving her, even when he was dead.

'How long will you be staying, signor?' asked the hall porter.

'Only a few days,' John told him.

'It is the end of season,' the hall porter explained. 'We have only these people.'

He made a gesture towards the terrace and the pool where the young tearaways could be heard screaming and laughing.

'Hooligans,' commented the hall porter, reaching to a rack and taking down a key.

'I show you to your room,' he said and, before John could stop him, he had picked up the heavy suitcase and hauled it up the stairs.

Fortunately John's room was at the top of the stairs on the first floor. The old man was breathing heavily as he held out his hand to take John's generous tip.

Once alone in the room, which was only adequately furnished, John began to unpack his suitcase and put his shirts in drawers and so on. There was no telephone in the room so he would have to rely on the booth in the hall. It was now or never, he decided. When it happened he presumed the old man downstairs would ring the number in England that he gave him. He imagined a uniformed policewoman calling on Julie and telling her the sad news. He couldn't help it. She had to be told outright. She would be angry with him for not warning her, and it had to happen this week.

With this firm intention John left the room and made his way down the wide staircase to the terrace. He paused at the hall porter's desk.

'Could I have a drink on the terrace?' he asked.

'*Si, signor,*' the man replied. 'What would you like?'

'Whisky and soda.'

'*Si, signor.*'

John went on his way to the terrace and the swimming pool area. The three young people were the only other residents and they were still round the pool. Two boys and a girl. What were they doing in a dead and alive place like this? It didn't seem to be their scene at all. Rome, yes. Not here. The girl, attractive and nubile in her one-piece swimsuit was standing waist deep in the water at the shallow end of the pool. She was shivering and tearful, John noticed.

'Please let me get out,' she cried.

As John took his seat by one of the terrace tables he could see that the two boys, clad in swimming trunks with towels over their shoulders, were guarding the steps thus preventing the girl from getting out of the pool. As soon as the girl made an attempt to climb out of the side of the pool one of the boys ran round and trod on her fingers. The two boys were close-cropped, street-wise thugs and John wondered what such an odd trio would be doing in a place like Vacchio and at such an unseasonable time of year.

'Let me out!' the girl screamed.

'We're not stopping you,' said the fair-haired boy.

'Yes, you are.'

'No, we're not. Are we, Dave?'

So the dark boy's name was Dave.

'No. Certainly not,' agreed Dave. 'Use the steps at the other end, you silly cow.'

'You know I can't swim.'

'Now's the time to learn,' said the fair boy.

'Please, Dave. Stan. I'm cold,' pleaded the girl.

So they were Stan and Dave and an unsavoury couple of young layabouts they looked and sounded, John decided. The girl stood in the water shivering with her arms round her shoulders. John could imagine how cold she felt. Stan picked up a towel from the table beside him and threw it to the girl, making sure that it fell in the water. The girl made a grab for it and fell over. She scrambled frantically to her feet, spluttering and gasping. She held up the wet towel.

'What's the good of this?' she cried.

'Oh, Stan! You are awful,' mimicked Dave.

The girl, by hanging onto a rail below the edge of the pool and which went all the way round it, managed to make her way midway round one side. Dave hurried to the point that the girl was making for and just as she was scrambling out of the water he put his foot on her head and pushed her back again. She still held onto the rail and pulled herself back to the shallow end of the pool. She reached the steps and was about to climb out when she hesitated, suspecting a trap.

'Dave! 'Elp the lady out!' cried Stan.

Dave hurried to the girl and offered her his hand, which she took. He began to pull her up the steps when suddenly he twisted his hand free and the girl fell back into the water with a terrified shriek.

201

John watched the antics of the boys with a smouldering revulsion.

The two boys were convulsed with laughter as they watched the girl unashamedly weeping.

'Ow! Stop blubbing,' cried Stan. 'You can come out now. Come on. We won't stop you.'

Timidly the girl climbed up the steps and began to dry herself with another towel.

'How did we ever get lumbered with her?' asked Dave. 'I said we should never have brought her.'

'Oh, she's all right,' muttered Stan.

'You wait till I get home,' said the girl, threateningly.

'What does that mean?' challenged Dave.

'You know very well what it means,' answered the girl.

Dave turned to Stan and spread his arms in despair.

'See?' he exclaimed. 'What did I tell you?'

Dave approached the girl, menacingly.

'You open your mouth, my girl,' he hissed. 'It'll be the last thing you do. I'll cut you to pieces.'

'Chance would be a fine thing,' cried the girl, defiantly. 'Once I've finished with you.'

Dave advanced on her again and she backed away in fear.

'What did you say?' he snarled.

The girl backed further away, really frightened now.

'No, Dave. No,' she wailed. 'I didn't mean it.'

Stan joined his friend, seizing the chance to torment the girl further.

'She wants teaching a lesson,' he said.

'Yes,' agreed Dave. 'A swimming lesson.'

They both made a grab for the girl who had no time to run away. One of them took hold of her arms, the other her legs, and began to swing her over the edge of the pool.

'No!' screamed the girl in abject fear. 'No! Please! I can't swim! I'll drown!'

Ignoring her pleas, Dave said, 'On the count of three.'

The two boys counted as they swung the struggling, screaming girl over the pool.

At this juncture John, who had sat watching with only a half interest, got up from his seat and walked slowly over to the boys. They were on his side of the pool, the terrace side and he calmly stood in front of the swinging body of the girl.

'Just a minute,' he said.

The boys stopped swinging the girl and stood holding her.

'What's up with you?' asked Stan, aggressively.

'Don't you think your little joke has gone far enough?' asked John.

'Wipe your snotty nose and clear off,' said Dave.

'Can't you see the girl's terrified?' John insisted. 'She might drown before you can save her.'

'That's all right, Dad. You can save her.'

They started to swing the girl again so John stood in their way.

'I can't swim either,' he said. 'So put her down.'

The swinging stopped.

'OK, Dave,' said Stan, with a wink and a conspiratorial signal. 'Do as the old geezer says.'

The two boys dropped the girl on the ground unceremoniously. She scrambled up and ran away as fast as she could into the hotel. Satisfied, John turned to take his seat at his table but Dave and Stan caught up with him, grabbed his arm and turned him round.

'Not so fast, Dad,' warned Stan.

'How about a swimming lesson for you?' threatened Dave, grabbing John's arm.

'Take your hands off me,' cried John, thrusting the boy away.

Dave reeled back, letting out a cry of pain as his bare foot caught a table leg.

'Get him, Stan,' he shouted.

Stan made a vicious blow at John who was not so easily overcome. When Dave recovered himself and joined his partner John was on the point of being hauled into the pool. At that moment the hall porter came onto the terrace with John's drink on a tray. He put the tray down quickly and hurried to John's assistance.

'*Basta! Basta!*' he shouted as he grappled with the boys who immediately released John and made out it was only a joke.

'I told you before,' the hall porter warned. 'I call the police.'

'Oh, piss off, Garibaldi!' muttered Stan.

John sat at his table and picked up his drink while the hall porter, in spite of his age, remonstrated with the hooligans. The old man returned to his post in the hotel just as the girl, now dressed in shorts and tank-top, joined the two boys and laughed with them as though she had never been the victim of their taunts and torture. Dave and the girl turned into the hotel, laughing and hugging each other.

'We'll be in our room,' Dave called out.

Stan sauntered over to John's table, put his hands on it and leaned towards him, aggressively.

'What's your name, mate?' he asked.

'I don't think that's any of your business,' replied John.

'Please yourself.'

Stan lifted the table suddenly so that John's drink fell into his lap. John stood up quickly, grabbed Stan by his throat and slapped his face.

'Have you no manners?' he cried.

Stan was so shocked and surprised that he staggered back, one hand held to his face. He thought of attacking John but was not too sure of himself without his partner, so he comforted himself with a threat.

'You'll pay for that,' he sneered.

'Any time,' said John, casually.

Stan slunk away still with a hand to his cheek. John dried himself and decided not to replace his drink. He sat watching the sunset and wondering what to do next. With a smile he realised that if the trio of hooligans had thrown him into the pool it might have been the answer to his problem. If they had walked away and left him to drown

Julie would have got her money and that would have been the end of it. Now he would have to devise some plan to do away with himself and do it quickly because there wasn't much time. He was now out of touch with his office and his home. He did not intend to phone Julie again. To all intents and purposes he had now vanished and the next news they had of him would be of his death. Julie may suffer some anxiety between now and then, an anxiety which he would gladly save her if he could but it was inevitable in the circumstances.

Julie was certainly puzzled. She didn't mind John having a break by the sea. He worked hard and deserved it. She just hoped that he was safe and well. By rights he should be with her, she thought, as she made her way next morning to pick up the newspaper from the front door mat. She went into the kitchen to make herself some coffee.

The newspaper headline screamed at her in large black letters:

ASHLEY DUKES DEAD

So what, she mused. With all his money, the richest man in the world couldn't keep himself alive. Wasn't he one of Tony's patients? She seemed to remember hearing him talk about him. He'll miss those nice fat fees, no doubt. She did not bother to read the story but turned instead to the female pages. There was only one letter when the postman called. It was addressed to John and, although they opened each other's letters, she decided to leave it for when he got back. It was an official-looking letter from an insurance company so it couldn't possibly be of any interest to her.

Julie dismissed the news of Ashley Dukes' death as just one of those things but her friend, Tony Bradley, was certainly concerned. He could not understand it. There was nothing wrong with the man so why should he die suddenly? The newspaper was spread out on his desk as he spoke to Ashley Dukes' lawyer on the telephone. He spoke quite emphatically.

'I tell you his X-ray was perfectly clear.'

'You're sure of that?' asked the lawyer.

'I'd stake my reputation on it.'

'You may have to.'

There was a silence while Tony absorbed the implication of that remark.

'What does the American doctor say?' he asked.

'Fatal haemorrhage from a bronchial carcinoma,' the lawyer recited from a transatlantic fax.

'Rubbish,' declared Tony, turning to Helen as if for confirmation as she came into the office carrying X-ray pictures.

'That's all very well, Doctor Bradley,' said the lawyer.

'I can't imagine what else it could be,' insisted Tony.

'But I'm damned certain it wasn't a carcinoma. I gave him a perfectly clean bill of health.'

'That's no guarantee of anything,' countered the lawyer.

'I know it's not.'

'I haven't had the full report yet.'

'Well, let me know when you do.'

'I'll give you a ring.'

'Right.'

Tony put the phone down and turned to Helen.

'Ashley's lawyer trying to tell me I don't know my job. Those the X-rays?'

He took the envelope from Helen and put the X-rays on the viewing stand. Helen stood beside him. He put his arm round her waist, such was their present relationship.

'Nothing there,' mused Tony. 'Nothing at all.'

Then, after further scrutiny, he said, 'Wait a minute. What's this?'

'What's what, dear?' asked Helen.

Tony pointed to a spot on the X-ray.

'That,' he said.

'Looks like a calcified cyst to me,' Helen decided.

'Exactly,' agreed Tony. 'Harmless as an old boot.'

'Not like you, eh, sweetie?' Helen suggested.

Tony turned away from the screen and sat at his desk. Helen sat on the desk itself, facing him, legs crossed provocatively.

'Half the population's got a calcified cyst somewhere,' he declared. Then, as he ruminated, 'I don't remember Ashley Dukes having one, though.'

He stared into space. Helen uncrossed her legs and crossed them again, aware that she was showing a lot of thigh.

'Wait a minute,' said Tony, suddenly.

'What?'

'John Suter.'

'Your friend?'

'That's right. Get his X-rays.'

Helen got off the desk with a wiggle and went out of the room. She was conscious of a sudden change in Tony's manner and she was fearful that the sexual familiarity between them was not going to stand her in such good stead as she had imagined. She had a fear that the X-ray she was collecting was somehow going to seal her fate. Memories of her first morning in the job came flooding back. She found John Suter's X-ray and took it into Tony's room. He was still sitting at his desk staring into space. She handed the film to him.

'Put it on the stand,' he said, without looking up.

Helen fixed the X-ray film onto the illuminated viewing frame. She stood looking at it. Tony joined her and stood beside her. She put her arm round his waist but he took it away without looking at her.

'Christ All Bloody Mighty,' he exclaimed.

'What?' asked Helen, vaguely, puzzled.

'Notice anything?' he asked.

'No.'

Tony pointed to a part of the film.

'There's Dukes' carcinoma.'

'So it is.'

'And the film is labelled John Suter.'

Helen peered at the corner of the film.

'Well? Isn't it?' asked Tony, fearfully.

'Yes. You're right,' admitted Helen.

'You put the wrong name on it.'

'Did I? Well, yes. I suppose I must have done.'

Tony returned to his desk and sat down, wearily.

'It was your first morning here,' he said. 'You were an hour late. Remember?'

Helen walked provocatively towards the desk and sat on the edge of it, showing plenty of leg as usual, her stock in trade.

'Yes,' she said. 'I remember. You were very sweet about it and took me to bed that night for the first time. The first time for us, that is,' she added with a smile.

'You put the wrong name on the plate,' said Tony, coldly. 'Doesn't that mean anything to you?'

'You can't blame me,' protested Helen.

'Why not?'

She leaned over towards him.

'You took both sets of X-rays before I got here. I have a memory, too, you know. You didn't mark the cassettes so how was I to know which one was which?'

'I told you precisely which one was on the right.'

'That depends where you're standing, darling.'

'If you weren't sure why didn't you bloody well ask?'

'Now wait a minute.'

Helen got off the desk and was prepared to battle with the doctor over who was to blame for the cock-up of the X-rays.

'Do you realise what you've done?' accused Tony.

'What I've done?'

After a pause, during which Tony let his temper calm down, he said, 'Get him on the phone.'

'Who?'

'John Suter. You can't phone Dukes.'

Helen picked up Tony's personal telephone directory, a crocodile-covered book with the doctor's initials impressed in gilt letters and looked for John Suter's telephone number. She dialled the number and waited.

'Mr John Suter, please,' she said at last.

She waited again as she was obviously being put through to his secretary.

'Mr John Suter, please,' she said again.

John's beautiful black secretary was only too pleased that someone wanted to speak to her boss. It was always dreary when he was away.

'Who wants him?' she asked, tentatively.

'Doctor Bradley.'

'He's not here.'

'When is he expected?'

'As a matter of fact he was supposed to be back in the office a few days ago. We don't know where he is. He's due back from his European trip but he hasn't turned up yet.'

'You haven't heard from him?'

'Not since he phoned in from Rome. He's left the Excelsior and according to our Italian agent he hired a car and went off towards the coast. That's all I know.'

'I see. Thank you.'

Helen replaced the receiver, thoughtfully.

'They don't know where he is.'

'Get me his wife.'

Again Helen consulted the personal directory and dialled a number. She waited.

'At least you don't get music while you wait,' she muttered. Then, 'Mrs Suter? Doctor Bradley for you.'

Tony took the phone.

'Hello, Julie. Where's our wandering boy?'

Helen raised her eyebrows in mute criticism and crossed the room to look out of the window onto the Harley Street traffic. She remembered John Suter going off in a taxi the evening he learned of his condition.

Julie was sitting at the kitchen table as she spoke to Tony.

'All I know is he's taking a bit of a rest somewhere by the

sea. I don't know where. He didn't say. He usually phones me but he hasn't phoned for a couple of days. I thought of calling the office today and having a word with Jane.'

'Who's Jane?'

'His secretary.'

'I've been on to her. She doesn't know where he is. That's why I'm phoning you.'

'Why do you want him?' asked Julie, suddenly.

'No particular reason,' Tony hedged. 'I just wondered when we could meet up.'

'If I hear from him I'll let you know.'

'Thanks.'

Tony was worried when he put the phone down. Helen turned from the window and went back to the desk.

'No news?'

'No. It's not like John not to contact his wife.'

'He'll turn up,' said Helen. 'I don't know what you're worrying about.'

'You don't?'

'No.'

'It doesn't worry you that a man's going around mistakenly thinking he hasn't got long to live? There's no telling what he'll do.'

'What do you mean?'

'He might commit suicide.'

'Do you think he would?'

'I don't know. Nobody knows. But it's a possibility. And the man is already behaving out of character.'

Tony got up and began to walk about the room. Helen hurried after him. She put her arms round his neck.

'Don't worry, sweetheart.'

Tony pulled her arms away and pushed her aside.

'Don't worry. Is that all you can say? Apart from John Suter being missing, what do you think this Ashley Dukes business does to my professional reputation?'

'Oh. I see,' declared Helen, accusingly. 'That's what's really bothering you. Not Ashley Dukes or John Suter. Just your reputation. What about my reputation?'

'You don't count.'

'Except to sleep with. Is that it?'

'As far as I am concerned, Miss, you are an inefficient radiographer.'

'And as far as I'm concerned, Doctor Bradley, you are an inefficient lover.'

'What?'

Helen laughed.

'I thought that would puncture your ego,' she said.

'I think you'd better take a week's notice,' said Tony, as he returned to his desk.

'Thanks. I will,' replied Helen.

'I'll give you a reference, naturally,' muttered Tony, making a note on the papers in front of him.

'I wish I could say the same,' said Helen, as she went out of the room.

'Cow!' declared Tony, looking up at the closed door.

Julie rang John's office and spoke to Jane. But there was no news of John's whereabouts. Jane was as puzzled as Julie and the boss of the company, Aunt Annie, was beginning to wonder what John was up to. It wasn't like him not to keep in touch.

Julie decided to open the letter that was addressed to John in the hope of finding some clue to his odd behaviour. It was the letter from the insurance company. She had difficulty in fathoming the contents but one figure stood out. The figure of five hundred thousand. She read the letter and discovered that John had insured himself against an accident for half a million pounds. He had never done such a thing before. She knew that much. Insurance during flight can be anything and anyone like John, flying so often, was inclined to put in a high figure in case of a plane crash. But this was for an accident at any time that he was away. What did it mean? Would Jane know? She picked up the phone and dialled a number.

'No, Mrs Suter,' said Jane. 'I know nothing about it. I did the usual travel insurance. That must be something he did himself.'

211

'He didn't say anything to you about it?'

'No.'

Julie was now more puzzled than ever.

'It's a pity you didn't go with him, Mrs Suter,' said Jane.

'I know,' admitted Julie. 'But Mr Seymour's word is law, isn't it?'

'Mr Seymour?'

Now Jane sounded puzzled.

'Mr Seymour?' she echoed.

'Yes,' Julie went on. 'I was going until he vetoed it.'

'Mr Seymour didn't veto anything,' declared Jane.

'My husband asked him if I could go and he said no. Something to do with economy.'

'No, Mrs Suter. That's not right.'

Julie suddenly felt frightened. She felt a sinking sensation in the pit of the stomach.

'What do you mean?' she asked, nervously.

'Mr Suter originally asked me to book two tickets as usual. He said you were looking forward to it. Then he changed it to one.'

'Are you sure?'

'I'm positive. In fact, Mr Seymour asked him why you weren't going.'

'What was his answer?'

'He said something about your sister being ill.'

'Are you sure?'

Julie realised that she was repeating herself.

'I'm sorry,' she explained. 'I keep saying that. But it's so strange. Why should he make that excuse? My sister wasn't ill. He suggested I went down and I stayed with her only because John didn't want me to be on my own. He phoned every morning and seemed quite normal. Until just now.'

Julie hesitated.

'It could be another woman, of course,' she admitted.

'I doubt it.'

'When did you last hear from him?'

'We had a fax saying he was taking a few days off and going to the coast.'

212

'He'd never done that before, had he?'

'No. You've been with him on all the other trips.'

'Yes. Of course.'

'I'm sorry I can't help you, Mrs Suter.'

'I know. I'll just sit and wait. He's bound to turn up sooner or later.'

'I'll let you know as soon as we hear anything.'

'Thank you.'

Julie put the phone down and walked slowly to the window looking out onto the garden. What was she to think? Why should John act so strangely suddenly? She did not think seriously about the idea of another woman. He wouldn't have gone to such lengths for a mere liaison. He would have had plenty of opportunity for that sort of thing at the hotels where he stayed. Some kind of mental aberration must have occurred. Perhaps she should try to contact Seymour's European agents herself and ask them if they have any idea of John's whereabouts. Would that incriminate them in any way with the company? Perhaps it would be better if Jane phoned them. They would be more forthcoming with her, especially if another woman was concerned. She returned to the phone and rang Jane again.

'Jane,' said Julie, without any preliminary chat, 'do you think there is anything to be gained by ringing the European agents?'

'Yes,' said Jane. 'I could do that. It's a while since he was in Paris but I could ring Rome. That's where we last heard of him.'

'Thank you. That's very kind of you.'

Sensing Julie's anxiety, Jane said, 'Don't worry, Mrs Suter. I'm sure there's a perfectly simple explanation.'

'Let's hope so.'

'I'll ring you back.'

'Thank you.'

Again Julie wandered over to the window and looked out in the garden that she didn't actually see, so occupied was she with thoughts of John.

213

John, in fact, was sitting on the hotel terrace reading an out-of-date English newspaper. He was quite alone. The two English yobos and the girl had gone out in a car. He wondered about them. He got the impression that they were hiding out for some reason. He turned to the newspaper and read that Ashley Dukes, one of the richest men in the world, had died suddenly in New York. He chuckled to himself. Poor Tony. His best customer had passed out on him. He remembered that the great man had turned up at Tony's surgery for his annual check-up when he'd called on him about his cough which, strangely, had vanished. But another and more menacing ailment had taken its place. He didn't feel ill in any way. In fact, he felt quite well. What was Julie thinking? She must be puzzled, poor dear. And what were they thinking at the office? He had left everything in order and sent in his report on his visits to the agents so there could be no problem there. His main worry was Julie and the anxiety he was causing her. She would understand once he had achieved his objective, something he mustn't lose sight of. Instead of languishing on the hotel terrace he should be out trying to find a way of killing himself. He folded the newspaper and stood up. He remembered seeing a railway level crossing somewhere on his way to the hotel. There was no gateway, he noticed. He would explore the location. It could prove useful.

Tony Bradley had been ringing John's office frequently but without success. He wanted to tell him that his diagnosis of terminal cancer was a false alarm, that the X-rays had been mixed up. He didn't want to talk to him at home in case Julie became suspicious, not that it would matter so much now. All he could learn from John's secretary was that his return from the Continent was overdue and that he should have been back some days ago. In desperation he rang Julie, who hurried to answer the phone thinking that it was either John or his secretary ringing.

'Julie? Tony.'

'Oh. Hello.'

214

'You don't sound very happy.'

'I'm not. I'm worried about John.'

'So am I.'

'Why should you be?'

'I can't tell you over the phone. Can we meet?'

'Of course. Come round for a drink after surgery.'

'Right. I will.'

It was not unusual for Tony to visit John and Julie. They often went to the theatre together and had dinner together. To Julie he had sounded rather mysterious on the phone. Why couldn't he tell her what he wanted over the phone? The phone rang again and Julie hurried to answer it. It was Jane. She had no news of John's present whereabouts but she recited a chapter of accidents that had occurred on the trip, beginning with the collapse of the balcony at the hotel in Paris and including John's strange behaviour in Athens when he climbed to the top of the ruins and had to be rescued and ending with Emilio in Rome seeing him off in a fast sports car in the belief that he was heading for the coast to give himself a bit of a holiday, all of which was so alien to John's nature that it was something more than puzzling. All this information came from agents who had phoned in. Apart from the strange behaviour in Athens and Rome, it was unlike John to give himself a holiday of any sort without consultation with the company. As for climbing ruins, he'd never even bothered about them when he'd been there previously.

John sauntered out of the faded hotel and made his way to the car park. The red, open Ferrari was a splendid-looking car and he wondered if it wasn't a little too noticeable for his purpose. The original purpose, of course, was to crash the car at high speed but the opportunity had never occurred. Or did he funk it again? His idea now was connected with the railway crossing he'd seen on his way to the hotel. He remembered that there were no crossing gates but there were traffic lights to control the road traffic. He climbed into the car and drove away. Once on the roadway he thought he'd have a look at what, in seaside towns, was known as The Front. The calm, flat sea was kissing the shore and running away again. It was a very lethargic effort on the part of the waves not like the rough buffeting the English shore suffered. There weren't many people about. It was very much the end of season but such people as pedalo and surfboard owners were still plying their trade. He stopped near the pedalo station and sat watching. Nobody was using the machines and a young seafaring type was sitting on a hard-backed chair beside the cash booth. He looked as if he was asleep. Here was another idea, John decided: take a pedalo out to sea and don't bring it back, keep pedalling far out to sea and it wouldn't matter if you fell off and drowned. That would be the end of it. The sea was too calm to tip you out. He didn't know what it was like further out. No good trying it yet. It was only midday. Best wait until late afternoon and then pedal until it was dark.

He drove back to the hotel, all thoughts of a level-crossing fatality banished from his mind by the prospect of an attempt with a pedalo. He went to his room and stretched out on the bed, relaxed. At least, he thought, he would be able to promote a real accident. He could not think of any way in which anyone could interfere. He would just pedal out into the darkness and no one would be able to find him. He realised that he couldn't swim and if the sea didn't tip him out of the machine then he would slip off it. Once he was out of sight of the shore, of course. He decided that four o'clock in the afternoon would be a good time to start. The evenings were drawing in quickly now and by four o'clock it would be getting dark.

While he was setting out on his latest experiment with death, Tony Bradley and Julie were sitting in the garden room at Newbury Cross, drinks in hand.

'You sounded very mysterious on the phone,' Julie began.

'Sorry about that,' Tony admitted. 'But you will understand in a minute.'

'Good.'

'You know he had that annoying little cough.'

'He came to you with it and it went straight away,' Julie chuckled. 'Very clever of you.'

'That's right. I X-rayed him.'

'You didn't find anything.'

'No. But the stupid girl mixed up the plates.'

'What do you mean?'

'When he came back that evening he read the report that should have applied to Ashley Dukes.'

'Ashley Dukes? The man who died?'

'Yes. He had what John thought he had, what I told him he had.'

'Oh Lord.'

'So John's been going around thinking he hasn't got long to live.'

'But he would have read about Ashley Dukes. It's world news.'

'He wouldn't know the plates had been wrongly titled.'

'No. Of course not.'

'That's why I'm anxious to contact him.'

'I wonder if that's why he's gone into hiding.'

'It fits. Particularly in view of the insurance you told me about.'

'Poor John. That's why he behaved so strangely in Athens and Rome and Paris. But it was Andre Fleury who nearly fell to his death in the hotel. Not John.'

'How do you mean?'

'Andre says he walked out onto the balcony while John was in the bathroom.'

'You mean Andre Fleury walked into the trap that John had probably set for himself.'

'We don't know that.'

'No. But it's suspicious. He's insured himself heavily

against an accident that he's been trying to make happen. That's how I see it.'

'That doesn't sound like John.'

'It sounds like John wanting to protect you. To leave you more than comfortably off.'

'Don't say things like that. I can't bear to think about it.'

'We've got to find him, Julie.'

'If anything had happened we would have heard by now.'

'How?'

'The police. They'd get in touch with next of kin and all that. So nothing could have happened yet.'

'He'll have identification on him, of course, because he'd want you to collect the insurance.'

'Don't.'

Julie did not cry. She wouldn't do that in front of Tony, anyway. She cried when she went to bed, in those moments when sleep won't come. It was then, too, that she prayed and touched the wood of the bedside table for luck.

'Do you think the newspapers could help?' she asked.

'How?' queried Tony.

'You often read about some Briton missing somewhere abroad.'

'There's usually some mystery about that sort of thing.'

'There is here. John's vanished.'

'Because he wants to.'

'Mistakenly,' Julie persisted. 'What if the papers said he was wandering about thinking he was dying when he wasn't?'

'They'd come on to me as his doctor and I'd have to admit a wrong diagnosis.'

'Oh, yes. I'm sorry.'

'Oh, I don't mind. If it would help. Ashley Dukes' lawyers are after me as it is.'

'I don't know any newspaper people,' admitted Julie. 'Do you?'

'No. I suppose you can just phone them up.'

'It's an idea.'

'It certainly is,' enthused Tony. 'Have you got today's paper? There'll be a telephone number on it.'

Tony was resigned to the bad publicity that would be heaped upon his practice. He knew that it would come eventually. While Julie was looking for the daily newspaper Tony wondered what his other patients would make of the exposure. He wondered, too, how much he could blame his radiologist. If she was contacted no doubt she would make the most of their brief affair. More damning publicity.

Julie found the telephone number of the newspaper and recited it to Tony who went at once to the phone.

'Wait a minute,' cried Julie.

'What?'

'Shouldn't we check with Jane? The company may not welcome the publicity.'

'There is that.'

Tony endeavoured not to show his relief.

'I'll see if Jane's still at the office,' said Julie, dialling a number.

She was.

'Jane. Julie.'

'Oh. Hello. Any news?'

'No. But I was wondering if it would be a good idea to let the newspapers know.'

'How do you mean?' asked Jane, cautiously.

'Well, you know how you read about a lone Briton lost in the Sahara and that sort of thing? I wondered if we could let the papers know about John and what the Seymour company would think.'

'I can't speak for the company. They've all gone home. But John's not lost.'

'He is if we can't find him.'

'We don't know if he wants to be found.'

'Oh, don't say things like that, dear.'

'Well, judging by his behaviour...' Jane began.

219

Julie interrupted the girl.

'Jane,' she insisted, 'what you don't know is that John thinks he's got terminal cancer.'

'What!'

'But it's all a mistake. Doctor Bradley is with me now. Evidently John's X-rays and the X-rays of Ashley Dukes got mixed up and it was Dukes who had the cancer, not John.'

'Oh, my God,' exclaimed Jane.

'We can't reach him to tell him, you see. We think he's trying to fake an accident so that I get the insurance. That's why he insured himself for such a high figure.'

'Yes. I see. It also accounts for his odd behaviour while he's been away.'

'Exactly.'

'In that case,' admitted Jane, 'perhaps it would be a good idea to let the papers know.'

'But what about the company? I don't want to get them involved in unwelcome publicity.'

'I won't be able to do anything about that until the morning.'

'No. I understand. Thank you, anyway.'

'I can see now why he didn't want you to be with him,' said Jane.

'Yes. So can I. Poor dear.'

When Julie returned from the telephone she found Tony studying the Italian copy of the Michelin Guide which he had discovered in the book shelves. He was searching the slim red volume for a map of Italy.

'Let's check,' he said. 'Seaside towns near Rome. That's what he said, wasn't it?'

'Oh, it's like looking for a needle in a haystack,' protested Julie, frustration causing her to become short-tempered.

'Naples,' said Tony. 'That's not all that far from Rome. He could drive there easily, in just over an hour. I've done it. Do you think it would appeal to his sense of humour?'

'Naples?'

'See Naples and die.'

'Oh, Tony. Please.'

'Sorry.' He shut the book. 'There's another small sea-side resort only about half an hour from Rome. If I can take this book with me I'll ring them all up and ask them if they have a John Suter staying there.'

'Would you?' asked Julie, eagerly.

'It'll be a start.'

Tony put an arm round Julie's shoulders.

'I know it's a trite thing to say, but don't give up hope.'

'It's a question of catching him in time. Not hope.'

'I know. I'll tell you how I get on with the hotels,' he said, waving the book.

'Good luck.'

While all this was going on John Suter was making his way to the pedalo station on the beach. Wearing shorts and singlet, in keeping with the style of a holidaymaker, he drove the car which he intended to leave by the shore, deserted. It was late afternoon but the station was still operating in a lackadaisical kind of way. The young attendant, leaning against the wooden hut and smoking a cig-arette, obviously wished he was somewhere else. During the winter months, like most of his kind, he worked in the hotels in Rome. Anywhere that he could meet the girls who had all gone from the coast by this time.

John approached the lethargic young man and asked him if he could take a pedalo out.

'On your own?' queried the young man, whose English was perfect, putting John to shame.

'Yes,' said John. 'If that's all right.'

'Up to you,' said the young man.

John paid the young man the money for an hour's trip. He had no intention of returning the machine within the hour. His intention was to pedal straight out to sea as far as he could go and to hell with the young man and his lovely white pedalo. If he capsized so much the better. This time, he was sure, nothing could go wrong. He would be out of sight and only a helicopter would be able to find him and he doubted if the young man would go to that extent for the sake of one pedalo. He might fret and fume because he wanted to shut up the station and go home. He wouldn't be able to call him back, not even with a loud hailer.

Once on the machine and launched onto the water John lost no time in pedalling energetically out to sea. He pedalled as fast as he could, looking back occasionally to see what distance he had made from the shore. The sea was calm and still and he made good headway.

The young man in charge of the station was not watching him. Customers usually pedal up and down the shore line among the bathers. That is about all they ever did. He hoped the eccentric English gentleman wouldn't be long because he wanted to go home. He called him eccentric because he thought most English were and to want to take out a pedalo at this late hour was certainly eccentric. It was getting dark so the man shouldn't be long, he decided.

Dusk began to settle on the sea. John was a long way from the shore. He could only just see it. He looked down at the sea beside him and could almost feel its huge depth as it heaved quietly, menacingly, around him. This is what he planned, to slip into the water and let it do what it liked with him. He wouldn't struggle. He'd drown. He knew that. He couldn't swim and he expected to choke a bit as he swallowed water. Could he trust himself to sink calmly to the bottom? What was it like at the bottom? He would probably be dead by the time he got there, he presumed. So long as he lost consciousness as soon as possible he wouldn't mind. That would happen, he supposed, as soon as his lungs filled with water. Nothing can go wrong this time, Julie, he said to himself. There's no one about, no interfering guide, no one. Thank God.

What was that? He could hear a sound like a motor bike in the distance. He looked round, strained his eyes to survey the gathering gloom. He couldn't see anything. Then, as the sound gradually increased, he could make out a speed boat coming out to sea in his direction. As it came nearer he could see that it was being driven by someone in white trousers and singlet. Bugger, he thought. It was the young man from the pedalo station. Another interfering bastard. He pretended to have fallen asleep and slumped back in the pedalo chair and closed his eyes. He'll say he had no idea he'd drifted so far out. Inside himself he was furious. At this rate, he thought, Julie will never get her money.

The speed boat pulled alongside the pedalo and the boy shouted, 'What do you think you're doing?'

John pretended to wake suddenly.

'Oh. Sorry. I fell asleep.'

The boy threw a rope to John.

'Catch hold of that and tie it to the rail in front. I'll pull you back.'

John dutifully attached the rope to the front of the pedalo and as the speed boat pulled the pedalo away he tucked his feet out of the way of the fast-revolving pedals. He felt like a guilty child. When they reached the beach the Italian boy made no attempt to conceal his anger.

'That was a stupid thing to do,' he cried.

'I fell asleep,' said John, lamely.

'You could have drowned yourself.'

'I'd have woken up by then,' said John, trying to make light of the situation.

'I'll have to charge you for taking the boat out.'

'Of course,' admitted John. 'I understand.'

He paid the boy the money that he asked, extortionate though it was.

As he made his way to his car he realised how cold he felt. He promised himself a stiff whisky when he got back to the hotel.

At home, Julie had suffered a set-back in her efforts to trace her husband. Jane telephoned to say she'd had a word with the chairman of Seymour Products and he was not at all keen to let the newspapers know about John's disappearance. He understood the situation but felt that the newspapers would only cause Julie more anxiety. He was quite sympathetic towards John and would welcome him back if and when he returned. Julie had to agree that the invasion of the national press and TV cameras could prove troublesome.

Julie was in the garden room with Tony Bradley when she took the call and she passed the news on to him.

'Not very helpful,' he muttered.

'Do you think I should go over?' she asked.

'To Rome, you mean?'

'Yes.'

'I don't know. We've drawn a blank at the hotels we've phoned. Unless he's staying at one that's not in the Michelin.'

'Would there be such a place?'

'In any case, you're not going on your own. If he hired a car the garage people would know the number and we could ask the police to help us find the car. If we pitched them the story about a man thinking he's going to die. My Italian is no better than yours, but this agent chap...'

'Emilio.'

'Emilio. He could get the police on our side and once we've found the car we've found the man.'

'We hope.'

'We hope.'

Now everything happened at once for Julie. Tony telephoned the Excelsior and booked them in, then he phoned British Airways and got them on the very next flight to Rome, which was at midnight. Tony went home to pack a few things and Julie went upstairs to do the same. He picked her up in a taxi and off they went, complete with John's Italian telephone contacts.

Unaware of such sudden activity, John felt frustrated right

and left in his efforts to get rid of himself. But he was determined not to be outdone. On his way back to the hotel after his latest dismal failure with the pedalo he noticed that he had to drive over the level crossing where the railway line bisected the road. This was the one that had no gates. He pulled onto the roadside and stopped the car. It was a very minor road and there was hardly any traffic. He got out of the car and walked to the crossing. He studied it in all its aspects. He looked up and down the road. There was no accommodation for a crossing keeper. It must be a matter of luck or local knowledge that avoided a fatal accident. Except for the usual road signs to warn motorists, there was only a wooden post with slats at the top in the form of a cross which was planted in the embankment. John was now desperate. He hadn't achieved his objective yet and time was still ticking away. The level crossing presented a Heaven-sent opportunity. He had used it several times since he'd arrived at the hotel but he'd never seen or heard a train. It would be just his luck if the line was discontinued, particularly as, in this instance, there couldn't possibly be any outside interference. Here was the answer to his problem right under his nose. It might be a bit painful but so would the balcony in Paris and the ancient monuments in Athens and Rome. He got back into his car and drove to the hotel.

He asked his friend, the hall porter, 'Have you a railway timetable?'

'Where for, signor?'

'Oh. Local.'

'Ah!'

The hall porter rummaged among the papers and books under his counter and produced a small, much-thumbed paperback book.

'Here, signor.'

'That it?'

'*Si, signor.*'

'Thank you.'

As John walked away the hall porter called out, 'You want me to book you somewhere, signor?'

John paused on his way to the terrace.

'No, thank you,' he replied. 'I'll have a look and let you have it back.'

Strange man, mused the Italian as he watched the eccentric Englishman make his way to the terrace. What does he want with a local timetable when he has that beautiful sports car outside?

He did not see John extract some figures from the timetable which he copied into his notebook. Satisfied, he got up, returned the timetable to the hall porter and went out to his car. He drove to the level crossing and parked the car by the side of the road with the engine running. He took out a piece of paper from his notebook and put it on his knee. He sat waiting, eyes on his wristwatch. He heard the whistle of a train. He took a pencil and prepared to write down a figure. As the train thundered over the crossing he made a note of the time. He then raced the car across the rails, stopped on the other side and made a note on the paper. Satisfied, he turned the car round and headed back to the hotel. On his way he opened the window and threw the screwed up paper out of the car. Then a thought struck him. He stopped the car, got out and retraced his steps until he found the piece of paper which he put in his pocket. He returned happily to the hotel. At last he was getting somewhere. Tomorrow he would do it. Definitely. He felt relieved.

As he sat on the terrace he could only half hear the conversation between the teenage thugs and the girl.

'What a dump this is,' moaned Shirley. 'Why don't we go home? There aren't even any men worth looking at.'

'What about Dad,' suggested Dave, indicating John at a nearby table. 'He looks worth a scene. A sucker if ever I saw one.'

'Yeah,' admitted Shirley. 'I wonder why he's on his own.' Then quite suddenly she said: 'Ere! He could be a detective.'

226

Her remark seemed to galvanise the boys into some kind of alarm.

'Why don't you belt up?' hissed Stan.

'Put a sock in it, girl,' added Dave.

'Then why is he on his own?' persisted Shirley.

'Because he smells,' said Stan.

'Because he's a queer,' said Dave.

Shirley became somewhat subdued but couldn't help continuing with her idea.

'I still think he's a detective,' she went on. 'I think we should move on. I don't feel safe with him here.'

'Aw! Shut up!' commanded Stan.

'Anyway, I want to go home,' she moaned. 'And if you don't take me...'

'You'll what?' asked Stan, menacingly.

'I'll tell that detective why we're here,' she replied, defiantly.

Stan gave a little threatening laugh.

'You're a devil for punishment, aren't you?'

'Well!' pouted Shirley. 'This place is driving me mad.'

'We'll go home when I say so and not before,' decided Stan, who seemed to be the leader of the trio.

'I can hitch-hike back. I don't need you to take me. Plenty of men would be glad of the chance.'

'If they ever got it,' said Stan.

Dave decided to join in the dispute.

'Why don't we lock her in her room, Stan,' he suggested. 'She's a menace. If she opens her trap we've had it.'

'Good idea,' agreed Stan. 'We'll lock her in her room and feed her like an animal.'

'Oh, no you don't,' said Shirley, getting up and moving away.

Stan grabbed her wrist and forced her to sit down again.

'Stan!' she complained. 'That hurts.'

'Come on, Dave,' said Stan. 'Let's lock her up.'

'No,' cried Shirley. 'Stop it. Don't be daft.'

'No, Stan,' said Dave, winking at his partner. 'I don't think that's a good idea.'

227

'Oh, all right,' agreed Stan. 'Have it your own way.'

He released Shirley's wrist from his grasp.

'Go on, slut,' he encouraged, giving her bottom a slap as she went away.

'What's the idea?' asked Stan.

'You'll never get her to her room without a fuss, especially in front of him.'

Dave nodded his head towards John's table.

'What's your idea, then?' asked Stan, grudgingly.

'Let her think you're going up there for the usual and once she's fallen for it, nip out and turn the key.'

'Good idea. I'll go up.'

Stan stood up.

'Wait a minute, Stan. Not so fast.'

'Eh?'

'It's my turn, I believe.'

'No, it's not.'

'Toss you for it.'

'OK.'

Stan took a coin from his pocket and tossed it in the air.

'Heads,' called Dave.

Stan caught the coin and slapped it onto the back of his hand.

'Tails,' he announced. 'See you.'

Stan hurried away leaving a resigned Dave sitting on his own.

Stan knocked on the door of Shirley's bedroom.

'Come in,' she called.

As Stan entered the room he looked her up and down. She was completely naked and not at all embarrassed by it.

'Why didn't you ask who it was?' questioned Stan.

'Don't be silly. It could only be you or Dave.'

'Don't you care which?'

'Of course.'

'Well?'

Shirley approached him and put her arms round his neck.

228

'It's not your turn, you know;' she said, affectionately.

'I know,' Stan chuckled as they fell on the bed.

After they had made love Shirley lay dreamily on the top of the bed while Stan dressed himself.

'Don't go,' said Shirley.

'I must.'

'Why?'

'Dave's waiting.'

'Let him wait.'

'I can't do that. He wants to go to the casino.'

'Losing some more of that lovely money you've got?'

'He feels lucky.' Stan went to the bed and gave her a kiss on the forehead.

'Get dressed, you slut.' As he went out of the room he quickly took the key out of the door, slipped out and locked it from the outside. Shirley leapt off the bed and ran to the door.

'Here!' she cried. 'What's the game?' She struggled with the door, trying to open it.

'Open this door, you rotten bastard!'

She banged on the door with her fists.

As Stan came down the stairs he was approached by the hall porter.

'What is that noise?' he asked.

'I'm sorry, mate,' explained Stan. 'The lady's had too much to drink. It takes her like that. But don't worry, sport. She'll fall asleep in a minute.'

'I hope so,' muttered the old man as he shuffled away.

Stan came whistling onto the terrace and slapped Dave on the shoulder.

'The bird is in the cage,' he announced.

'Took you long enough, didn't it?' commented Dave.

'Yeah,' admitted Stan. 'I must be getting old.'

'Come on, then,' said Dave, getting out of his chair.

'Let's get down to the casino.'

Shirley dressed herself hurriedly. There was no telephone in her room so she could not phone for help. She went to the window and saw Stan and Dave drive away. So they'd left her locked up. She decided to climb out of the window. She went about the room gathering her belongings, such as passport, money and handbag and put them in her small backpack which she slung over her back and climbed out onto the parapet. The casement window of the next door room was open so she made up her mind to go in there and find her way out from there. Climbing along the parapet wasn't all that hazardous for her. She'd done the same sort of thing many times.

She came out of the neighbouring bedroom into the hotel corridor and made her way cautiously down the stairs. The hall porter watched her come down and cross the hall and go out to the car park. He didn't think she looked very drunk.

Once outside the hotel Shirley made for the line of parked cars. She singled out John's red Ferrari, opened the door and got in the back. She stretched herself out on the floor, out of the view of any driver, and settled down to wait.

Some time later a determined John came out of the hotel and got into his car. Shirley crouched down lower as he got in so that she couldn't be seen. She heard the engine start up and felt the car move away. John drove out of the car park and onto the road. He drove grimly towards his final destination, the level crossing.

Shirley found the car slowing down and stopping as John parked the car at a vantage point where he could watch for the train. He kept the engine running and an eye on his wristwatch, the second hand of which moved slowly round the dial.

On the floor of the car at the back Shirley was puzzled to know what was happening as she could hear no other traffic.

When the second hand of John's watch reached a certain position he put his hand on the gear lever and prepared to move forward. At the same time the whistle of a train was heard in the distance. Shirley thought that this was the cause of the delay and was relieved. But she was horrified to feel the car move forward and gather speed as John put his foot down hard on the accelerator pedal.

The car was travelling at great speed as John looked up briefly in the driving mirror. His expression froze in horror as he saw the terrified face of Shirley kneeling in the back of the car. He jammed on the brakes as hard as he could and wrenched the steering wheel over to the right. He came to a standstill as the express train thundered by. With a scream of terror Shirley was thrown to the floor.

In a fury John got out of the car, opened the back door and shouted in his rage, 'You bloody little fool!'

He pulled the girl out of the car.

'What d'you think you're doing?' he demanded.

Shirley suddenly sobbed in wailing hysteria, sank to the ground and covered her face with her hands.

John looked down at her helplessly. He crouched down beside her and put a hand on her shoulder.

'How long had you been there?'

Shirley twisted round and glared at him accusingly. Her face distorted and puffy with tears.

'You tried to kill yourself, didn't you?'

John was taken aback.

'No. No. I...' he mumbled.

'You're mad!' she sobbed.

John helped her to her feet as she began to tidy herself up and adjust her make-up. He went to the car, got in and backed it onto the road again. He rejoined Shirley.

'It still goes,' he laughed. 'No damage done.'

'You're a mad, crazy driver. At your age, too.'

'Why did you hide in the back like that?'

'If I'd asked you wouldn't have taken me.'

'Taken you where?'

'Home. Back to England. I wanted to get away from those two.'

'There are trains and planes. Couldn't you...?'

'I haven't enough money. They keep it all. And I could tell you where they got it.'

'If you really want to get away from them I'll give you the fare and put you on the plane.'

'You want to get rid of me, don't you? So you can try again.'

'I wasn't trying anything. I thought I could get over the crossing.'

'Then why did you stop and wait?'

'You put me off.'

'You waited for the train to come. You were afraid I might get killed with you.'

'Come on. Let me get you to the airport.'

'You were waiting for that train, weren't you?'

'None of your business. Come on.'

He helped her into the front seat of the car.

'As a matter of fact,' he explained, 'I was conducting an experiment.'

'Yeah. With death. Who you kidding?'

He slammed the door shut, got into the driving seat and roared away.

Julie and Tony Bradley were in conference with Emilio and the proprietor of the garage which supplied John's car. Having ascertained the registration number of the car Emilio picked up the phone and informed the police. He also asked them to apprehend the driver. Then Emilio remembered a rather scruffy hotel on the coast where he would sometimes take a lady. He rang the number and asked if an Englishman with a red Ferrari was staying at the place. There was. But he was out in the car at the moment.

At this exciting news Julie suggested leaving at once to find him but Tony decided to leave a message which he dictated to Emilio as he spoke on the phone to the hall porter. It took a little time for Emilio to get the hall porter to write in English: Regret X-rays mixed up. You're clear. Don't do anything rash. Tony Bradley.

After that Tony and Julie got into Emilio's car and he

drove them to the coast, pleased with himself and chatting away happily.

The Italian car that drove into the hotel was driven by Dave with Stan asleep beside him. They were returning from the casino where they had lost a lot of money in spite of staying on in the hope of winning some of it back.

'Come on, Stan,' cried Dave. 'Wake up.'

Stan roused himself sleepily.

'I don't know how you can sleep after losing money the way you do,' accused Dave.

'I'm hungry,' muttered Stan, getting out of the car.

'These dumb wops have never heard of breakfast,' complained Dave.

'Let's wake Shirley up,' said Stan.

They stumbled into the hotel and made their way up the stairs. Dave fumbled for the key of Room 13.

'She's very quiet,' said Stan.

'Probably asleep.'

Dave opened the door and they both walked in. The room was empty.

'She's gone!' exclaimed Stan.

'How can she? I locked her in.'

They searched the room.

'She's taken everything.'

'I bet that bleedin' porter let her out.'

'Come on.'

They hurried out of the room and down the stairs.

Just as the hall porter was coming out of his lodge, with the counter flap already lifted up, Dave and Stan rushed up to him and pushed the flap down again hard.

'Where is she?' demanded Stan.

'Please,' said the porter. 'I do not understand.'

'You let her out, didn't you?' accused Dave.

'I don't understand. What do you want?'

'Where is the lady from Room 13?' asked Stan.

The hall porter turned to look at the rack of door keys.

'No,' said Stan. 'The key's not there. I've got it. Where is she?'

He grabbed the man by the lapels of his coat and held a flick knife to his throat.

'I said where is she?'

'I saw her go out.'

'Did you let her out?'

'No.'

'Then how did she get out?'

'Never mind that, Stan,' said Dave. 'Where is she? That's the point.'

Stan released the old man who shrugged his clothes straight.

'Where did she go?'

'I don't know. I saw her get in the red car.'

'What red car?'

'The one the Englishman drives.'

'Ah! The old geezer.'

'Was he with her?' asked Stan.

'No. He came down much later and he drive off.'

'All right, old man,' said Stan. 'We'll wait for him to come back.'

'*Si. Si.*'

Stan and Dave walked away towards the terrace.

The hall porter waited for them to be out of earshot then he picked up the phone and said one word in Italian, '*Polizia*'.

As Stan flopped down into his chair he said, 'The cow.'

'If she's gone off with him she could let the cat out of the bag,' suggested Dave.

'When I get her up in her room I'll give her the biggest hiding she's ever had.'

'If it's not too late.'

'We'll soon find out.'

'How?'

'From him.'

They did not have to wait long before they saw John

Suter come onto the terrace. They got up at once and went towards him.

'Hello, Dad,' said Stan.

'Hello,' replied John, puzzled.

He made to move away to a table on his own but the two boys blocked his way.

'What's the matter?' he asked.

'Where've you been, Dad?' asked Stan.

'I don't think that's any of your business,' said John.

'Don't you?' asked Stan, taking out his knife.

Dave also produced his knife.

'I think you'd better sit down, Dad,' said Dave, pushing him forcibly into a chair.

John at once tried to get up but the boys pushed him back roughly.

'Now look here...' he began.

'Where's Shirley?'

'How should I know?'

'You went off with her.'

'No.'

'The porter saw you.'

'He may have seen her get into my car. She hid in the back. I didn't know she was there.'

'What she do that for?'

'She wanted to get to the airport.'

'And you took her.'

'Yes.'

'Very kind of you.'

'Anything to oblige.'

The boys stood looking down at him.

'Now, if you've quite finished...' John said as he began to get out of the chair.

The boys pushed him back again.

'No,' said Stan. 'We haven't quite finished.'

'What did Shirley talk about, Dad?' asked Dave.

'I have no intention of reciting our conversation to you,' said John.

'You haven't, eh?' said Dave.

He hit John across the mouth with the back of his hand.

John jumped to his feet but was knocked down again and this time found a knife held at his throat.

'What did she tell you?' demanded Stan.

'She told me that you were a couple of bastards and I'm inclined to agree with her,' moaned John.

'What else?' asked Dave.

'Oh, she prattled on,' said John. 'I don't know what she was talking about. Robberies and coshing old ladies. I don't know.'

Stan and Dave looked at each other.

'What did I tell you? She's opened her trap,' said Dave.

'Fat lot of good it will do her,' replied Stan.

'What shall we do with him?' asked Dave, pointing his knife at John.

'I think I know.'

He turned his attention to John.

'You did say you couldn't swim, didn't you, Dad?'

'That's right. Why?' John answered.

'Come on, Dave,' said Stan. 'Let's take him up the deep end.'

Together they pulled him out of the chair and frog-marched him to the deep end of the pool and led him to the edge.

'You see that water, don't you, Dad?' said Stan.

'Yes. I see it,' replied John.

'Deep, isn't it?'

'Very.'

'And you can't swim, can you?'

'No.'

'Well, Dad,' Stan went on. 'If you don't come across and tell us what Shirley told you you're going in there head first. It'll be just one of those unfortunate little accidents. See?'

John brightened visibly, his voice eager.

'Accident?'

'That's right. An unfortunate accident in which you will be left to drown.'

'Well, you know,' said John. 'That's something I've been looking forward to for a long, long time.'

'What?' asked Stan. 'What are you talking about?'

'Cut the wisecracks, Dad,' urged Dave. 'Tell us what she said.'

'As I'm not going to tell you,' said John, 'I suggest you throw me in now.'

'Why, you stupid...' Stan began to threaten.

'Look out,' warned Dave, suddenly.

They could see the hall porter approaching with a piece of paper in his hand. They held their knives at John's back.

'Any tricks, Dad,' hissed Stan, 'and you get it.'

'Excuse me, Mr Suter. A message for you.'

'Thank you,' said John, taking the paper.

'You all right, Mr Suter?' asked the hall porter, anxiously.

'Yes. Yes. I'm fine,' said John, with a smile.

The hall porter went away, looking back now and again, puzzled.

As John was about to open the paper Dave snatched it out of his hand.

'I'll have that,' said Dave.

'Yeah,' said Stan. 'It may be from Shirley.'

'It's meant for me,' complained John.

'So what?' said Dave, reading the message.

'Oh, I forgot,' said John. 'Other people's property has an attraction for you, hasn't it?'

'There you are!' exclaimed Stan. 'The bitch 'as talked.'

Dave was puzzling over the message he was reading.

'What's this all about?' he asked.

He read the message:

'X-rays mixed up. You're clear. Don't do anything rash. Tony Bradley. What sort of code is that?'

John suddenly realised the meaning of the message and brightened considerably.

'Let me see that,' he said.

He took the message and read it.

'What's it mean?' asked Dave.

John looked down at the deep water of the pool. Then

he looked at Stan and Dave and realised what a dangerous position he was in.

'It means,' said John, 'that there has been a terrible mistake and an accident is no longer necessary.'

He suddenly made a move to run away but Dave and Stan grabbed him and twisted his arms behind his back.

'Oh, no, you don't,' said Stan. 'Unless you tell us what Shirley said to you you're going in that water.'

'But I can't swim,' protested John.

'That's your look out, mate,' said Dave.

'Listen,' said John, pleading. 'I didn't care before. I wanted an accident to happen. But it's different now.'

'One,' said Stan, counting.

'I took her to the airport. That's all. She didn't tell me anything.'

'Two,' said Stan.

John braced himself, pushed back on one of the boys and kicked out at the other. He was free for a moment but only as long as it took Dave to double round in front of him and cut off his retreat. He turned back, dodging between the tables towards the shallow end of the pool.

'Round the other way, Dave!' shouted Stan.

Dave doubled round the pool and came up behind John so that he was between the two of them. Dave and Stan converged on John so that he could only go one way and that was towards the deep end of the pool where they cornered him. His only escape was the high diving board. He turned and began quickly to climb to the highest point.

'After him!' called Stan.

They climbed up the ladder after John.

Once at the top John waited for the boys to get near. He kicked out at their hands as they tried to mount the high diving board, but it was an unequal struggle. Stan and Dave got onto the board and John backed away towards the open end and the water.

'Get ready to rush him,' said Stan as they made their way slowly towards him. 'Both at once. One. Two. Three!'

The boys rushed at John who kicked out at the menacing knives. He lost his balance and Stan and Dave watched as he clawed the air in panic and, with a scream, hurtled into the deep end of the pool.

'Quick!' cried Stan. 'Scarper!'

'What's the panic?' asked Dave. 'It was an accident, wasn't it?'

They made their way down the ladder to the terrace and sauntered casually towards the hotel.

In the hotel foyer they were met by the hall porter and two policemen, behind whom stood Julie, Tony Bradley and Emilio.

'Where is he? Where's my husband?' cried Julie, pushing past them all and making for the terrace, followed by Tony Bradley and Emilio.

The three of them stood on the terrace anxiously looking about.

'John?' called Julie.

She moved nearer to the pool where she could see something floating on top of the water.

'Tony!' she cried in alarm.

As soon as Tony saw the body he stripped off his jacket and dived in, followed by Emilio. Together they recovered the body and propelled it to the side of the pool where Julie helped pull it out. Tony immediately set about resuscitation, pumping water out of the body. Suddenly he sat back on his heels.

'Phew! That was a near thing,' he breathed.

'Why have you stopped?' asked Julie, fearfully, as she knelt beside John.

'See for yourself,' said Tony.

Julie could see that John was breathing. He opened his eyes, looked up and saw Julie.

'Hello,' he said. 'I must be in Heaven.'

Julie clutched John's wet body to her.

'You very nearly were,' she sobbed.

Tony and Emilio got to their feet.

'Better get him upstairs before he catches his death of

cold,' said Tony, helping John to his feet and moving with him, Julie and Emilio to the hotel.

John thought to himself: Thank God for interfering bastards.